A Hidden Cryptid History

You may not have ever seen them, but you know them: Bigfoot, Mothman, chupacabras, the Jersey Devil, and Nessie, the Loch Ness Monster. Cryptids exist everywhere around the world—on land, in the air, and under the water. Some creatures are recent discoveries; others date back centuries. But where did they come from? What is their hidden history?

Collected in this anthology are twenty short stories featuring a wide variety of cryptids as well as the cryptozoologists who discover them, hunt them, study them, or shelter them. Alongside the classic creatures of legend and lore are pixies, aliens, lizard men, and doppelgängers—plus a few original and newly discovered cryptids that will capture your curiosity. With genres ranging from fantasy and science fiction to historical fiction and romance, there is something for everyone to enjoy. As an added twist, each story utilizes at least one form of epistolary writing to help tell the story, including text messages, podcast interviews, newspaper articles, and journal entries.

So tune in to Bigfoot's podcast, write a love letter to Nessie, and then pick up a pair of tickets to the grand opening of the Cryptid Zoo. The world around us is full of the weird and the wonderful, and the creatures that were once long hidden are ready to come out of the woods.

Weird Wilderness: A Cryptid Bestiary is the tenth anthology edited by Lisa Mangum and the first co-edited by Jessica Guernsey and published by WordFire Press. Profits support the various scholarship funds for the Superstars Writing Seminar.

WEIRD WILDERNESS

A CRYPTID BESTIARY

WEIRD WILDERNESS

EDITED BY
LISA MANGUM
WITH
JESSICA GUERNSEY

Weird Wilderness: A Cryptid Bestiary
Edited by Lisa Mangum and Jessica Guernsey

WEIRD WILDERNESS
Copyright © 2025 WordFire, Inc.
"Out of the Woods" © 2025 CL Fors
"A Study in Pixies" © 2025 Azure Arther
"Grand Opening: Cryptid Zoo" © 2025 Katherine MacEachern
"Accounts Payable Denies Your Request" © 2025 Sixth Moon Press, LLC
"Night Contractors" © 2025 Rebecca J. Carlson
"The Gurt Dug of New Bannockburn" © 2025 Jason Kristopher
"The Vision Serpent" © 2025 Jamie Sonderman
"Dear Nessie" © 2025 Bonnie Elizabeth
"On the Trail of the Swamp Soggon" © 2025 Mark Leslie Lefebvre
"Hunting the Headline" © 2025 Sara Itka
"Working the Salt Mine" © 2014, 2025 Sam Knight
"Best Foot Forward" © 2025 Aaron Fors
"Surviving" © 2025 Janessa Keeling
"Nessie's Morning Cup of Coffee" © 2025 Angelique Fawns
"The Leeds Devil" © 2025 J. Thompson
"How to Be Friends with a Human" © 2025 Annmarie SanSevero
"Treading Eggshells" © 2025 John K. Patterson
"The Alien Hunter" © 2025 John M. Campbell
"A History of Hodags in the City" © 2025 Darren Lipman
"Faceless" © 2025 Tanya Hales

All rights reserved. No part of this book may be reproduced or transmitted in any form or by any electronic or mechanical means, including photocopying, recording or by any information storage and retrieval system, without the express written permission of the copyright holder, except where permitted by law. This novel is a work of fiction. Names, characters, places and incidents are either the product of the authors' imagination, or, if real, used fictitiously.

The ebook edition of this book is licensed for your personal enjoyment only. The ebook may not be re-sold or given away to other people. If you would like to share the ebook edition with another person, please purchase an additional copy for each recipient. Thank you for respecting the hard work of these authors.

EBook ISBN: 978-1-68057-746-4
Trade Paperback ISBN: 978-1-68057-747-1
Dust Jacket Hardcover ISBN: 978-1-68057-748-8
Library of Congress Control Number: 024945252
Cover design by Miblart
Kevin J. Anderson, Art Director
Vellum layout by CJ Anaya
Published by

WordFire Press, LLC
PO Box 1840
Monument CO 80132
Kevin J. Anderson & Rebecca Moesta, Publishers
WordFire Press eBook Edition 2025
WordFire Press Trade Paperback Edition 2025
WordFire Press Dust Jacket Hardcover Edition 2025

Printed in the USA
Join our WordFire Press Readers Group for
sneak previews, updates, new projects, and giveaways.
Sign up at wordfirepress.com

Contents

Out of the Woods *by CL Fors*	1
A Study in Pixies *by Azure Arther*	16
Grand Opening: Cryptid Zoo *by Kate Dane*	33
Accounts Payable Denies Your Request *by Julia Vee*	40
Night Contractors *by Rebecca J. Carlson*	52
The Gurt Dug of New Bannockburn *by Jason Kristopher*	63
The Vision Serpent *by Jamie Sonderman*	78
Dear Nessie *by Bonnie Elizabeth*	93
On the Trail of the Swamp Soggon *by Mark Leslie*	106
Hunting the Headline *by Sara Itka*	118
Working the Salt Mine *by Sam Knight*	135
Best Foot Forward *by Aaron Fors*	150
Surviving *by Janessa Keeling*	162
Nessie's Morning Cup of Coffee *by Angelique Fawns*	169
The Leeds Devil *by Jeff Thompson*	173
How to Be Friends with a Human *by Annmarie SanSevero*	188
Treading Eggshells *by John K. Patterson*	198
The Alien Hunter *by John M. Campbell*	210

A History of Hodags in the City *by Darren Lipman*	224
Faceless *by Tanya Hales*	238
About the Editors	259
If You Liked ...	261

Out of the Woods
by CL Fors

The mailbox was crammed full. Three weeks of traveling would do that. Laura wedged strong, sinewy fingers between the thick sheaf of letters and food ads and the hot metal of the mailbox. Stuck. Whoever decided metal mailboxes in Arizona were a good idea was a sun-fried idiot. She braced herself with a foot against the sun-weathered wood of the post and pulled. The red post was a mess of paint, with splinters peeling and flaking into the hot sand, decorating the spikes of her dusty-green aloe vera plants like blood spatter.

The same as her walls would look. Chupa had been alone for weeks; who could blame him?

The box released its grip, and Laura tumbled back onto her gravel driveway, cursing and catching herself with her hands. She didn't need a fall at her age. *Sixty-five and still spry*—the words came as an echo of her grandmother's lively voice, only she'd said it at every age until she'd given up the ghost at ninety-six. Laura had at least thirty-one years ahead of her, and she was going to make sure she could get her job done.

That thought brought a spike of panic that she tamped down before it could take shape, though a greasy stain of unease clung to her insides. Thirty-one didn't seem like much, laid out next to the sixty-five already spent. Was thirty-one enough time to set all her affairs in order when they spread across the whole continental US?

She didn't even have a good count of how many charges she had depending on her to keep them hidden and safe.

Laura ignored the stinging in her palms, grateful her hands caught her without a broken wrist or a dislocated hip. Now that she was sitting, the setting sun a winking red eye over the Sierra Vista mountain ranges that ringed her high desert home, she may as well open the mail.

The first half was credit offers. She ripped and tossed them into her messenger bag, then separated out the expired ads before a familiar address and name caught her eye. There weren't many people who liked to use snail mail anymore, real paper letters, but Laura's clients were different.

The smell hit when she opened it: the resinous tang of deep woods and damp growing things. She upended the envelope and shook out a single sprig of blue spruce, still fresh and pliable, into her hand, its sharp scent wafting. She couldn't help but smile, which loosened the crease between her brows and softened her worry lines. Cither writing letters meant some sort of trouble, but he knew about the magic of small gestures. He knew to buy his asks with giving: a bundle of fresh morel mushrooms discarded by a hiker scared off by his sudden appearance, a choice stick with all the right bends and just enough straight bits, a sprig of spruce sent into the desert.

Cither Saturn
Potters Creek Rd
Point Pleasant, WV 25550

Dear dearest Laura-laur,

>*If you will ...*
>*I implore*
>*A visit*
>*A tête-à-tête*
>*Perhaps more?*

>*A new composition just for you! I hope you like it. But at the risk of being crass: on to business! Some others and I have spoken, and we share*

a deep discontent, one too many centuries in hiding, dear Laur, and I, for one, am finished. The sentient among us agree.

Even Honey agrees, and before you ask how I know, the Louisiana swamps are a short flight from my old home, and Honey wasn't hard to find. (He was regaling a little enclave of Cajun youths in the swamp while coaxing them away from an alligator's reach on the edge of the river.)

Honey hoped it would be the start of a new day for him. Dare he hope for friendship, acceptance? But Honey made the mistake of finding the little brown mushrooms the young ones had come looking to ingest. They tasted the colors of the trees and wouldn't believe Honey was real, and Honey's feelings were hurt when they mixed him up with Bigfoot. (Honestly, their range doesn't even overlap.) He is more resolved than ever. There are others. (See the signatures attached.) You have always aided our obscurity, now we would rejoice in your aid to come out of the woods.

Safe flights and warm tailwinds,
Your Cither

Laura snorted a laugh at the rhyme at the start of Cither's letter. He was making use of the poetry volumes she'd left him. Hopefully, they were a good outlet, a distraction for the rest of mating season, that season of holy hell among the near-extinct clients she tended to. The poem's tone made her raise a brow and blush a little. He better not mean anything by the last line—*Perhaps more?*

Mating season comes around, and they all lose their furry minds, she thought.

The rest of the letter made her laugh out loud, but uneasily. Every other decade, Cither had a new want, a new passion, and he would burn himself out like a moth crisping against the scorching glass of an antique light bulb. *Dzzzt!* It was funny because it was so predictable, and because humor was the only way she could watch that flurry of manic energy followed by bitter disappointment.

This letter had to be another one of his phases, the mention of others agreeing with him an exaggeration. She didn't look at the signatures; she could do that later and suss out how much was fiction and how many she'd need to talk down. For now, Chupa was waiting.

Laura ignored the knot of worry forming in her gut and folded the letter. She tucked it into her bedraggled travel bag, a tattered, trustworthy old thing still sporting the telltale fraying patches from the sixties, along with several new ones. Her favorite was a circular patch depicting a winding path through dark woods with the bold letters: "All those who wander are not lost ... But I sure as hell am!"

She stood and brushed the sand off her behind. Some of it crawled against her hands—ants—so she brushed more and stomped her feet on the cement slab that passed for a porch. It was too dark to see the insects, but this was the Arizona desert, and she knew her critters even by feel. These fat-bodied fellows with large heads were the biting kind, but not fire ants like the South had.

Chupa was squealing at the door by the time she got the keys out; he had been since she'd pulled up in her battered truck—battered like her bag, her mailbox, her joints. She liked the little reminders around her that a thing could be battered by time and wear and even misuse, but still be good, so long as they weren't falling to pieces.

"Alright, alright, Chups." Damn lock was stuck again, and his high-pitched whine was bordering on frantic and wavering into registers that she could *feel*. It vibrated the bones of her skull, making her dizzy, disoriented; she had to put a hand against the door. Chupa's whining ability was good for slowing down prey, but not good for getting the door open faster.

The lock gave with one more jerk, and she pushed hard when the jamb seemed stuck too. How many times had Chupa body-slammed it in her absence? And then he was on her, all 150 pounds, with forepaws propped next to her cheeks and a long, wet prehensile tongue bathing her face.

Laura's throat tightened as if not only her heart but all her organs had risen into her chest. He was okay. Weeks of worry pushed down as she did what had to be done—making the rounds, covering poorly hidden tracks, spreading cover stories, discrediting sightings—all washed away with Chupa's tongue-bathing. He was okay, if a bit thin, but he'd fatten quickly. Chupacabras put on weight fast. His mother wouldn't have had any milk for him. They weren't mammals after all. No, a Chupa neonate needed blood from the beginning, a mother's blood. Laura knew what she was getting into when she'd rescued him. Some of the angry, pink scars along her arms were still healing.

He'd moved on to pigeons and goats when she could get them. There was a cooing coming from somewhere in the dark of the small house, so one bird had made it this long. But Chupa was hungry; she could smell it on him, a sharp musk with an undertone of that sickly sweet signature smell of a chupacabra, rotting fruit and old blood. He nuzzled the underside of her arm, nipping and whining for permission. She almost caved even as her body recoiled. He wasn't a neonate anymore, and his adult teeth were in, rows of canines like thick medical needles for taking bone marrow.

She pushed him off ... or tried. That high-pitched whine rose an octave and oscillated, and her thoughts grew confused, muddled, until she doubled down. Weaning a child was hard. This might be even harder. It felt like rejection, like withdrawing her love. *Just a little might be okay.*

She bit down on her tongue and drew blood, spitting it into her palm. She offered it to Chupa, who lapped at it, taking the blood in one greedy swipe of the tongue and then stepping back, paws on the ground again. Laura sighed and reached for the rough-scaly body, wrapping her arms around Chupa's massive rib cage and resting her head on his shoulder. Long spines stood up from his back, and she scratched and stroked along the sensitive ridge until he let out a chuff of approval.

Two hours and several pigeons later, Chupa slept, curled around her on a scratched, brown leather love seat worn smooth by decades of bodies shifting and settling into it. The glow from her laptop lit her face and strained her eyes. She wiped at their corners and pressed on, categorizing the sightings by urgency. Some were absurd enough to ignore for a while, others were in another Crypwatcher's jurisdiction. She could leave those unless someone reached out for help.

An alert flashing on her screen got her attention. A normally credible blogger with no history of cryptid sightings. Laura skimmed the blog for essential info. It was the location that caught her first.

New Orleans.
Sasquatch sighting.
Honey Island Swamp monster.
Tracks found with locks of thick, shaggy fur embedded ...

If those were Honey's tracks, then the fur couldn't be an accident. It wasn't shed season. It was mating season, and Honey would have a thick, glossy pelt right now, shaggy and swamp-colored, at its best. Unless Honey, who was usually so meticulous, had done it on purpose and wanted to "come out of the woods" like Cither claimed. *Shit.*

Another ding, another alert. This one from Point Pleasant, West Virginia. Laura blinked at the article, once, twice.

The Cryptid Creep Newsletter
The Next Generation of Mothmen?

Sighting alert! The first of its kind in six decades. Spring has sprung, and someone in the West Virginia woods has been very busy! A dozen sightings, ranging from April 1 through April 12, of what some are describing as moths the size of large house cats, dark in color, with red eyes and dark, fur-covered wings the span of a small buzzard. The critters are drawn to car headlights, and several collisions have been reported, but no specimens recovered.

Could it be that Mothman has returned to the Virginia woods after a sixty-year absence and found a mate? As you can guess, I've been patrolling the roadsides after dark with a headlamp, and I won't quit until I can confirm the sightings.

Signing off,

Your very own Cryptid Creep patrolling the wilds so you don't have to.

Ron Roach

She read it a third time and then pulled out Cither's letter. He'd sent it from Point Pleasant, West Virginia. What in the sweet spruce woods was he doing back there? He'd sworn on his good right antenna not to go back there. And what sort of memories could have enticed him back? She had no good ones; the business with the bridge eclipsed all the others.

Another sighting flashed on the screen: *Moth-child captured!*

A spike of adrenaline sent her body upright, jostling Chupa. He let out a single sharp whine that resonated in her skull and kick-started another migraine—or maybe that was Cither's fault. But Cither had mentioned nothing about mothlings in the letter.

Laura exhaled as the image loaded on her screen. The supposedly captured moth-child was made of clay and feathers with glossy resin eyes—skillfully done but still a fake. Okay, not a *crisis* but an *emergency*, definitely a code orange.

She looked down at Chupa, heart constricting. She'd just come back, and he was thin, clinging to her in a way that made her feel sick and angry at herself.

So much for your promise, whispered the little voice in the back of her head.

But she'd made promises to Cither, to Honey, to all her charges, plus her oath to the Crypwatch. She'd hoped this thing with Cither would blow over, that she could tuck it away like the letter. No such luck. Still, she couldn't leave Chupa again. And turning him loose wasn't happening either—reintegration was a slow and careful process. There was nothing for it. She had to travel across the South with a largely untrained chupacabra, pick up the Honey Island Swamp Monster along the way for suicide watch, and talk some sense into the Mothman.

Airports were out of the question, and staying off-road would be too much for her beat-up truck—the '90s were farther away than she or the truck wanted to admit—so I-64 West it was.

Thirty-two hours, several hour-long rest-stop naps, and many caffeine top-ups later, Laura crossed the Ohio River on the Silver Memorial Bridge, a death grip on the steering wheel. She knew she was taking years off her lifespan white-knuckling it for 1,280-plus miles, which included picking up Honey, but the alerts on her phone had kept coming, with a dozen more sightings of moth-babies in Point Pleasant, and the Cryptid Creep's followers were converging on Point Pleasant from across the country. She couldn't afford to drag ass. Cither could be missing, hurt ...

She tightened her hands on the wheel, despite the pain in her swollen, arthritic knuckles, and hit the gas.

She almost ignored it when the warning whoop of sirens went off just behind her, but the flash of red-and-blue across her dash meant business. She glanced at Chupa in the front seat with a chest harness and seat belt. Only his scaly muzzle and seven-toed paws stuck out of the Cowardly Lion costume she'd dressed him in, the fluffy mane obscuring his otherworldly face just enough, she hoped. Honey was in the back seat—a swamp monster wearing khakis and a button-up shirt patterned with tiny jazz instruments and the words *The Big Easy*. His mottled gray-green skin, hanging with heavy fur, resembled Spanish moss more than anything else.

The officer's siren whooped again, and Laura slowed, pulled over.

"Right then." She did a quick rifle for license, registration, and insurance, hoping her preparation would speed the process and prevent the questions she wanted to avoid.

The officer tapped the window, and she rolled it down, holding out the documents before he could ask. "License and registra—"

Shit.

He'd dropped his shades, revealing blue eyes gone wide, staring out of cheeks and forehead that had burned and tanned and burned again. He was looking at Chupa and Honey, eyes flicking back and forth between the two.

"Your dog, he's a—" The officer tried to clear his throat, but it seemed to have gone dry.

Thankfully Chupa was faking sleep, smart boy, his face half covered by his over-large paws. Those claws were a lot to explain, but a good, fast lie should suffice. "He's a Xoloitzcuintle, very rare."

The officer nodded as if he knew the breed, but she could see in his eyes he just wanted to look away and let it go. Honey, though, was harder to ignore, with his broad grin, oversized yellow teeth blunt from a lifetime of chewing dense roots and other vegetables, and a full body of swamp hair like an unwashed Wookiee.

"Gonna need some ID from your passenger." He nodded toward Honey, then handed Laura her paperwork back. Laura groaned inside. Two hurdles crossed, only to trip on a third.

But Honey passed his counterfeit ID forward, heavily swamp-stained, and she relaxed.

"You heading to a, uh, a concert or something?" the officer asked.

Laura knew what was happening in the officer's head. It was the same thing that happened with most sane people, the ones who were ignorant and happy to remain so. Aliens, vampires, chupacabras, and swamp monsters named Honey who liked jazz and long walks on the riverbank, had no place in their very urban existences.

"Right, yeah. The Mothman Festival." She almost slapped herself as soon as the words spilled out. *Too tired, dammit.*

The officer's brow screwed up in skepticism. "In April?"

The Mothman Festival was in September. She knew that. Now, here she was, blowing it when Cither needed her. Another lie tumbled out to build on the last. "Yep, that one. We're setup crew. Planning happens all year—you know how meetings are—more work than the event itself." Laura watched his face shift as the mental gears turned. This one wanted to believe her. She dug into her background in law enforcement, from both sides of the cuffs. "Training exercises all year."

That got him. The officer handed Honey's ID back and grinned. Shook his head.

"Don't I know it. Well, drive safe. Even when the signs are a bit hard to see, you're expected to slow down." He gave her a wink that said, "This is your warning," and then tipped his hat before trotting back to his vehicle.

Laura pulled back onto the road. Honey's heavy hand squeezed her shoulder, triggering an unexpected emotional reaction. It was the stress of the moment, the hours behind the wheel; that was all. It would take another hour at this lower speed to hit Cither's old haunt, an hour of scouring the woods bordering the road for critters that might be there and might not.

That last hour felt like twelve as she fought her fatigue by guzzling the last of the cold, road-stop coffee. The freshly painted lines with shiny new reflectors made ghost lights in her eyes when she blinked, and the woods remained too dark to see what she was looking for. She turned on her brights, slapped her cheeks to keep her eyes open, and finally opened the driver's side window.

Chupa was whining again before long—hungry or aching from the long drive—and it drilled into her skull.

"No! Chupa, no whining." Her voice was sharp, the kind she'd used with recruits in training when they broke rifle discipline and pointed their weapons up-range or, worse yet, at a battle buddy. Her tone was too harsh for Chupa, and she regretted it immediately. But Chupa didn't stop and instead let out a series of chuffing snarl-whines, like glass in an active garbage disposal. He tried to stand in the front seat, but the harness held him back, so all he managed was landing his front paws on the dash, an excited Cowardly Lion with a faux-fur mane blowing around his reptilian face in the cold night air.

Then something basketball-sized flew through the driver's side window and slammed into his head. Another followed it, and another, until one collided with Laura's face, and the truck went off the road, clipping a tree and spinning out into the ditch.

Laura groaned and felt around her for whatever had hit her. Her ears rang and her vision had grayed out, coming back in as static. She could hear Chupa whining, wrestling with something, and Honey moving around in the back. They were okay—for now. Three of the somethings were in her lap, flopping and twitching, covered in soft fur. The first things she saw when her vision cleared were eyes—golden moth eyes the size of teacups, pinprick pupils fixed on her, or maybe on the light of the truck's cabin above her head.

Blink, blink, blink. They blinked in sequence like a wave, antennae twitching and brushing her face like waving cattails. Moth-babies. They were actual, honest-to-weirdness moth-babies.

And Chupa was trying to eat one. Laura snapped to and put a hand on Chupa's muzzle, pushing back against the smooth scales and making eye contact. A shake of the head. "No, Chupa. You can't eat Cither's mothlings."

A whine.

"No. Not even one."

Cither was where she expected him to be, and where he absolutely should not have been if he knew what was good for him. He'd returned to the abandoned fireworks plant he'd furnished with antiques and discarded collectibles from bygone eras. He wasn't sick. He wasn't missing. He was just negligent, and he greeted her with a placid smile on his very human lips. Cither was more human than the myths made him out to be, smoothly muscled with a man's face —if a bit pointed around the chin—and a long nose that stretched down instead of jutting out. It was the downy black-and-brown stripes of moth fur that covered his body and the wings that marked him as something inhuman. His soup-bowl eyes stretched and filled the top of his head. They were glossy, luminous, and amber-colored in the lamplight but would gleam red in the headlights of her battered truck if he came out.

The truck, scuffed and worse for wear, limped along once Honey had shoved it out of the ditch with very little help from her. It wouldn't make it back to Arizona, but it didn't matter. What mattered was that it had gotten her here so she could set Cither straight. She couldn't think about the truck, or Arizona, or how she hurt all over from the crash, not while she collected a gaggle of mothlings and strapped them to her chest with her jacket sleeves, then stormed up the factory steps with Chupa and Honey in tow.

The door creaked open like a backwoods memory, and Mothman sat just inside, silhouetted by the dim lamplight. Reckless —always leaving doors open as if his "enjoyment of the night air" came before safety.

Laura slammed the open factory window shut and pulled four puppy-sized mothlings out of her makeshift sling. She plopped them on the dust-covered Victorian desk in front of Cither, where he was writing with quill and ink on antique paper. It was an affectation that she'd found charming in years past, but now it expanded her anger like a bellows. All four of the mothlings pressed their faces close to the colorful Tiffany lamp on the desk, one just like the several others broken on the debris-covered floor of the old factory. They drooled on the rainbow glass, little tongues darting out to taste the fake flowers.

"You came!" Cither stood with open arms. He didn't seem to notice her scowl.

"You set moth-babies loose in the woods! They're colliding with cars! Was that the plan? To force me back here? To talk about your declaration of—what? Of insanity? Of leaving the woods? Because that *is* insanity!"

Cither glanced at the mothlings on the desk and tapped one chubby hand before it could grab the bulb. He shook his head with a stern look, and the mothling withdrew its curious fingers.

"To bring you here? Honestly, no. Life events aren't always well timed, and I assure you, their mother was quite the willing partner until the eggs emerged and were, well, mothy instead of human. And numerous. I think that scared her. I did tell her, of course, but seeing is believing. You know that better than anyone, Laura."

"Numerous?" Laura glanced at the four tumbling humanoids on the desk and then back at Cither, eyes widening in realization and growing alarm. "How many, Cither?"

"Thirty by my count, although they're adventurous little things, not always here all at once."

Laura gripped the graying hair on both sides of her head and then dropped her hands, tightening the slack she'd made in Chupa's leash. The chupacabra was pulling toward the mothlings, and she had to rein him in, but his whine wasn't helping her think.

"Laura, I think you should sit down, sleep maybe. There's a bed in the loft …"

Sleep? He thought she could sleep with twenty-six moth-babies loose in the woods and Cryptid Creep's pack on the prowl?

She sat down in the chair he offered. "Okay, this is what we do. With enough light and butterfly nets—I have big ones in the kit in the truck—we can get them all inside. At your growth rate, they'll calm down in, say, three to six weeks. In the meantime, we go far north. Canada maybe, and then—"

Honey mumbled behind her chair, forgotten. "Canada is cold."

Cither cleared his throat and pitched his voice low. "I'm not leaving Point Pleasant again."

"What? Why?" She was frantic. "There's nothing here we can't set up somewhere safer, somewhere they won't look for you." The tightness in her throat made it hard to talk.

"Good memories."

"Good memories? Not possible. We took down Silver Bridge. All those cars trapped in the water. All those deaths because they crowded on to see you in broad daylight."

"I met *you* here, Laur."

"You tried to warn them, but it didn't work because people are stupid. Stupid and dangerous." She didn't process what he'd said until her own words were out, fear-fueled words she'd tried not to say out loud.

Cither shook his head, and she saw disappointment in his eyes as his pupils dilated with hurt. "Well, I don't think so. I think people are mostly good—I know *one* who is—if you give them a chance. I aim to do that, and I'm asking you to help me."

"I *am* trying to help you. I'm trying to keep you safe!" It came out a shout. She covered her mouth and then grimaced. Where was her old military bearing now?

Cither frowned and motioned with his pointed chin to Chupa, straining at the leash and harness. "Are you keeping him safe too? Keeping Honey safe by being the only person he can talk to? Will you be there the next time the void calls his name?"

"I—It's my job. Yes, I can. I saved Chupa. And Honey's better —" She glanced back at Honey, trying not to see the dark ink of depression that never seemed to entirely leave his eyes. She looked down at the chupacabra on her leash, stubbornness warring with the judgment Cither seemed to level at her: She was the problem and not the solution.

Several dark shapes stepped out, and her breath caught. She'd never read the signatures on Cither's letter. A lycanthrope named Barry; Hannah, a reptilian from Los Angeles; and two others from another Crypwatcher's jurisdiction. They were all in their holiday best, ready to meet people respectably.

Laura felt panic rising. Her back was against the wall; she was outnumbered. She came around the desk and whispered to Cither, the fur of his chest tickling her face as she leaned up. "Cither, please don't ask me to risk this. Think of all of them—all your mothlings."

"Oh, I am, Laur. I'd rather they self-immolate than hide for their whole lives like I have."

Realization hit her like a hurtling moth-baby. She'd hid him, kept him safe like she kept Chupa and Honey and all the others safe. So safe she'd smothered out their lights like a campfire at the end of the night, doused under layers of dry soil. Safe, always safe.

"Oh," she whispered.

He took her hand and tucked something into it. "If you could keep us hidden for so long, I think you can figure out how to reveal us. The safe Laura way. The smart way." She knew what he was doing, bandaging her ego after breaking it down so she'd see she'd been lying to herself. And why would he do that? Because he was good. He was the best, lifting the good bits of her and his fellow Cryptids into the lamplight. She just hoped he was right about people, and if he was only half-right, like she thought, she hoped she could reach that better half and keep her friends just safe enough.

Laura took stock of the pulled muscles in her arms, her throbbing head, the bone-deep fatigue she wouldn't have felt years ago, even after a drive like that. *Thirty-one years.* If that. Not long enough to keep them hidden forever. But maybe it was long enough to help them come out of the woods.

She looked down at the paper Cither had pressed into her hand. There were names and phone numbers and a press release.

> To Whom It May Concern,
> One Cither Saturn (Mothman) invites you to attend the Cryptids Ball, our Coming Out of the Woods and into Polite Society Party. Expect light refreshments and deep conversation. All open-minded questioners are welcome.
> September 16, 8:00 pm—or when streetlamps are lit!

Laura pressed the letter to her chest, the corners of her lips trembling as she searched for words, then patted the underside of Chupa's drool-wet muzzle. "I have some phone calls to make." She nodded and forced a smile, turning on her heel before the tears could come.

Cither called his thanks after her. She heard worry in his voice, worry for her, so she raised a hand as if to wave without turning, stepping out into the humid dark of West Virginia woods.

She had a long drive back. She'd have to sleep in the truck, but there was planning to do before September. A chupacabra to acclimate and release into the wild, hard goodbyes, and a lot of closed minds to open. One couldn't just spring a real-life Mothman and thirty moth-babies on people. She'd have to bring them into the light slowly, carefully. There wouldn't be any self-immolations on her watch.

About the Author

CL Fors is a speculative fiction author, illustrator, and publisher and considers herself a friend and protector of all creatures, slithering, crawling, or creeping, including cryptids should she ever meet one. Cherrie Lynn (to her friends) lives in the California desert with her author husband, four human kids, a large animal menagerie, and a foundling cat named Lucifer who snuggles like a moth-baby and bites like a chupacabra. She is a recent winner of Illustrators of the Future and author of the Primogenitor Series, a science fiction epic of humanity stolen and reclaimed. Book one, *Cradle of Mars*, can be found on Amazon or at www.clforsauthor.com along with the rest of the series.

Follow her graphic novel on Patreon:
patreon.com/OrionsFlight.

A Study in Pixies
by Azure Arther

Compilation of Case Notes for Ingen Pixie Studies: The following are the compiled documents, notes, and known sundry for Dr. Anne Ingen, current location unknown. Case numbers begin with 01 and follow.

CN001

Delouth Dictionary Definitions
Pixie /pi/x/ie/ noun
Also known as pixy, pisky, a pox on your house
Delouth Dictionary definition of PIXIE
1
a: an animal, usually found living in flowers or wilderness biomes
~~b: an imaginary or strange kind of creature both fantastical, mythical, or legendary~~
A pox on that. We know they're not imaginary.

CN002

Dear Anne,

    I saw you on television last week, right after the Reveal. I felt a bit of comfort knowing that I know you, even if we haven't spoken since the kids were young. I tried to ring you up, but the phones aren't working. Just a quick note to say I'm glad you're next door, and I do hope you'll extend whatever magical protections you received to my house too.

    Anyway, it's nice that those Dictionary company people bought up all those labs. I think they'll be a real help at some point, right?

    Your neighbor,
    Carol

CN003

From: Delouth Labs <j.hofstader@delouthdictionary.org>
To: Anne Ingen <a.ingen@delouthdictionary.org>
Sent: Monday, April 4, 2033 at 02:43:30 PM CDT
Subject: Pixies: lab approval needed

Hi there Anne,

I hope this finds you well and summer safe! I am following up as our records show that we need a copy of your lab approval sheet and/or non-approval notice and submittal of your security deposit of $500.

Mail security deposit by check of $500 to

Delouth Dictionaries
Attn: Lab Program
PO Box 000010001
Santa Fe, NM 87502

If you have submitted these before, please forward proof to me. any questions, let me know!
thank you
j

CN004

Artifice Securities Message Board

11:00 Neil—Hey, Barney quit the Ingen barn. Said the pixies are attacking.

12:00 Walen—Oh noooo … a 4-inch bat is swooping at me. Ha.

12:07 Barney—It's not like that. You go out there then.

12:13 Walen—As much as they pay, I will.

CN005

Anne,

Thank you so much for your help last week. I really wasn't sure what to do about that pesky Sasquatch issue. It is cryptozoologists like you who run the world now. Have you ever thought that maybe, since all of these creatures have come out, that you should petition to be president? Maybe of the whole world? Ha. That would be fun.

I really wish we saw each other more. I feel like you've been avoiding me and only helped with the Sasquatch because we have a fence line together. I know I used to call you crazy, but I was one of the first to believe you when the creatures started showing up.

Anyway, I would really like to have a chat with you over our fences like we used to, maybe pick your ear on protection techniques. Ha, maybe you could even come over and help me ward the house, now that you have magic? It's kind of unfair that only people who believed in these monsters BEFORE they came out got magic.

We've been neighbors for decades. Our kids went to school

together. I know Bobby didn't always treat your Gene the best, but kids will be kids, right?

Neighbors should help each other!

Your friend,

Carol

CN006

Artifice Securities Message Board

```
1:27 Neil—Hey, Barney. Walen quit the Ingen barn.

1:35 Barney—I TOLD YOU

1:44 Walen—Sorry, bro. You were right.

2:09 Neil—Maybe we can send the new guy? He's a little mage, right?

2:21 Walen—Matthew? Mark? What's his name?
```

CN007

Rachel Jensen, Human Resource Manager
Delouth Dictionaries
555-508-3405 | r.jensen@delouthdictionary.org | Seattle, Washington 98128

July 1, 2033

Anne Ingen, Sr. Lab Mage
555-456-7890 | a.ingen@delouthdictionary.org | Elbert, Colorado 80106

Dear Anne Ingen,

It is my pleasure to introduce Kari Yemen as the Jr. Lab Assistant and Apprentice for your lab. Kari has seven years' experience working with creatures, and I have seen her magic for myself. She is on track to be a powerful mage. Kari developed her magic at the same time as everyone else, but as she was still a teenager at the time, she appears to be growing exponentially stronger as she ages. She would do well with a more experienced mystic who has a more tangible understanding of cryptozoology and mystical means.

During her short tenure at Delouth, Kari has displayed valuable talent with coaxing smaller creatures into appearance. As the leaders in monsterology, cryptozoology, mysticism, and magic, Delouth Labs Headquarters believes that Kari is best suited for your lab location. You can review her resume and published portfolio in the attachments.

She will arrive on Sunday, August 14, 2033.

We would appreciate it if you lowered your defenses and would prefer that Miss Yemen survive the wilds of your location intact. Your bonus for taking on an apprentice will be provided monthly.

If you need more information, please don't contact me. This is a nonnegotiable requirement, particularly since you are already on notice for your inability to control Queen Mab, whom you introduced to Delouth.

Sincerely,
Rachel Jensen
Human Resource Manager

CN008

Laboratory Record
Patterns of Myosin Phosphatase in Pixie Muscle
Anne Ingen
Department of Cryptozoology & Molecular Mysticism
Delouth Dictionary
Elbert, Colorado 80106
(555) 721-3092

4 Sept 2033

Title: Primary Culture, Pixie pectoralis and supracoracoideus muscle

Purpose: To understand pixie wing anatomy

Introduction: I believe pixie wing anatomy is inherently different in comparison to regular flying creatures (e.g., birds). I need to dissect a pixie to be sure, but I have had issues navigating and negotiating for one in the past. I hope to receive one of the newly dead from their latest war.

Materials and Methods: The pixie queen has agreed to provide to me as many dead as she can, in the hope that I will learn enough about their wing structure that I will be able to assist with reattachment or suturing when magic is not enough.

Procedures: Due to a recent agreement, I received three newly deceased from Queen Mab.

NOTE: One pixie is male. The other two are female. I am already noticing a difference in male and female biology.

Cleansed deceased with both aseptic solution from lab and cleansing spell learned from a recent copy of Delouth's Home Protection Manual.

NOTE: I was in the process of using #10 scalpel to cut away back surface of male pixie when the family arrived and took all three cadavers. Queen Mab is unreachable. Apparently, there is a pixie mutiny due to her agreement with me. Lab location may be unsafe.

CN009

Anne,

I saw that young woman go onto your property last week, but I haven't seen her since. Who is she? Is she alright? I thought about calling the authorities to check on you both but realized you probably have more control over them than I do. Ha. How the tables have turned.

Not that there was ever a bad table, mind you. I always believed in equal rights for people like you, but we were young once. You know how the world was, and I wasn't a person to stand up to anyone. I was timid back then.

But I never thought we were enemies, yet that's how you treat me! And I really wish you wouldn't.

Like last week, when you drove by when that hippogriff was destroying my fence and eating my flowers. You could have helped.

Or when I saw you in town. I know it was you. No one else local has that distinct salt-and-pepper afro. You didn't have to disappear the second we made eye contact. That was pretty clever, though.

I heard your farm is now considered a lab. Do you think you could give Bobby a job there? He's still at home, and he could walk over to work. He moved here after the divorce. Did I tell you my granddaughter, Mazie, has magic? She's only thirteen, and we don't see her much because of how wicked her momma is. The things I could tell you about that girl and her lies on my Bobby. You'd think he didn't rescue her from over there. One of them Asian countries. I always forget which one.

Anyway, I really wish phones still worked. I heard those with magic still get all kinds of technology through ley lines and the like. Is that true? It'd be nice to just call you. Though, now that I think of it, I don't think I have your number! Funny that. Neighbors for thirty years at least, and I don't think we ever shared numbers. I guess it's because we always saw each other on the street.

I can't seem to catch you at home these days.

Write back, will you?

Oh, and do consider Bobby for a job? He can do just about anything.

Your friend,
Carol

CN010

Artifice Securities Message Board

```
8:04 Neil—Okay, look. I think we should
just send Ingen a recommendation for
Euless Security.

9:00 Barney—Whoa, you'd rather give
Useless the booking than keep sending
folks there?

9:22 Neil—For the short of it, yes. For
the long, we don't have anyone else to go.

9:46 Walen—I heard Mark's in the hospital.

10:00 Neil—Yes.

10:01 Barney—Useless it is!
```

CN011

From: Delouth Labs <j.hofstader@delouthdictionary.org>
To: Anne Ingen <a.ingen@delouthdictionary.org>
Sent: Thursday, December 1, 2033 at 04:03:10 AM CST
Subject: Pixies: Lab Change Request

Hi there, Anne,

Christmas is coming! Or should I say Happy Yule? Winter Solstice? All the holidays! Happy holidays!

I am following up with your recent request to change your lab location. While I can respect the prompt payment and proper paperwork, we do not currently have a location suitable for your lab, particularly with the healthy pixie community that would likely follow. Also, we both know Jensen will likely disagree. I already know "there would be a large expense for moving as much equipment" as you are listed to have. I am returning your deposit forthwith ... in person!

Due to the urgent nature of your request, we here at Headquarters (basically me) feel that an in-person inspection is needed.

So, holidays and all, I'll be there before Christmas! The destruction of so many train systems has made exact days a bit difficult. But I should be there soon ... ish!

See you in a bit,

Jerry

CN012

La*blog*ology - La*magic*ology - La*crypto*ology
the best online resource for and about magic and laboratory professionals

Welcome to the Danger Zone:
How One Mage Is Making Big Waves

(Note: This is a partial interview.)

Where the world used to solely rely on medicine and the skilled labor of scientists, doctors, and other medical professionals, we have now added the powered hands of magicians, mages, and other professions to the mix. The global Reveal (colloquially called "The Reveal") of newly discovered creatures —creatures we once considered nightmares, dreams, folklore, and monsters—has changed our international engagement with how we look at the outside world, particularly as our status as apex predator has become tenuous at best.

However, Delouth Dictionary, once a fantasy and science fiction conglomerate, has become a moving force, ensuring international training, constantly updating manuals, and growing a workforce that can seamlessly integrate into hostile environments and help the local population with communication, protection, and navigation in this new world.

I discussed the importance of understanding pixies (and how she went about creating the current truce with them) and analytical techniques with cryptozoologist, Anne Ingen, MS, MLS, DDS. When it comes to laboratory experience, Ingen is a powerhouse. She started as a lowly lab assistant in 1995 while working on her associate in science and rose in the ranks as she furthered her academic career. We've previously discussed Anne's accomplishments in cryptozoology ([here](#)), but we haven't spent any time with the mage herself. As one of the leaders in the community of cryptozoology and magic, and the official leader in pixie anatomy, we sat down to have a face to face with the famed cryptozoologist.

Orion **(O)**: Hi, Anne! Thanks for speaking with me today.

Anne **(A)**: Hello, Orion. Well met.

O: Well met, indeed. So, let's get into it. Can you describe a typical day in the life of Anne Ingen?

A: Ha. Well, I'll skip past breakfast and a shower and jump straight into lab work.

O: Ha. Indeed.

A: I usually begin by looking at samples from our latest cadavers or inspection of lab notes from my assistants.

O: When you say cadavers, do you mean the pixies?

A: Sometimes. It depends on what gets delivered. Even though I am located in the Americas, my lab is considered international property. Every country has its criteria for being able to practice medical science, and not many labs have both the certification for international creatures and a medical scientist in place to run the lab, so I often get cadavers or live specimens from all over the world. But mostly cadavers.

O: Is it all delivery? Do you get into the field often to acquire your own creatures?

A: Hmm. Queen Mab has decided that I can't talk to you right now. *[sighs]*

O: Does Queen Mab run your lab or do you?

A: When it comes to a pixie autopsy site, I negotiate as I can. We are learning a massive amount of—oh, dear. She is destroying my latest samples. Perhaps we can interview again at a later date?

As you can see from the abrupt end to our interview, not everything is easy peasy when you're a cryptozoologist, particularly a medically trained one! But we all know you had to believe in magic to receive magic, and the stronger the belief, the greater the power. Anne Ingen is one of the most powerful magical scientists out there. I will update this blog when we finish our interview.

—Orion Langley, MD, CTZ, is currently a magical nurse at Hollymoon Teaching Hospital. She freelances for La*blank*ology, *Slayer Magazine*, and others. She has an upcoming book, *Why Beastly Is Problematic*, with Cryptid Press. You can find out more about her at her website cryptidali.com.

CN013

Anne,

    I would like you to know that I no longer consider you a friend. Bobby told me he saw your Gene and his wife just float by on one of those fancy magic-driven contraptions, and Gene WAS TALKING ON A PHONE. My Bobby said he tried to flag Gene down and his wife, that weird little Latin girl who used to wear all black (including lipstick), stuck her tongue out at him! Those kids have to be at least in their mid-thirties, if not older, because my Bobby is forty-two, and they not only ignored him, but when they did acknowledge him, it was to laugh at his—at our—misfortune.

    I believe I have been a good neighbor all these years. I didn't join in when they would talk about you when you kept trying to join the country club, and I could have. It definitely would have made me look better. And I really did think we could be friends in these new times, but I don't think I can be your friend if you can't get your child under control. Now, I sent Bobby over with this note, but I do hope you'll talk to him about that job I asked you about and about getting us a phone!

    Be a good neighbor. Be a responsible mage. Be the change.

    Your soon-to-be-former friend if you can't fix these problems,

Carol

CN014

Text stream between Euless Security members

Peter Dang (PD): yo i'm not doing this anymore find someone else

Jamarcus Johnson (JJ): what happened now?

PD: damned pixies turned my skin purple hair green

PD: then one of um compelled me to sing nursery rimes in town squar

PD: when I wasn't screaming, I was yelling like I was batshit long live Queen Mab

JJ: LOLOLOLOL! Bro. Send me a picture.

PD: Also no.

CN015

February 3, 2034

Microbiology Case Study: Seventy-three-year-old male with "starry-eyed" syndrome

Case History

A seventy-three-year-old male presented to the emergency department with a two-week history of star-gazing all night, mouth open, staring up at the stars. His past magical history was notable for communication with aliens (possible pixie or fae kidnapping) and a loss of two decades prior to the Reveal, during which time no one knew where he was. Patient returned after the Reveal.

Oral history indicated that the patient was foul-tempered prior to the disappearance, but returned with a much milder temperament and demeanor. Family does not want a return to previous, potentially abusive behavior from patient but would like for patient to stop spending nights outside, occasionally screaming at the stars.

Magical Identification

Blood cultures were procured for culture workup, magical ritual, and creature identification. No creature identity was established, but traces of magic indicate pixie dust in patient's eyes. Requested laboratory consideration from Ingen Lab through Delouth Dictionary.

Solution

Dr. Anne Ingen has requested the patient be transferred to lab for study.

CN016

Rachel Jensen, Human Resource Manager
Delouth Dictionaries
555-508-3405 | r.jensen@delouthdictionary.org | Seattle, Washington 98128

April 1, 2034

Anne Ingen, Sr. Lab Mage
555-721-3092 | a.ingen@delouthdictionary.org | Elbert, Colorado 80106

Dear Anne Ingen,

    I have recently received Jerry Hofstader's recommendation that you be allowed a new laboratory location due to constant interference with your work from Queen Mab's defectors. However, I fail to see how a four-inch creature (or two) could possibly cause enough issues to warrant the exorbitant cost required to move your lab. As such, please take this letter as an official denial from Delouth Dictionary.

    On another topic, please notify your lab assistant, Kari Yemen, that she has not contacted me, and she should, as I am concerned for her welfare. To be clear, I am her aunt, and a position with your lab should have guaranteed her safety. Tell her that I know she resented being sent there but not to be rude.

Basically: I do hope you haven't allowed something to happen to her.
Sincerely,
Rachel Jensen
Human Resource Manager

CN017

Anne,

We saw the fire go up in your barn. Haven't seen your car since. That little girl—Kari, was it?—ran into my Bobby, but she couldn't be bothered to stop and explain what happened. We still can't get past your barriers to the property, but that barn sure smoked for a long while. Can't say I'm surprised. People like you never worry about others, do you? You've always been like that. Snobby. Stuck up. Thinking you're better than others when we all know who the superior people are, don't we?

Anyway. I'm still waiting on one of those magical phones. I told Bobby if he got into the house, you wouldn't mind if he took one. I'm sending him back tonight, but thought it may be nice to let you know. I'm sure you won't mind, since it seems like you abandoned the property.

Thank you for being a good neighbor.
Carol

CN018

Transcript of voicemail, May 5, 2034
Recon Security Guard Randy Smith, Everest Security

"I just wanted to let you —ers know that —ck this job and everything about it. Y'all can kiss my —s. These —cking pixies! I know! I'm leaving! I'll never—I'm not the one that did that though! See! See, this is what I'm talking about! Can you hear them? I didn't do—Why did you send me here?"

CN019

From: Delouth Labs <j.hofstader@delouthdictionary.org>
To: Anne Ingen <a.ingen@delouthdictionary.org>
Sent: Thursday, May 4, 2034 at 02:43:30 PM CDT
Subject: Urgent

Anne, don't go in the lab. STAY AWAY.
j

CN020

Anne,
    WHERE IS MY BOBBY? You better answer me soon, or I swear that fire will be the last thing you need to be worried about.
    You know who this is from.
    Well, in case you don't. This is Carol. YOUR NEIGHBOR.

CN021

From: Ingen Lab <a.ingen@delouthdictionary.org>
To: Jerry Hofstader <j.hofstader@delouthdictionary.org>
Sent: Sunday, July 2, 2034 at 12:01:06 AM CDT
Subject: Relocation

Dear Jerry,
    Thanks for the warning. Even though I understand that she didn't believe in Queen Mab's power, her insistence that Delouth can do what they want and that my lab is Delouth property and should be open to them at all times was surprising. I still can't quite believe Jensen really tried to take over the lab. To expect me to be

removed from it, to be exiled to some backwater location at her behest …? Well, I feel sorry for the people she sent to go up against Q. M.

Anyway, the relocation went well. I set fire to the lab as instructed, and Kari stumbled through town and wailed. People really think my research died in that fire. She deserves an acting award. See about getting her one, will you?

I can't say I'm sorry to hear about what happened to Jensen later, really. Q.M. is not to be trifled with, and most of my lab findings have been very clear about that. To tell the truth, pixies, in general, should not be provoked, particularly by weaker species.

I'll send my latest findings to you as soon as Q.M. approves. We're making strides.

Anne

About the Author

Azure Arther is a college professor, mom, and all-around anxious creative. Her short stories and poems have appeared in dozens of publications, including *Aurealis, Uncharted Magazine, Andromeda Spaceways Magazine,* and *Writers of the Future.* You can keep up with her at azurearther.com.

Grand Opening: Cryptid Zoo

by Kate Dane

GRAND OPENING: CRYPTID ZOO
Come see the cryptids
Strange, unusual, and horrible monsters
Big and small! Swimming, walking, and flying!
From every corner of earth, we caught them
and brought them here for you!

Grand Opening Discounts
Don't miss the traveling cryptid zoo!!!!

The pictures on the row of holographic posters showed off giant sea snakes and swimmers, hairy two-legged creatures with snouts, horns, and gleaming eyes, four-legged creatures with fangs, and every environment—from snow to murky water, forests to gleaming lakes, bridges to swamps—in brilliant colors. All in lifelike 3D.

Dontay tugged on his mom's shirt. "I wanna go see the monsters."

Mom didn't turn away from the grocery checkout line. "Monsters will give you nightmares. I'll take you to the Bright Waters meet instead. You could cheer on your classmates. Racing is exciting, especially when they come down to the finish in a dead heat."

"I hate sports. Swimming from one line to another. It's not like they cross an ocean and fight off killer sharks." Dontay made shark-stabbing motions. "Besides, there's a discount."

"Spending money to see animals who wanted to live and hide in peace but are now trapped is cruel. You're supporting the hunters. That's cruelty, even if there *is* a discount."

"It's educational. I could write a school report. Please, Mom, please. The zoo travels. They'll leave, and I'll never get to see the cryptids."

"Well ..."

Well was almost a yes. "Some of those cryptids kill people and eat them. They've got claws and horns and fangs, and they move like eels. Swish-swish." Dontay made sinuous glides and a strike. "You don't want one of them to kill me, do you? I have to learn how to fight them."

"People are very rarely killed by cryptids. They hide. They will not attack you."

"See? Cryptids don't have good lives. They starve, they get hurt, and nobody looks after them. Now they have food and a warm place to eat, and people take care of them. That's an upgrade. I bet their food is expensive." Dontay looked up at his mom with the sad expression he used when he was in big trouble. "We can help feed them by buying tickets."

The checkout line moved ahead.

Mom chatted with the clerk and paid for her groceries.

They left the store.

Mom looked down at him. "If you promise you won't have nightmares—"

"Yes, yes. I promise so much."

"—*and* you'll write a report for school on one of the cryptids, not the whole zoo. You'll have to research that cryptid and how it lives in the wild. What it eats, how it hides, how it came to be. If you do all that, I'll take you."

"Yes, yes, yes!" Dontay spun in circles fast, faster, fastest. He was going to see a cryptid. They probably had models and maybe habitats or puzzles or holograms. Mom would buy him something to show at school. "You're the greatest mom ever."

Mom and Dontay arrived at the traveling cryptid zoo.

The souvenir shop had adult and baby cryptid models with fins and arms and legs that moved and eyes that flashed and mouths that opened with enormous teeth and fangs and fake fur that didn't get icky when wet. You could buy little trees and caves and fake food for your cryptid toy. There were pictures, too, and a booth where you could get a hologram of yourself with a cryptid hiding and watching you.

"I want one of me and my cryptid," Dontay said. "That one. Loch Nessie is giant, and I'll be jabbing at her with a sword."

"We paid to see a lot of cryptids. We'll look at them first." Mom moved toward the entrance. Cryptid enclosures lined a curving walkway, some higher, some lower, some filled with water, some dry land. "You're going to choose one. They might not have the Loch Ness Monster here. These are less-famous cryptids."

The enclosures had plaques on them with descriptions of what the cryptids ate and graphics showing their habitats.

> The Beast of Bray Road is a furred wolf creature able to walk on two legs. When the enclosure lights dim, you will see its eyes glow yellow. The Beast favors wooded areas and eats meat, preferring live meals. Its original habitat is the middle part of the continent.

"I don't like the fur."

The creature was way bigger than Mom and looked angry, like a smoke demon covered with fur. It stalked back and forth in its enclosure, paws big and toes splayed out like fins, slashing clawed hands through the air. Those claws could slice someone's throat. The Beast had a pointy muzzle and ears that poked up. It bared its teeth and growled, the sound blasting out of the enclosure's speakers.

The roar hurt Dontay's head. He backed up. "Wet fur gets matted. Like my Sasquatch toy, Oooky."

"Some fur sheds water." Mom clicked her teeth. "Cryptids might find shelter in caves. They might be smart enough to build roofs and walls."

The lights dimmed, and the Beast's eyes glowed an eerie yellow. They focused on Dontay, not his mom, as if considering how meaty he would be. The Beast snapped the air.

Dontay backed up more. The Beast's gaze followed him, and Dontay hurriedly moved on. "I'm not doing a report on him."

Mom followed. "What about the moose? It's white, an unusual color for a cryptid, and it only eats plants."

> The Specter Moose is three times the height of an average moose, ghostly white, and impervious to bullets, arrows, and knives. This herbivore's reported ability to avoid injury was tested repeatedly until it was determined to be a cruel investigation of an animal in captivity. Its ability to avoid serious injury appears to be a limited time-temporal shift out of phase with the hunter/investigating scientist, which allows weapons and projectiles to pass through the area occupied by the moose without inflicting injury.

"That's pretty cool." Dontay pressed his face against the enclosure's transparent barrier. "Except he only eats plants. I bet if a T. rex were alive, he would chomp the moose into beef bites."

The moose seemed to shimmer in place and moved its antlers down and up the way a bull might size someone up before charging.

Dontay moved away, keeping his gaze fixed on the moose. "If he can make weapons miss him, do you think he could walk through the wall? What keeps him locked in place?"

"I don't know." This time, Mom moved ahead. "If you don't want fur, what about one that flies?"

> The reptilian Snallygaster eats livestock and sometimes children. The Snallygaster has a metallic beak that can crush or pierce most natural substances. Tentacles hold prey for easy kills. The wings are leathery. Many specimens have only one eye. Snallygasters were captured from the Appalachian area of the United States. They may be difficult to observe in the enclosure since they spend much of their time camouflaged by trees.

Dontay peered around for several minutes. "I can't see any of them. This is no fun." He sped on, glancing at one enclosure, then another. Monsters were supposed to be exciting. These weren't.

Lots more fur, creatures doing boring swimming things, creatures on top of branches or lying in swamps, mostly gray and black and blue. No Loch Ness. The white moose was looking like his best bet.

Then another land enclosure caught his eye. He stopped. "This one."

Mom stopped behind him. "Are you sure? They don't look very special."

"They're wearing clothes." Dontay exhaled bubbles. "They're pretending to be people."

> Self-identified as "humans," these cryptids lived throughout the Earth. They acted like hive creatures, creating multi-storied living structures to protect themselves from the elements. Hive decoration varied by region. The names they assigned to various species of other cryptids are used in reference materials here, since the colonies engaged in extensive classification and literature. The hives also engaged in transportation of people, food, and materials in pseudo-commerce. The widespread nature of this cryptid demonstrates what coordinated effort can achieve despite a lack of aquatic abilities and intelligence.

The creatures stared at Dontay and his mom, eyes big, and vocalized as if trying to communicate. A range of higher- and lower-pitched sounds grated on Dontay's hearing organs.

Water ran down the face of a bigger, bulkier one.

A smaller, deformed one, with a bulging top and bottom, made wild gestures, pointing to the controls at the edge of the enclosure, grimacing and holding out cupped hands.

"They're weak. Most of the cryptids have weapons to attack. These don't. But they were the most powerful lifeforms on Earth until we arrived." Dontay swam closer. "They'd drown in our spaces. Don't you think they're fascinating?"

"They're disgusting." Mom read the more detailed notes. "Their skin would tear if it brushed coral. They use fire on their food. They would not survive without clothing or their hive structures. The zoo maintains a limited temperature variation for them to survive and provides a specialty diet. Do you really want to report on these feeble creatures?"

"Yes." Dontay plastered his tentacles against the plexiglass and flared his fins before the creatures called humans. "Take a selfie of us so it looks like my tentacles are crushing their heads and my fins are slicing their feet. I'm going to argue they're intelligent."

"Oh, Dontay. How can they be?" Mom smacked her teeth. "They grew up on land where animals screech and honk and twitter. They didn't need to build a civilization underwater. Intelligence is driven by adversity."

"You're right, I guess." Dontay's fins relaxed to their sleek form, and he spun to face his mom. "Can I have some as pets, though? They couldn't escape because they'd drown."

"I'll think about it," she said. The tone of her voice said this was a *no*, not a *maybe on the way to yes*. "Maintaining their habitat and diet would be expensive."

Dontay twirled back to the humans.

They stared at him, shoulders slumped, farther away from the enclosure's wall than they had been.

When Dontay waved three tentacles, they jumped back.

"They're afraid of me. They're smarter than the others. I bet we could make videos of them doing things. Like Zomber the lillygoo. He was worth a fortune. Let me try, please?"

Mom moved closer to the enclosure, colors swirling across her midsection while she pondered.

The humans were emitting sounds, taking turns instead of barking in unison.

"We can see what the zoo would charge. Only two of them, though, and the same gender. I don't want a litter of humans."

"Okay." Dontay somersaulted with joy, exhaling a complicated figure eight of bubbles. "I'll do the coolest report ever and make a fortune."

About the Author

When she's not writing, Kate Dane can be found curled up reading. She has a published collection of speculative fiction stories, *Plus or Minus Forever*, and her stories can be found in anthologies. Kate is always dreaming up new characters and new worlds. She writes offbeat stories with heart.

Accounts Payable Denies Your Request
by Julia Vee

From: Jim Liu <james.liu@flm.cryptidconservation.gov>
To: Karen Higgenbotham <khiggenbotham@accounting.forestry.gov>
Date: April 15, 2024
Time: 8:03 p.m.
Subject: Re: Budget Increase Request

Dear Ms. Higgenbotham,

    We tried to place an order for more hay, alfalfa, barley, and oats with the approved vendor Enchanted Horn Hay. Unfortunately, the requisitions department informed us we had exceeded our budget line item for feed supplies. I am writing to increase the department's annual budget by $25,000 for feed or a reallocation of the transportation expense line item to be applied toward the feed.

Sincerely,
Jim Liu, Forest Ranger IV
Forestry Land Management & Cryptid Conservation Division
Department of Forestry and Management

Accounts Payable Denies Your Request

From: Karen Higgenbotham
<khiggenbotham@accounting.forestry.gov>
To: Jim Liu <james.liu@flm.cryptidconservation.gov>
Date: April 16, 2024
Time: 7:58 a.m.
Subject: Re: Budget Increase Request

Dear Mr. Liu,

   The budgeting deadline has passed. If you wish to apply for an exception, please submit Form A-182793x, with a cc to Finance Director Marvin Sanchez <msanchez@accounting, forestry.gov>.

Best regards,
Karen Higgenbotham, Senior Clerk III
Accounts Payable
Department of Forestry and Management

From: Jim Liu <james.liu@flm.cryptidconservation.gov>
To: Karen Higgenbotham
<khiggenbotham@accounting.forestry.gov>
Cc: Marvin Sanchez <msanchez@accounting.forestry.gov>
Date: April 16, 2024
Time: 5:11 p.m.
Subject: Re: Budget Increase Request

Dear Ms. Higgenbotham and Mr. Sanchez,

   Attached please find the completed Form A-182793x. We are running low on feed for the horned cryptids and would appreciate you expediting this request.

Sincerely,
Jim Liu, Forest Ranger IV
Forestry Land Management & Cryptid Conservation Division
Department of Forestry and Management

From: Karen Higgenbotham <khiggenbotham@accounting.forestry.gov>
To: Jim Liu <james.liu@flm.cryptidconservation.gov>
Cc: Marvin Sanchez <msanchez@accounting.forestry.gov>
Date: April 17, 2024
Time: 9:01 a.m.
Subject: Re: Budget Increase Request

Dear Mr. Liu,

Thank you for submitting your budget increase request.

After careful review, we regret to inform you that your request does not meet the requirements for an exception.

We encourage you to submit a proposed budget for the next fiscal year.

Best regards,
Karen Higgenbotham, Senior Clerk III
Accounts Payable
Department of Forestry and Management

From: Jim Liu <james.liu@flm.cryptidconservation.gov>
To: Karen Higgenbotham <khiggenbotham@accounting.forestry.gov>
Cc: Marvin Sanchez <msanchez@accounting.forestry.gov>
Date: April 17, 2024
Time: 7:53 p.m.
Subject: Re: Budget Increase Request

Dear Ms. Higgenbotham,

As per my email on April 15, if we could just reallocate $25k of the transportation expense line item to the feed expense line item, we would still be within our total budget for the fiscal year.

Please reconsider the request so that we can get the feed ordered. The unicorns and karkadanns in particular are running through our supplies at a tremendous rate. The qilin are omnivores and have jaws like wolves, so they can hunt the local rabbit population to supplement their diet. However, we need to get feed to the karkadanns or there will be a severe impact on the surrounding environment.

Sincerely,
Jim Liu, Forest Ranger IV
Forestry Land Management & Cryptid Conservation Division
Department of Forestry and Management

From: Karen Higgenbotham <khiggenbotham@accounting.forestry.gov>
To: Jim Liu <james.liu@flm.cryptidconservation.gov>
Date: April 18, 2024
Time: 10:32 a.m.
Subject: Re: Budget Increase Request

Dear Mr. Liu,

Line items cannot be reallocated after the budgets are finalized. If you wish to apply for an exception, please submit Form A-25641s, with a cc to Finance Director Marvin Sanchez <msanchez@accounting.forestry.gov>.

Best regards,
Karen Higgenbotham, Senior Clerk III
Accounts Payable
Department of Forestry and Management

From: Jim Liu <james.liu@flm.cryptidconservation.gov>
To: Karen Higgenbotham <khiggenbotham@accounting.forestry.gov>
Cc: Marvin Sanchez <msanchez@accounting.forestry.gov>

Date: April 19, 2024
Time: 9:21 p.m.
Subject: Re: Budget Reallocation Request

Dear Ms. Higgenbotham and Mr. Sanchez,
    Per my initial email of April 15, I asked for a line reallocation and was told to fill out and submit Form A-182793x, which I did. Nonetheless, attached please find the completed Form A-25641s.
    I cannot emphasize to you enough how urgent this request is. After the last delegation "gifted" us with a small herd of karkadann, our feed provisions were clearly not sufficient to sustain this additional herd. The karkadann have the build of a buffalo and eat three times the amount the unicorns do. Furthermore, they become aggressive when hungry, which agitates the qilin pair. Qilin can fly and when they become startled, they launch into the canopy, damaging the enchanted silver mesh enclosure that surrounds the cryptid habitat.

Sincerely,
Jim Liu, Forest Ranger IV
Forestry Land Management & Cryptid Conservation Division
Department of Forestry and Management

    PS I am also forwarding the requisition request to Enchanted Horn Hay. Please approve and expedite.

From: Jim Liu <james.liu@flm.cryptidconservation.gov>
To: Karen Higgenbotham <khiggenbotham@accounting.forestry.gov>
Cc: Marvin Sanchez <msanchez@accounting.forestry.gov>
Date: April 19, 2024
Time: 9:22 p.m.
Subject: Fwd: Supply Order from Enchanted Horn Hay Req. No. 8521637-5214
From: do-not-reply <orders@req.forestry.gov>
To: Jim Liu <james.liu@flm.cryptidconservation.gov>
Date: April 15, 2024

Time: 9:30 a.m.
Subject: Supply Order from Enchanted Horn Hay Req. No. 8521637-5214

Your order to vendor ENCHANTED HORN HAY has been received. It will be confirmed once finance approves the budget variance.
Order status: PENDING

Requisitions and Supplies
Department of Forestry and Management

From: Karen Higgenbotham <khiggenbotham@accounting.forestry.gov>
To: Jim Liu <james.liu@flm.cryptidconservation.gov>
Cc: Marvin Sanchez <msanchez@accounting.forestry.gov>
Date: April 20, 2024
Time: 11:29 a.m.
Subject: Re: Budget Increase Request

Dear Mr. Liu,
Thank you for submitting your budget reallocation request.
After careful review, we regret to inform you that your request does not meet the requirements for an exception.
We encourage you to submit a proposed budget for the next fiscal year.

Best regards,
Karen Higgenbotham, Senior Clerk III
Accounts Payable
Department of Forestry and Management

From: Marvin Sanchez <msanchez@accounting.forestry.gov>

To: Karen Higgenbotham <khiggenbotham@accounting.forestry.gov>
Date: April 21, 2024
Time: 8:04 a.m.
Subject: Re: Jim from Cryptids

Karen – got a bunch of angry voicemails from some ranger named Jim over in Cryptids. Said something about unicorn food. Would you take care of it? Thx.

Marvin Sanchez
Finance Director
Department of Forestry and Management

From: Karen Higgenbotham <khiggenbotham@accounting.forestry.gov>
To: Marvin Sanchez <msanchez@accounting.forestry.gov>
Date: April 21, 2024
Time: 8:05 a.m.
Subject: Re: Jim from Cryptids

Marvin,
    I've been responding to Jim Liu about the budget guidelines. He's hopelessly late, and he's asking for a 50% increase in the feed line item—it's overreaching and fiscally irresponsible.

Best regards,
Karen Higgenbotham, Senior Clerk III
Accounts Payable
Department of Forestry and Management

From: Karen Higgenbotham
<khiggenbotham@accounting.forestry.gov>

ACCOUNTS PAYABLE DENIES YOUR REQUEST   47

To: Jim Liu <james.liu@flm.cryptidconservation.gov>
Date: April 21, 2024
Time: 8:07 a.m.
Subject: Re: Budget Increase Request

Mr. Liu,

    Kindly do not bother Mr. Sanchez with your budget issues. We have a process we all need to follow.

    I direct you to the internal FAQ located here.

Best regards,
Karen Higgenbotham, Senior Clerk III
Accounts Payable
Department of Forestry and Management

From: Jim Liu <james.liu@flm.cryptidconservation.gov>
To: Karen Higgenbotham <khiggenbotham@accounting.forestry.gov>
Date: April 21, 2024
Time: 9:11 p.m.
Subject: Re: Budget Increase Request

Look Karen,

    I've tried to follow all your processes, but you don't seem to understand that I have hungry cryptids on my hands. They eat literal tons of hay and oats, and we are about to run out. Do you know what is standing between you and a herd of rampaging karkadann and their poisonous horns? A thin piece of silver mesh, which the agitated qilin are currently destroying.

Sincerely,
Jim Liu, Forest Ranger IV
Forestry Land Management & Cryptid Conservation Division
Department of Forestry and Management

It has been 3 days since you received this email. Respond?

From: Jim Liu <james.liu@flm.cryptidconservation.gov>
To: Karen Higgenbotham <khiggenbotham@accounting.forestry.gov>
Date: April 21, 2024
Time: 9:11 p.m.
Subject: Re: Budget Increase Request

Look Karen,

 I've tried to follow all your processes, but you don't seem to understand that I have hungry cryptids on my hands ...

From: Karen Higgenbotham <khiggenbotham@accounting.forestry.gov>
To: Jim Liu <james.liu@flm.cryptidconservation.gov>
Date: April 25, 2024
Time: 7:59 a.m.
Subject: Re: Budget Increase Request

There is no need for hostility.
 I direct you to the Code of Civility located here.

Best regards,
Karen Higgenbotham, Senior Clerk III
Accounts Payable
Department of Forestry and Management

From: Jim Liu <james.liu@flm.cryptidconservation.gov>
To: Karen Higgenbotham <khiggenbotham@accounting.forestry.gov>
Date: April 25, 2024

Time: 11:28 p.m.
Subject: Re: Budget Increase Request

Give me the food budget, Karen.

Sincerely,
Jim Liu, Forest Ranger IV
Forestry Land Management & Cryptid Conservation Division
Department of Forestry and Management

From: do-not-reply <transportconfirmation@flm.cryptidconservation.gov>
To: Marvin Sanchez <msanchez@accounting.forestry.gov>
Date: April 26, 2024
Time: 5:00 p.m.
Subject: Your Oversized Overnight Express Package Is On Its Way!

You can follow the tracking of this package here. Please be available for signing during business hours on April 27, 2024.

Oversized Transportation & Hauling
Forestry Land Management & Cryptid Conservation Division
Department of Forestry and Management

From: Marvin Sanchez <msanchez@accounting.forestry.gov>
To: Karen Higgenbotham <khiggenbotham@accounting.forestry.gov>
Date: April 27, 2024
Time: 8:21 a.m.
Subject: Re: Delivery?

Karen—Did you order something? Someone needs to be there to

sign for it today, but I've got a dentist appointment this afternoon. Could you take care of it? Thx.

Marvin Sanchez
Finance Director
Department of Forestry and Management

From: Raj R. Mehra <rrmehra@req.forestry.gov>
To: Marvin Sanchez <msanchez@accounting.forestry.gov>
Date: April 28, 2024
Time: 9:07 a.m.
Subject: Re: Supply Order from Enchanted Horn Hay Req. No. 8521637-5214

Hey Marvin,

    I am writing to follow up on the pending order for Enchanted Horn Hay that awaits finance approval. I have left you a vmail as well. I wrote to Karen earlier this morning, but received the autoresponder that she was out on leave indefinitely.

Raj R. Mehra, Vendor Relations
Requisitions and Supplies
Department of Forestry and Management

From: Marvin Sanchez <msanchez@accounting.forestry.gov>
To: Raj R. Mehra <rrmehra@req.forestry.gov>
Date: April 28, 2024
Time: 11:09 a.m.
Subject: Re: Supply Order from Enchanted Horn Hay Req. No. 8521637-5214

Hi Raj,

Sorry I missed your call earlier. Played nine holes this morning with the VP.

Karen had an incident yesterday when a pair of qilin were delivered to the office. Apparently, they started flying everywhere and left their calling card all over Karen and her cubicle. Also got into the oatmeal in the staff room. She's out on medical leave for a while.

Anyway, I approved the order. Go ahead and get that feed shipped over to Jim Liu, pronto!

Thx.

Marvin Sanchez
Finance Director
Department of Forestry and Management

About the Author

Julia was that Gen X kid who rode their bike to the library or bookstore and spent all day there. On the way home, she drank out of people's garden hoses. Now her life looks nothing like that, but she still spends a lot of time in bookstores and libraries. She remains largely unsupervised and gets paid to make up stuff. She writes with her childhood friend Ken Bebelle. Together, they have written over a million words and their books include the Seattle Slayers series and the Phoenix Hoard series.

Night Contractors
by Rebecca J. Carlson

Hi Alan,

Thanks for your interest in my property at 56-019 Kamehameha Hwy. You asked why I'm selling it at below market value.

Full disclosure.

I've always wanted to move back to Hawaii. All my best memories happened there, in the years before my family moved to Arizona when I was ten. I'd been watching, and saving up, and when this little two-story vacation rental with a manager's apartment came on the market, I jumped at the chance. It's way out on the northwest shore of Oahu, right between the highway and the beach. There's a long, sandy driveway through a dense stand of sea grapes and ironwood trees, and then a clearing with the ocean right there in the backyard. Paradise! I've attached a few photos so you can see what I mean.

I bought it sight unseen, so I expected a few issues. Nature isn't friendly to anything you build on a tropical island. Big ferns choked the rain gutters, moss ate its way up the fascia, rust bled from the bolts on the stair railings. Nothing I couldn't handle, though. I cleaned the place up, gave it a fresh coat of paint, took pictures, and posted on VRBO. Two hours later, I had my first renters sign up, and by the end of the week, I had the whole summer booked out. It was a good thing too. I'd basically sold my soul to get the place, and without renters coming in right away, there was no way I could cover the mortgage.

Only one problem. To get my business license as a property manager in Hawaii, my property had to pass an inspection.

The inspector showed up in this white pickup that came bouncing along my sandy driveway. The truck pulled to a stop and a huge Polynesian guy in shorts and a polo shirt hefted himself out. He strolled up, not smiling. From the look on his face, I knew what he was thinking. *Here's one ha'ole from the mainland trying to make a buck, get rich off all the tourists come to trash our island.*

Not me. I belonged here. I was only trying to find a way to stay.

We said good morning and shook hands.

"Where you from?" he asked with a glance at his clipboard.

"Just moved from Arizona, but I was born here."

His voice warmed a little. "Oh yeah?"

"I'm Hawaiian on my mom's side," I said, trying to score some local-boy points. "My dad worked at a military base here before we moved away."

"Oh yeah, what base?"

"Schofield."

"Yeah, my cousin works out there."

This kind of small chat went on as the inspector circled the property, then shone his flashlight into every nook and cranny on the inside of the house.

When we weren't talking, I got to thinking about my *tutu*, my Hawaiian grandma. I wished she'd lived long enough to see me move home to the island. I remembered her stories, like the one about her uncle who almost ran into the Night Marchers, torch-carrying warriors who would take your soul if you so much as looked at them. Then there was the one about her cousin, who saw our family's owl spirit-guardian by the side of the road and slowed his car down just in time to avoid being hit by a runaway truck. My mom would always smile and shake her head at these stories. Mom might not have believed they were true, but I could tell Tutu did. A small part of me still believed too.

Maybe it was that kind of magical thinking that had me hoping the inspector would give me a break. No such luck. When we got back outside, he shook his head as he wrote on his clipboard. "So this place, sorry, brah, not in good shape. Maybe better to knock it down and start over."

Cold disbelief tumbled my insides like I'd been tossed by an ocean wave. Sure, maybe the roof was sagging in that one spot, and the stairs wobbled a little, and there were some water stains on the ceiling I hadn't painted over yet, but it couldn't have been that bad. Besides, I didn't have the cash for any kind of major construction work. I was already going to be short on grocery money until my first renters came. I'd been wondering if I'd have to go up in the mountains and hunt pig for food.

"If you can get these repairs done, you're open for business." He tore a yellow sheet from his clipboard with his meaty paw and handed it to me. "Good luck."

I kept my eyes on the paper, gripping it tight. Repair roof, replace rain gutters, rebuild deck, reinforce stair posts, install hurricane ties—the list went on. I muttered a few choice words, the kind that if my tutu had heard coming out of my mouth, she would have whacked me up the head with her slippah.

I didn't know how to do any of the stuff on the list, and no amount of YouTube videos was going to teach me. Sweating despite the cool sea breeze, I climbed the stairs to my apartment, flipped open my laptop, and looked up local contractors. All of them seemed to be out in Honolulu or Kaneohe, almost an hour away. As I called down the list, not one of them could make it out in less than a month. I finally got one who said he'd come in a few days, but then he didn't show up and wouldn't answer my calls. I guess nobody wanted to drive an hour down a long, winding, pot-holed highway out to the edge of nowhere. Not that the drive isn't absolutely worth it. The vacationers know it. They come out in droves. Like I said, I had no trouble finding renters. I just couldn't line up a contractor.

It was only two weeks until my first renters were due to arrive, and I was going crazy. I could not afford to cancel on my customers. After another round of fruitless calls, I threw my phone onto my bed and walked out to the beach. The cool salty air, the rumble of the surf, all that blue. I couldn't believe I might have to give it up because of some stupid building inspection code.

One of my neighbors came down the beach, strolling across the sand with a surfer's easy grace. His dog, a low-slung yellow mutt with big, pointed ears, pulled on his leash and sniffed at the crab holes. My neighbor stopped to talk, and pretty soon I was telling him my problems.

"So you know anyone who does contracting work up here?" I asked. "I got all these repairs to do, and I can't get anyone to come from town."

He said nothing, seemed to weigh me. "I know some guys," he said, his brown face serious.

"Great, can you give me their number?"

"They don't got one, but I'll tell you how to get them to stop by your place. One thing, though. They don't like anyone to watch while they're working, and they want their pay in advance."

That sounded shady. I didn't like it. I almost said no, but I was desperate. "Yeah, sure, I'll talk to them."

He smiled like I'd said something funny. "No need. Just leave them a list."

"That's all? How fast do they work?" I asked.

"Real fast," he said, still with that smile. "They do good work too."

"So, what do I got to do?"

He told me.

I kept asking if he was serious, and he kept shaking his head and saying, "That's what you gotta do."

"Who are these guys?" I asked.

"Some local boys," he said. "Been here a long time. Trust me, they do good work."

It was weird. So weird, I wasted three more days trying again to find a contractor before I gave up and took my neighbor's advice. All I could think was that the guy wanted to prank me.

I went to the grocery store and bought some bags of poi. I never liked poi. It's like cold, runny, purple-gray mashed potatoes. You make it by pounding taro root to mush, then leaving it out on the counter to get sour. I guess the Hawaiian in me never reached my taste buds because I can't stand the stuff.

Next, I went to L&L Barbecue and ordered ten shrimp plates.

"Having a party?" the girl at the register asked me.

"Yeah," I said with a smile, though I could feel my ears heating up. Party for no one. A party with no guests. My neighbor was almost for sure trying to pull one on me.

When I got home, I put the poi in a big bowl and set the shrimp plates out on the porch. This was their pay, my dog-walking friend had explained. All they wanted was a good dinner. I pinned the yellow paper the inspector had left me to the porch with a big chunk of rock so the wind wouldn't blow it away. The whole time I thought that my dog-walking friend was watching to see if I'd really do it, and then he'd come and grab everything and go have *himself* a good dinner.

Fine.

I was desperate, like I said.

I went upstairs to my apartment and shut the door. I wanted to keep an eye on the driveway to see if anyone came, but my friend had warned me not to watch. It seemed more suspicious every minute, and those shrimp plates had not been cheap.

I watched Netflix for a while, and just before I went to bed, I heard growling outside. Dogs! That's who had come to dinner. I almost went down to chase them away, but I was too tired and angry to clean up whatever mess they were making, so I went to bed.

When I went to check the damage the next morning, the porch was perfectly clean except for two things: the big metal bowl that had been full of poi, and my list still under its rock. The Styrofoam boxes of shrimp were nowhere in sight. Not a scrap, not a grain of rice anywhere. A thin film of water coated the bottom of the bowl, seawater from the smell of it.

And, of course, none of the work had been done.

If that guy ever walked his dog past my place again, I'd have a few things to say to him. He must have come and taken all the food. Maybe that was his dog I'd heard growling.

Then I noticed the paper. It had been turned over, and someone had written on the back in what looked like thick charcoal pencil.

It was a list of building supplies.

They needed supplies so they could do the work. They were going to do it if I got the stuff for them.

Oh, man. Did I go for this or not?

I went for it.

In town, I loaded my pickup with everything on the list. Wood, paint, shingles, gutters, bags of cement. That was another few thousand on my credit card, and I topped it off with another two hundred by picking up dinner again.

I unloaded all the supplies, left the food and the list on the porch, then went upstairs to my apartment. This time, I sat by my window and listened. Everything was quiet. I dozed off and on in my chair until morning came. By then I was feeling thoroughly stupid. Nobody had come. If they had, and they were working, I would have heard the noise.

When I went downstairs to check the porch, the food was gone, just like the first night, and the building supplies were gone too. Great. I'd been robbed.

Then I glanced up at the front windows. Instead of cracking paint and decaying wood, the frames were all new.

I walked around the house. Rain gutters replaced. No more termite damage on the porch. Roof repaired. I couldn't believe that I hadn't heard hammers or anything. The crack in the cement pad under the carport was patched. They'd even done some things I hadn't put on the list. All in one night!

And all for a pickup load of building supplies and a few hundred bucks' worth of food.

This was the best deal ever. Who were these guys? No wonder they didn't advertise. Everybody would use them.

I started thinking of what else I wanted done around the place. The repairs were great, but I had some improvements in mind. First thing, I called the inspector to tell him he could come back any time. Then I made a new list and headed to town for more building supplies. On the way home, a roadside pop-up canopy was selling lau lau plates, so I picked up twenty.

"Having a party?" the woman asked as she handed me the Styrofoam boxes.

"Big party, Aunty," I said.

The next morning, every last scrap of food was gone, the plates were in the garbage, the bowl was rinsed out, and my place looked amazing. My guys had put in a wooden walkway from the house to the beach, installed an outside shower so guests could rinse the sand off before going inside, put in a koi pond with a fountain, and a gazebo with a swing. The place actually looked like the million bucks it had cost me, even by mainland standards. I'm telling you, Alan, it is, without a doubt, the very best deal on the market in the neighborhood.

That's when it hit me.

There was another story my tutu had told me, about little people who lived in the mountains and loved to build things. They'd left their mysterious stone walls snaking all over the islands and gone into hiding when the first Hawaiians arrived in their canoes thousands of years ago.

Menehune.

It was crazy, but what other explanation did I have? No one in their right mind would do all that work just for a few plates of food, and no one ever worked that fast!

So, how much more would people pay to vacation in a place that had been fixed up by real menehune? Maybe if I set out one more feast, not asking for any more work, they'd let me get a picture. I imagined a shot of them posing on my porch, all throwing a *shaka*. It would be the perfect promo picture. Sure, people would think it was a fake, you know, Photoshopped or something. That didn't matter. It just had to get people's attention. This was going to be great.

As I went to pick up dinner for that night, I kicked around in my head what to call the place. Menehune Lodge. Menehune Cove. Menehune Beach. None of them had the right ring.

I put out the food again, more than ever. It was my "thank you" for all the work well done. After waiting upstairs, listening for hours, I heard the soft growls that I'd thought were dogs on that first night. I grabbed my cell phone and opened my front door as quietly as I could.

The noises from down by the porch fell silent. They'd heard me.

I paused at the top of the stairs and almost went back in. If these guys didn't want to be seen, then what was I doing messing with them like this? I could almost see Tutu giving me that warning glare of hers. But I wanted my picture, so I took the first step down the stairs. As soon as my slippah touched the step, there was a rustle, a thumping of many small feet, and a crash in the bushes around the far side of the house. I ran down to the porch, but by the time I got there, all the food boxes were gone along with my big metal bowl of poi. And there was not a single menehune in sight.

The next day, I went to town and got one of those surveillance camera systems. Maybe I couldn't get a good staged shot, but I might get something. I hid the camera up high under the eaves of the house and pointed it toward the porch. Then I went and got more food.

"Didn't I see you here yesterday? You got a family reunion going on or something?" the kid at the grocery store deli counter asked me.

"Something like that."

That night, I watched my security camera monitor. Nothing happened until 1:17 in the morning.

Something came onto my porch. It looked like a kid, maybe two years old, but he didn't move like a kid. He had a stealthy, powerful walk, an unruly bush of curly black hair, dark brown skin, and a skirt of green leaves. My camera was too high up to see his face. He stood and surveyed the food with fists on his hips. A second curly black head moved into the frame, then out again. I got the sense that this first one was the leader, and he was making sure everything was safe. I double-checked that my camera system was recording. This was the best. Absolutely amazing. I could create a whole new social media account just to post my menehune videos.

As if he'd heard me thinking about him, the menehune chief whipped his head around to stare straight at the camera. Fury blazed in his bulging eyes, and his white teeth flashed. It was the most terrifying jump scare I'd ever seen.

He vanished so quick I didn't see which way he went.

With a little pop, the lights in my room flared and went dead.

It took me a long time to remember where the circuit breaker box was in my new place. I wandered around in the dark with my phone's flashlight, scanning the walls. When I found the box, every breaker in the place had been tripped. I switched the power on again.

My camera was completely fried, and the SD card that was supposed to be recording the footage had absolutely nothing on it.

Okay, I got the message.

The next morning, my porch was clean except for my metal bowl, which they'd been kind enough to bring back. Lying in the bottom of the bowl, pinned under a chunk of coral, was a paper napkin from one of the food boxes. Thick charcoal lines spelled out four words:

TONIGHT
BEACH
BRING CAMERA

It was the same handwriting as that first supply list, so I knew it was the menehune. Maybe they'd talked it over and decided that a few of them wouldn't mind being photographed after all. I'd fed them for nearly a week now. It was the least they could do, wasn't it?

I made sure to charge my phone.

Of course, it crossed my mind that maybe it would be better not to go, but I kept thinking about how much attention I'd get with the story that menehune had fixed up my place. I'd be the most popular vacation rental on Oahu's North Shore.

When the sun set, I was on the beach.

The wind picked up, and clouds covered the sky. It wasn't long before I was wishing I'd brought a jacket. The waves reflected the gleam of my back porch light, but along the beach it was pitch-dark. Wind and surf filled my ears. I wanted to go back to the house and get something warmer to wear, but I didn't want to miss the menehune.

Should I have brought them food? Of course I should have. It's Hawaii. Always bring food. But even if I had brought them something, it would have been hard to keep it from blowing away. The wind was wild.

Over the wind, I heard another sound.

Drums.

My first thought was that it was the sound of the show at the luau down the beach, but that was too far away. Besides, the sound came from the direction of my house. I strained my eyes, peering into the wall of shadow that was the jungle around my property.

Flickering lights appeared deep in the trees, too orange to be car headlights from the highway. The lights grew brighter, came closer. Torches. A long line of them stretching like a net coming toward the beach.

The Night Marchers.

To look at them was forbidden. You'd die on the spot and your soul would march with them forever.

If you ever hear them coming, run and get inside, Tutu had said.

Too late for that. I couldn't get to my house. Running inside would take me straight toward them. They were almost out of the trees. They'd see me for sure.

Tutu's voice rang in my head. *If you can't run, lie down flat on your belly, hide your eyes, and don't look up until they gone.*

I flopped to the sand, propped my forehead on my arms, closed my eyes tight, and waited to die.

The drums came closer, thundering louder than the surf. Wind pelted me with icy cold sand that stung like needles and blew into my ears. Still, the drums pounded louder. Marching footfalls thumped close by my head, and the salt air smelled of torch smoke. I tried to sink down into the sand and disappear.

Sudden rain drenched me. I shivered in the cold and the wind, wondering if I would freeze to death on a beach in Hawaii. I had a horrible, aching need to get warm, but I didn't dare move, not when I could still hear those drums and feel footsteps shaking the sand underneath me. My insides turned to poi, sour and pounded to death.

I never moved. Not even after the drums passed by and faded in the distance and it was only the wind, rain, and waves crashing angry against the shore. Not until the sky grew light and I heard a different kind of sound: the rattle of a chain and the quick footfalls of a dog walking across the sand.

I lifted my head, shocked to see it was morning. I couldn't remember dozing off. My eyes throbbed from being pressed shut. A faint gray dawn struggled through the thick clouds overhead, and the waves churned an ugly, lead-colored sea.

"Auwe!" my dog-walking friend exclaimed under his breath, "You okay, brah?"

I rolled into a sitting position. Every inch of my exposed skin felt like someone had gone over it with sandpaper. My phone lay half-buried, drenched, with sand wedged in every crevice. I didn't have to check to know it was destroyed.

I managed a nod.

My neighbor reached down and picked up my phone. He brushed it off and handed it to me. He knew what had happened. I could see it in the way he shook his head at the trees, the way his gaze followed the trails of large, barefoot prints deep in the sand.

"You lucky you still here," was all he said.

And that's why the place is going cheap.

Honest, I swear, it's in fantastic shape. Passed inspection with no problem, got the papers to prove it. Those guys do good work.

Looking forward to considering an offer from you.

Best,

Jim

About the Author

Rebecca J. Carlson lives at the end of a long, winding, pot-holed highway that leads to a beach with the most beautiful sunrises on the planet. "Night Contractors" is based on local lore from her hometown of La'ie, Hawaii. She's the author of the Barley and Rye books, a fantasy adventure series for young readers.

The Gurt Dug of New Bannockburn

by Jason Kristopher

They're here, finally, to cage me or kill me.

—TRANSMISSION BEGINS—

Subject: Expedition Log
Planet: New Bannockburn
Transmission Code: Epsilon-7
Commander: Captain Elena Voss-Ragen
Recipient: Galactic Exploration Authority, Central Command
Date: 3692.75 sidereal-2

Locals deny existence of [REDACTED: CLASSIFIED] species unit. Initiating search. Further information when able.

—TRANSMISSION ENDS—

  Legends are like that, sometimes.
  That's how it started with the scuttling, chittering tetrapods in the tunnel-town recesses of Ajax Beta. Who are really just lovely, once you get to know them, provided you stay out of their nests during mating season.
  And with the towering "faerie-fire dragons" of the Western Wastes on Grimnore VI, though they're only weather patterns

masquerading as puzzles for the biophysicists who continue scratching their heads and try to give meaning to the meaningless.

Point is, legends have to start somewhere. Mine started that way.

And for all of them, the same fate when caught: cages—or death, if they're lucky.

All *I* wanted to do, though, was forget the incessant wars and the horrors I inflicted on Ajax Beta and Grimnore VI and all the rest. So much pain, in so many places, to so many lives, mine included.

I just wanted to curl up here on this hillside, my tail under me and my snout on my paws, enjoying the serene blue sunset over the purple fields, with no one else anywhere nearby, canix or human or tetrapod or anything else.

I needed to forget.

Not easy to do when you're being hunted for your abilities. The abilities I never wanted, never asked for, and can't lose, even if I haven't killed anything or anyone in years other than fish and rodents.

Even now, as I record this holo, the scent of these humans following me wafts over the waving grass on the breeze that tickles my beard. My ears flick forward, and I snort softly as the quiet clink of gear and the rattle of dislodged stones tells me the soldiers are too close for comfort.

Time to move again.

—TRANSMISSION BEGINS—

Site located, abandoned. Scout reports inconsistent tracking capability. Locals unhelpful, insist subject nonexistent. Resuming search.

—TRANSMISSION ENDS—

They got close that time.

Some locals spotted them and caused a ruckus, throwing off their track-bot. The locals like me, though they were tough to parse at first.

"Scamper, did ye, aye? Yer a right braw 'un. Ye mine us ae the auld hame. Gaw'n hide; we-ul keep ye safe, hen."

I had to use my transcoder, but that's one of the reasons I chose this world. The locals come from hardy stock, back on Old Earth, as did my kind originally, or so these folk tell me. Even back then, they were sometimes unintelligible, distrusting of outsiders, and partial to the, shall we say, more *natural* forms of the universe.

Not that anyone would call me or my kind *natural* anymore. Not after what was done to us.

I scared them, at first, when I stepped off the transport. I'm certainly a bit much for most humans at first glance.

Even my distant cousins ran from me, though they eventually came over and said hello with much fuss.

I had no plans when I arrived, still shaking from the last battle, where I'd gone AWOL.

Where it had all gone wrong, for all the ones like me.

So I'd found the only room available to me, and the human was wide-eyed when she scanned the code on my cred-tag. Hardly surprising. Even during the wars, my kind weren't too prevalent in civilian areas, but eventually she just shrugged and pointed up the stairs to the guest rooms.

More than a week later, I finally moved on, tired of the crowds and noise and too many smells from too many humans in too little space.

She said she was sorry to see me go. I believed her.

That kind human and all her kin are long dead now, and I'm still roaming the hills. I've seen few of the human locals in many years, but occasionally I'll save one of their sim-sheep or other livestock, and they'll leave a little care package out.

That's how legends start. And now, apparently, those legends have called in the hunters.

As legends always do.

I shouldn't backtrack, ever, but I haven't been here in years, and I'm always careful to pack out what I bring in. One *good* thing the humans taught me. There's soft purple grass to lie on, some good springs a little further up the hill, and the views can't be beat.

Best of all, no humans. Or anyone else. Not for miles.

I can't stay, not for long, and not just because of Captain Voss-Ragen and her cronies.

Earlier, I snuck in and got to her lander when her squad was out hunting for me. The tech was updated, but my augment still worked, and I accessed her files and found what I needed.

It had been a long time since I *connected*, and I still hated it, except for these holos. But I can't deny the augment was handy.

I left no tracks or other evidence. I don't have much time left on my scent-masker, but that was as good a use for it as any the Corps gave me. The water of the loch was extra cold today, and the somewhat matted gray-and-white fur of my coat still dripped from my first bath in quite some time. I'm not sure that they're tracking me by scent, but every bit helps.

This cave is smaller than I remembered. I had to duck as I walked in, and my ears still brushed the top of it. Maybe I've grown since I've been here, or maybe it's just the memories that fill my time now, being distorted by distance and, well, time.

The sun is going down, and my paw is cramping as I hold this holo-pad. Even with the damnable mods, there are some things that just don't come easy. Time to rest for the night. The good captain won't move her team after dark. Not when she's hunting one of us, anyway.

At least the stories the Corps spread during and after the war—tall tales, at best—are helping with that.

—TRANSMISSION BEGINS—

Subject evading in real time, knows we're here. Message rec'd: "Voss-Ragen: I'm out. Don't make me hurt you."
Subject confirmed: [REDACTED: CLASSIFIED], Unit 007. Proceeding as planned.

—TRANSMISSION ENDS—

This one is different, this human captain. Different from the ones before.

She's not following the usual procedure for the Corps, or whatever the Corps has turned into now. I've been gone long enough that it's probably changed hands a couple dozen times and gone through fifty different mission statements.

One of the "benefits," I suppose, of the treatments they gave us. After all, can't have your most vicious fighters dying of old age just a few years into a war.

Even now, thinking of those treatments makes me growl low in the back of my throat and raises the even-grayer-now hackles on the back of my neck. Still, life and war taught me not to let some stupid human get the better of me.

I am a thinking being.

I am a thinking being.

I am a thinking being.

Just repeating the mantra that Lucas taught me back in the ward helps me calm down. He wasn't going with us to the front, but he was smart.

Too different, they'd told him. *Too unmanageable. Too new.*

The Corps was stupid, sometimes. Hell, *humans* were stupid sometimes. Lucas was the best of us, of all the breeds, and it warmed my heart that he was out there, still alive. Still forging his own path and lighting the way for the rest of us.

Even if some of us had retreated from the universe and all its horrors.

It's another new-old place tonight, one that's familiar but also feels like I've outgrown it. A scattering of old leaves and other windswept detritus provides a soft bed over the rough stone floor of the cave, and the scents are all old. Faded.

Like me.

Memories of my first few years here flood back now, when I still had hope that things would change back in the world. That one of the few good ones would come find me, come bring me home and tell me that everything was done and that I could just be happy for a while.

I snorted at the innocence of those days.

The pack came off my back easily tonight. The long hike did me good, even if my muscles and the pads on my paws were sore and I was panting more than usual. I hadn't run this far in a while, and it annoyed me again that I had to do it because of some human.

There's a bright light in the distance. Damn. This captain has a brain in her head.
Wonderful.

—TRANSMISSION BEGINS—

Subject eludes, but scout suggests may be using old paths. Confirm launch of sat-track system. Est 1-2 rotations for contact.

—TRANSMISSION ENDS—

I should've forged a new path, I guess.
Lucas did.
But you get complacent as you age, and even *we* age, albeit so slowly glaciers call us ancient. Whatever ones of us survived the wars, anyway.
I'm still here. Well, it's another place, but I'm still safe and in hiding with none the wiser as I record this. I'm worried about what happened today.
It was the smell that woke me, my nose and its thousands of scent receptors working overtime as always. The scent was familiar and invaded my dreams. Maybe it was the impossibility of the smell that did it.
Crestin cakes didn't exist here. The ingredients would have to be imported, and the cost! I'd be surprised if anyone here on Bannockburn even knew what a crestin *was*. To say nothing of wanting to spend the unimaginable amount of creds to bring one here, milk it, process the milk, and then wait two years for it to ferment.
No, this was the good captain, tempting the legend, the monster, the "spirit in the hills" with a tasty reminder of its past, sure to bring it out of hiding. She'd done her research; she knew the cakes were irresistible to us from our training days.
Yes, they were tasty, and yes, I loved them, but I was also a thinking, intelligent being, and I knew what she was doing.
Still, it had been a long time.
A *long* time.

More than one generation of humans had been born, lived, and died since I had one of the cakes. The drool leaking out of my jaws and down my gray-black beard was proof of that, if nothing else.

So I did what I knew I shouldn't.

I turned on my scent-masker again and crept closer, onto an outcrop of rock covered in grass turned just the right way, and spied on the human squad as they tracked me, or tried to. I'd been keeping tabs on them for days, of course, but this was as close as I'd gotten.

Most of the squad hid under the thick, leafy branches of some sodura trees, but I knew they were there, and not just by their scents, though those were harder to pick out than I'd expected. Scent-maskers must've been upgraded in my time away, but we were always better, anyway.

They'd left their mind-prints unshielded though, which was odd for the Corps. Perhaps there weren't enough sensitives still around for it to be an issue. There were only humans in this squad, except for the track-bot, and I was surprised by that too.

No Ixs? What had the Corps done with them? I knew they wouldn't have any of *us* with them, after what happened, but *no* Ixs? I stayed still, scanning the sky, but saw none of the avix—giant Earth condors, reborn for war as undetectable, organic aerial scouts. Nor even a whiff of the docile-yet-dangerous equix packers, ubiquitous on most Corps expeditions.

Captain Voss-Ragen—Elena—was out front, down on one knee as she put the crestin cake on an upturned ration lid and set it on a flattish rock at the edge of a small clearing. She glanced around, but I knew that trick and stayed perfectly still.

She wasn't tall, a little over a meter and a half, with short, dark hair and a sort of quiet gravity to her movements that I knew most humans would envy. A presence, someone who was *in* the world, not just walking through it, and she reminded me of my first trainer. She hadn't lasted long with us. If only because she hated what was done to "improve" us, to make us more *useful* in the wars to come.

Elena made a point of showing she was unarmed as she walked back to the squad, and that confused me to no end. Did she really think I was *that* desperate, to fall for such an obvious plot to trap me? I waited quite a while, until she sighed, shook her head, and trudged into the woods with the others.

And now, here I am, brushing crestin crumbs from my beard with a paw. In this old hideout, miles from my usual haunts. Maybe, *perhaps, possibly,* I was wrong about this human?

—TRANSMISSION BEGINS—

Contact made at level 1. No comms, but good news. Hoping for more tomorrow.

—TRANSMISSION ENDS—

The nightmares brought me back this time.

I couldn't wait until tonight to record; my training, for good or ill, is in too deep, and I need to get this out.

My fortieth mission, or my hundred and fortieth ... there was no real distinction, especially in the dream. Another planet, another mission to "eradicate the enemy," though no one ever explained to me who, exactly, the enemy was. Just that I was to use my augments and teeth and claws to eradicate them.

I did.

So much blood on my muzzle that it took an hour to wash it all off.

The copper taste was in my mouth when I woke, and the flecks of red on the ground meant I'd bitten myself in my sleep.

Again.

That hadn't happened in a long time, either. Longer even than the last time I'd had one of those cakes. The psychoses evident in the early canix weren't *supposed* to happen at all to us later gens, but not everything the gene-wizards dreamed up actually worked the way it was supposed to.

And they'd certainly never intended any of their mods to work for this many years.

It's funny, in a way. Their experiments with us didn't just reverse the dichotomy of our age differentials, though they did that too, at first. They ended up completely obliterating them, turning those of us left into living legends.

Is it really life, though, when you spend it wandering the grassy hills and dark, wet moors and gazing into the crystal-clear lochs? No one nearby, no one to talk to, no one to experience life with.

Certainly none of us, the few who survived the wars, now scattered to the galactic winds. And our psychic connections, the ones the best human minds never figured out, were tenuous at best.

Just enough to know that there were some of us still out there, still holding on, somehow.

I hated being a soldier. I didn't like the killing, or the blood, or the "rewards" that always made me feel so small and stupid no matter how many I got or what they were for.

I hated life in the Corps.

But I hate this life too.

And I'm so, so tired.

—TRANSMISSION BEGINS—

Brief visual confirmation of subject. Subject file indicates post-human intelligence. Sighting likely purposeful. Progress slow but within limits.

—TRANSMISSION ENDS—

It was a local who made the choice for me. Or rather, a local child.

Sometimes pups escape their elders, even with humans. And that's what happened with this one. There was a yowling series of screeches from the next glen, and I raced off, my pack tightened down, my paws and legs strong and sure after all the new exercise I'd been forced into.

It didn't take long for me to track them, and sure enough, this young boy had stumbled into a nest of one of the galaxy's more annoying insects, the macra-beetle. The nest lay in the middle of a small stand of trees, hidden for the most part, unless you were careful and knew how to spot them.

The beetle's sting was painful, especially in large numbers, but you'd have to be stung by a whole swarm twice over to suffer any lingering effects.

That didn't help this foundling, maybe seven or eight years old, from screaming when he'd been stung as many times. Or when a local legend comes to life in front of their eyes, charging out of the underbrush.

I'm intimidating. I was bred that way. It's literally in my genes.

But I also know how to deal with the reaction it provokes in humans. Because that's there too.

I bent down, lowered my ears, and snorted as I shook my head, then nuzzled the young one's arm as he held it with the other, grimacing in pain but no longer shrieking. His long blond hair fell to one side and his eyes shot wide, not believing what he was seeing.

It wasn't my first time.

I sniffed at the stings, then gently dragged the boy by the collar away from the nest to rest against a tree. I nudged his arm again and went looking for the plant the older humans used in similar situations.

It wasn't until I'd burst back into the glen, bitter, slimy leaves in my mouth, that I picked up what my nose had been telling me: more humans.

Captain Elena and I locked eyes across the little grove as her squad came through the trees, and we both skidded to a stop. The child, for his part, glanced back and forth so fast that he had to be dizzy, before finally spotting the leaves I carried and, whimpering, reached out for me.

I took a few cautious steps, and when Elena and her squad didn't move, I kept going.

Here's the summary: the kid got their meds, I wasn't shot or captured, and Elena and I went our separate ways, giving me much to ponder.

She never even made a move toward me. Just squatted down to watch me, and I picked up nothing but awe, strangely, from her mind-print.

I'm in a new place tonight. It's fine, but I'm keeping my pack on, just in case.

—TRANSMISSION BEGINS—

Subject saved local child. Still no comms. Nonaggression from both Expo Unit and subject. Excellent progress.

—TRANSMISSION ENDS—

She spoke to me today.

Or at least tried to. After I realized my transcoder must be busted, I stopped trying to understand and just listened to her tone and her emotions from her mind-print.

It's crazy, but I don't think she wants to capture me.

There weren't *any* weapons on her, not even any "no-kill capture" variants. At least not any obvious ones.

Only one of her three-person squad had some sort of updated stun pistol, similar to the ones used years ago, but they never reached for it.

This is not the Corps I knew.

I smelled that on them. They were different.

But different enough?

I want to come home.

I want to be loved again.

To not be alone.

I didn't realize until today how much I want that.

—TRANSMISSION BEGINS—

Closest approach to subject yet. Comms initiated; no response, no aggression. Will try again.

—TRANSMISSION ENDS—

A new transcoder awaited me in the glen I wandered into this morning.

A *random* glen.

Either she knew where I was going, or she put them all over. But that meant she knew where I was. And I was careful with my tradecraft. I even walked reverse in my own footprints at one point.

Do you know how hard that is for a canix?

What's more is the message she left on the transcoder: "We mean you no harm. We are not here to take you, unless you want to come. We just want to talk, to tell you what's happened. Will you meet?"

A set of coordinates. Close, but not too close, and a field I've been to before. Lots of room to run if I needed or wanted to.

Dawn. Early, but I was always an early riser.

I left the transcoder there. I'm certain it was trackable.

I doubt I'll sleep tonight.

—TRANSMISSION BEGINS—

Comms established (one way). Mission parameters set. Subject aware of intentions.

—TRANSMISSION ENDS—

Dawn broke with crisp, cool air, filled with scents of all types and kinds, coming down from the mountains and blowing across the field.

Life here has a certain smell, different from nearly everywhere else I've ever been. Everything else aside, it was beautiful, and I stood for a moment just inside the trees, screened from view, and breathed it all in.

Of course I came. How could I not? My kind always had, for humans, and always would.

When called by those worthy, at any rate.

She stood shivering in the growing light, no weapons, no equipment other than the throat-mounted transcoder most humans from off-world wore. And most importantly, her squad wasn't there.

No scents, no mind-prints other than hers and some lingering higher-order insects.

I took a deep breath, then another. It was time. I was tired, and I'd either go home or it would all end here in this field. Not for her, just for me. I knew the kill-tooth would still work. That was the whole point.

Hope is a dangerous thing.

I hoped I wouldn't have to use the tooth.

I hoped I could finally go home.

I hoped.

She flinched, just a little, as I brushed through the trees, my eyes meeting hers even from a few hundred paces away. I didn't blame her; a canix coming toward you was always a little unnerving for humans.

Even thirty-five thousand years of mutual evolution can only do so much to calm them down.

Soon enough, we were eye-to-eye, barely a meter apart. I hadn't interacted with another human in decades outside of the occasional rescue, and I knew she'd never seen one of us in person until the other day with the child.

Elena was far too young for that.

She spoke, and the transcoder fumbled for a bit, trying different dialects, even a screeching one that made my eyes itch and both of us wince. Eventually, the output was in what I thought of as Terran Standard, though apparently that had evolved too, over the years, judging by the delay in translation.

"I'm Captain Elena Voss-Ragen of the Galactic Exploration Authority. I've—" She paused, glanced down, and I was shocked at the tears in her eyes. "I've been looking for you for a long, long time. So many of us have."

I considered that for a moment, cocking my head first to one side, then the other as I studied her.

She laughed a little, startling me and causing an involuntary jerk back.

Her eyes widened, and she clapped a hand over her mouth. "Oh, I'm sorry." She spread her arms wide. "It's just so much like—It doesn't matter. I truly mean you no harm. We really *have* been looking for you."

I peered at her again, then stepped a smidge closer to give her a good sniff, just for my scent-receptors to line up with her mind-print.

I coughed and cleared my throat, startling her in turn, and tried to avoid grinning, happy to be talking to a human again.

Her transcoder changed my own growls into what passed for Terran Standard.

"No Corps?" I asked, nudging the unfamiliar symbol on her sleeve with my snout before pulling back quickly out of reach.

She shook her head and frowned. "No Corps. They're gone, now. Disbanded. More than a hundred years ago. After what they did. To you. To all of you." She paused as her eyes widened. "How long have you been here?"

"Long time," I said, and scratched with my hind leg at an errant insect. "What want?" I tried to keep my tone neutral, which the transcoder helped with, but the longing for home made it tough.

A longing I thought I'd put behind me.

The tears were evident again as she took a breath, and her mind-print settled somewhat. "We know what happened to you." She shook her head. "No, that's not right. What our people *did* to you. I'm only here—my *family* is only here—because of what you did on Tassilon. You saved us."

She took a deep breath and a small step forward. "I'm here to ask you to come home, with us. To see the others who've come home too. To see what we've built in your honor and because of all you sacrificed. There's so much—"

I had no idea what to say. My mind raced. She was telling the truth; she couldn't lie to one of us. No human could. We scented and sensed lies, and neither triggered.

"Home," I said, allowing myself to *feel* the word for the first time in forever.

But the past isn't wiped away that easily. I sat back on my haunches and glared at her. "Cage. Kill. Blood." I snorted and shook my head, but I didn't leave.

It was a test.

"I ... I know what they did to you. What they made you do. We don't do that anymore, and haven't since you. Our young forced change." She looked away. "It was hard, but needed." She stared at me, but not aggressive, and there was no lie when she continued.

"No cage. No kill. No blood." She shuddered at the first as much as she did at the last in my list.

She'd passed.

I tilted my head again, then gazed at the world where I'd chosen to live for so long.

But it had never been my home.

And I so wanted one.

"Okay," I said to her, looking back. "Home."

She beamed a huge smile at me, and before either of us knew what was happening, she had reached out and up a little and was scratching me behind the ears.

"Good boy," she said.

And, as all the old gods are my witness, and heavens help me, I wagged my tail.

About the Author

Jason Kristopher is the award-winning, multi-genre author of *The Dying of the Light* zombie series as well as the upcoming *Elwys* and *Steak Tartare*. He resides on the Florida panhandle with the love of his life and the dog that rescued him, planning his massive epic fantasy series. Read more of his work, including full chapters of works-in-progress, at patreon.com/thefireinourheads or at jasonkristopher.com.

The Vision Serpent
by Jamie Sonderman

The Journal of Dr. Richard Ansel,
Castle Aisling, Scotland
January 1, 1918

This journal serves as my leash to reality, to the moral bedrock I fear this war seeks to erode. My hope is to spare the world another means to end even more lives in ways never imagined. I know the risk I take and what awaits me if this journal is ever discovered.

Gone is the youthful zeal that once sparked at the idea of advancing my studies through the examination of living specimens—replaced now by a bone-deep dread. I am weary, even on the eve of the prospect of coming face-to-face with an animal I was sure never existed.

Eastern European folklore tells of the Wzrok Węża, a creature with many eyes along its serpentine body. Legends say it grants prophetic visions to those who meet its gaze, but it also brings unspeakable ruin wherever it goes. It is this darker aspect that has drawn the attention of the War Department.

Guided by fragmented lore, a research team ventured into the depths of the Wieliczka Salt Mine, near Krakow, and discovered what appears to be one of the elusive "vision serpents." Situated in the former Kingdom of Galicia and Lodomeria, a region under Austro-

Hungarian dominion, the mine lay deep in the heart of enemy territory.

Tonight, my universe is condensed into two beating hearts resting beside me. My beloved Jessica and my son, Erik, find comfort in dreams I can no longer share. I catch myself watching them, memorizing the lines of their faces, as I fear tomorrow.

Their proximity warms me, but the real reason for their presence here in the Scottish Highlands fills me with cold. They serve both as my ethical compass and as the implicit deterrent to the very thing I intend to do.

I learned of my charge through hushed tones and sidelong glances, a legacy left by a predecessor whose mind could not bear the weight of his discoveries. Once a man of biology, he had cut and chopped at the Wzrok Węża before going mad. Rumors suggested he escaped during the night, along with one of his lab assistants. Now, the War Department thinks a fresh approach, one built on my expertise, will take the project into its next phase. I don't know how or why.

I was once a teacher of comparative religions and folklore. The power of narratives consumed me—how they shaped civilizations, how gods and heroes wrestled with fate. One day, while standing before a hall packed with youthful faces, I saw futures overshadowed by conflict. I felt a profound disconnect between the tales of old and the pressing, brutal story unfolding across the ocean.

As war broke out, I chose to leave and turn theories of the human condition into experience. My boots would tread in the muck of that old tradition of the soldier poet. I would see the fiery eyes of men committed to my death, and I would know what it was like to not simply read the poem, but to *be* the poem.

I traveled and enlisted in the Canadian Expeditionary Force, leaving my burgeoning family in the care of my parents. This left my wife angry; a bitterness she still harbors. She expressed her displeasure in the arms of another man while I was gone. Now, she likens her presence here in Castle Aisling to more of a kidnapping than a reunion. Reconciliation from here will be hard-won.

I belted songs with my brothers-in-arms as we sailed to the shores of France, excited about the heroics we'd soon experience. Our bravado turned to smoke shortly thereafter, as flamethrowers blazed in the night, and gas clouds suffocated the dawn. My own Vickers machine gun barked and misted the air red, sending souls away. With each trigger pull, the melody in my veins turned to lead.

The trenches counterposed my former life and nurtured a desperation in me. I yearned for books on endless shelves where I could spend my time in comfort reading by a warm fire with the company of "fellow travelers" nearby, each engrossed in their own books. I fear I'll never again know the halls of learning I cherish.

It is an old lecture I once gave on the Wzrok Węża that pulled me from the front lines and stationed me here in Castle Aisling. I have not had time to reflect on whether my circumstances have improved.

Now, the War Department has demanded a new weapon from me. It's unclear how they expect my expertise in folklore to achieve this. They want the Wzrok Węża to be a tool of terror, one so terrible it would end all future wars by its mere existence. But I know better. Whatever we create, our enemies will use against us.

There's an unspoken torment here in the castle, an acknowledgment of the fate that befell those who dared to peer too deeply into the shadows. I pass weary men trudging the halls, while nameless others stalk the corridors, armed with Lee-Enfield rifles.

Numerous clandestine projects unfold within these walls, each designed to hasten the war's end through means psychological, biological, or even purportedly "supernatural." It is yet unclear which category my Wzrok Węża falls into.

Once a stronghold of chivalric pursuits, Castle Aisling is now a crucible of war's alchemy. I lament how curiosity, imagination, and discovery have become tools of pain and destruction amplified by science.

January 2, 1918

Today, I came face-to-face with the Wzrok Węża, an encounter more unsettling than I had expected.

Earlier, I met my lab assistants and their families for breakfast.

Anton and Roger both seem to be fine men, seemingly as unfamiliar with this place as I am. We passed around a dossier of the project as it currently stands. I had to guard the folder from my ten-year-old son's prying curiosity. It was in the dossier that I learned a third member of the team had burned all his research notes before dying from a self-inflicted gunshot wound.

A photograph of the man who came before me, of Dr. Victor Aldridge, his eyes bright with excitement, struck me. His expression mirrored the mirth I'd experienced before setting foot in the trenches for the first time. It is an expression I doubt I will ever duplicate again.

My initial descent into the laboratory felt like stepping back into an era when deep places were the realms of the unknowable. It felt worlds apart from the ivy-clad halls where I once taught young men about the myths that define us.

Carved into the castle's bedrock, the space melds ancient stone with concrete and modern necessity. Scientific instruments, my new allies in this clandestine pursuit, clutter the scattered workstations.

Amidst this, a distant clatter of a gargantuan steam engine pervades the space—a mechanical dirge acting as a constant reminder of the castle's dual heart: one of oil-fueled lamps above, the other of electric bulbs here below. I find myself paradoxically seeking the hum and rhythmic huffs, as they provide a welcome distraction from the adjacent lab's muffled cries of human screams that seep never-ending through the walls.

My enigmatic predecessor, Dr. Aldridge, driven by the same blend of curiosity and dread that now fuels my days, postulated that the Wzrok Węża's skin reacts adversely to salt. Ancient people kept the vision serpent in a jar made of salt and stored it deep in the Wieliczka mines. I concur that salt somehow mitigates the animal. Osmosis, as it affects slugs, comes to mind.

This hypothesis led to the creation of an intricate habitat—an "aquarium" of sorts, where layers of pressed salt are encased between thick panes of glass. Inside, the Wzrok Węża is free to move as its will would have it, while still being contained by the influence of salt.

If salt is the answer to confining the creature, there should be no escape. Yet, Dr. Aldridge seemed to have prepared for all eventualities, embedding flamethrowers within the tank's structure.

This is a feature I plan to exploit once I am away from the prying eyes of my assistants. They are here to aid me, but I do not presume they aren't here to keep watchful eyes as well.

The potential hazards of the Wzrok Węża escaping its confines are as yet unknown to me. This uncertainty also shrouds the other ventures housed within the crumbling walls of Castle Aisling. The piecemeal construction of this facility does little to quell my apprehensions. Certainly, the desperate needs of war have led designers to compromise where they thought they could.

Despite my feelings of anticipation here in the lab, the unveiling of the subject was devoid of ceremony. A mere drawing of a curtain revealed the beast. Instead of encountering the aggression I had expected in a potential weapon, I was met with a peculiar curiosity as the serpent slid gracefully up to the glass.

The Wzrok Węża defies simple description. Both flanks are covered with eyes, each of them various colors, from brown to green to bright blue, and placed haphazardly, devoid of any natural order. Each eye blinks independently of any other.

Except for these uncanny aspects, the serpent presented itself exactly as I had expected. Only there was more—a grotesque mass sprawled heavily across the tank floor. The part that resembled the fabled serpent crept out of this larger mass like a slithering appendage. Its mass, comparable to that of a horse as indicated by the tank's integrated scale, underscored an unnerving reality: The specimen had grown considerably.

And so, I pause, as the Scottish winds howl a mournful tune against the stone of Castle Aisling. Thus far, I have spared you the worst part of my initial meeting with the beast for good reason. I pen these words by flame safely removed from the lab, now darkened for the night. Aspects of me—the scholar, the father, the man who once found comfort in the structured debates of academia—wonder at the path that has led me here. The tragic fate of my predecessor, a man driven to madness by the very research I now continue, weighs heavily upon me. It's a sobering reminder of the fine line between discovery and damnation. Tomorrow, I must face the beast again.

Approaching the glass that first time, a part of me—a part I wished to deny—hungered for the prophetic visions promised by folklore. That same part feared my mind would be carried off to see the fate of a world ablaze from the never-ending expansion of the war. Yet, as I peered into the multitude of eyes, I saw nothing but my faint reflection on the glass. As I expected, any notions of prophecy were a construct of legend.

Anticipating many things, I had armed myself with skepticism and scientific rigor. As I reminded myself that the Wzrok Węża was an animal just like any other, relief washed over me. That was until the visceral, haunting moment when the creature's skin split, as if cut from within, birthing yet another eye along the serpent's body. I retreated from the tank, my mind churning with questions left unanswered by science and folklore alike.

The laboratory felt like a stage for a play too grand for any one man to comprehend. This is no myth, but reality, unforgiving, and we are but players, bound by choices whose consequences reach far beyond the confines of the castle's stone restraints.

That oozing eye had blinked injured blood away and then gazed into me with an unsettling awareness, a window into an intelligence that should not exist. I could not shake the feeling of being measured.

I am familiar with this eye.

January 20, 1918

Weeks have passed, yet our subject remains unchanged, a stagnant mass of flesh. It does not seem to breathe. Despite my intention to stall any actual progress, my curiosity itches like a skin I cannot shed, yet I resist the juvenile urge to poke the creature with a stick.

In an unsettling exchange with our chief of resources, I learned the specimen doesn't eat. Many other labs put in regular calls for items such as whole cows, bales of human hair, and "black milk." Yet, for our project, nothing. Not a whisper of sustenance. It feeds on something unspoken.

His jest about surplus enemy uniforms lingered uncomfortably in the air between us. He has more than he knows what to do with. I myself had stumbled upon several feldgrau woolen tunics and trousers in a bin in my lab, German field uniforms. Understanding washed away more sediment from my dwindling resolve.

My initial meeting with my assistants planted the seed of potential human connection with like-minded contemporaries. Yet, the undercurrents within our team thicken the air, which I fear dash these hopes. Anton, ever meticulous, found stimulation in piecing together the burned remnants of Dr. Aldridge's research. Roger, though, remains an enigma, his intentions as obscure as the mist-laden Highlands. We have exchanged heated words, as he is ready to cut into the beast. His words crept to the edge of accusations of stalling the project. And so, the presence of my assistants, once a mere professional arrangement with the hope of friendship, develops now into a complex weave of alliances and potential suspicions. I must take steps to cover my true intentions.

It is in the pieced-together lab notes where we found reference to the same word repeatedly: *Accretion*.

January 22, 1918

Each night, as Jessica and Erik lie in the deceptive peace of sleep, I am tormented by visions of the beast, expanding, consuming. Their innocence is a reminder of the world I have dragged them into—a world far from the laughter and warmth of our past life. The weight of their safety, the enormity of their well-being, presses down on me with an unbearable gravity. I've ensnared them in a web spun from my own obsessions and fears. I will never make things right between us.

In the weeks since I met the monster, I have never been alone with it. Now, my intention to spare the world another means of destruction was finally at hand.

Erik, my son, has taken a liking to my lab partner, Roger, and the two of them have bonded over a mutual love of baseball. They've been playing ball in the great hall of the castle. As I watched them play, my son's smile infected me with a pang of both joy and regret. I lamented I may never know my son the way I would have if this war had never taken shape. I plead with all that is holy that our relationship recovers from my time in the trenches.

In that moment, however, I used my son to divert attention away from my clandestine intent. If the ruin that accompanies the beast is to be stopped, I had to hasten. I did not know where Anton was or when he would return to the lab.

As I stood before the tank, the stillness of the subject gnawed at my will. Thoughts of Erik's laughter and Jessica's steadfast gaze intertwined with the grim task at hand. The valve to end it all lay within reach under a skin of safety glass.

Yet, I hesitated. What would the destruction of just one of these mad experiments do in a castle full of world-ending potential? I would put an end to all the unholy activity in Castle Aisling if I were able. This, combined with the prospect of my family navigating the aftermath of my actions, tightened the noose of indecision around my neck. Their faces, the embodiments of my heart's capacity for love, haunted me.

Still, this monster, this "Accretion," brings with it misery. I know what it did to my predecessor. What it would do to me.

My hand shook as it reached for the cover. If anyone were to come in now, my pantomime meant to justify my actions would have no oxygen. I raised the small hammer by its chain. My hand hovered over the glass as I rethought my actions one last time. This thing, once done, may bring me much-needed peace. If not peace, then depriving the War Department of at least one weapon would settle me. I wish I could take more from them.

I steeled my intention.

Voices in the hall warned me of my approaching lab mates. My face flushed and sweat gathered. I realized I still held the hammer in my hand as they entered. I quickly dropped it where it swayed on its chain. Despite my efforts to appear calm, my disposition remained jittery. If they recognized it, they did not say.

January 22, 1918

The fabric of my reality unraveled further tonight. Word reached me that my assistant Roger had requested I join him in the lab. As I entered, I was met with a vexing sight. He had brought my son, Erik, to look at the creature we now called the Accretion. The innocence in my son's eyes, reflecting the horror I sought to shield him from, shattered the last vestiges of my hope. Roger's warning glare, a sentinel of the War Department's ever-watchful gaze, stripped me bare, leaving me as exposed as the specimen we study.

When Erik asked me if he could visit the lab again, Roger answered for me, saying he could return whenever he wanted. Rage filled my vision like a river of violent red. If I had been armed, I would have destroyed him then.

Now, I shared something with the Accretion. We are both prisoners here. The difference, I fear, is that it harbors power in its passivity—a sinister potential that lies dormant, waiting. But is this really a difference between us?

January 24, 1918

The impossible greeted us this morning: an empty tank, the Accretion vanished. Panic seized us. This monster loose in the castle put lives at risk and made us incompetent custodians. Catching glimpses of my lab partners stumbling as we took action told me just how desperate we were to make this nightmare scenario go away. I swear, Anton looked underneath a chair, as if the solution could be found there.

Yet, beneath the hysteria, an admiration for the Accretion's cunning stirred within me. It had waited, a silent strategist, while I, in my hubris, believed myself to be in control. This is a lesson the War Department would do well to consider.

The tank held only bones, a pile of them, all human. From the number of skulls I counted, seven souls. One had been Dr. Aldridge, not escaped as was rumored but taken into the beast. It had been his eye I had recognized on that first day.

At this point in my research, I am certain I know what this thing is and how it grows. I can imagine the devastating effect it would have on the battlefield. I thought of all the people in this facility and the danger we were all in. My family's presence here now seems an unforgivable sin.

Roger opened the airlock door and stepped inside. He was going into the tank. I noticed it at that moment. Peering through the reinforced glass, my gaze fell upon the specimen's delicate form, now almost ethereal in its translucence. Tiny veins pulsed beneath a diaphanous membrane, the subject having stretched itself into an astonishing, nearly invisible, thinness.

My instinct was to shout a warning to Roger, but he had already opened the inner door of the tank. Transparent skin fluttered in the wind made by the opening door.

I suppressed my voice in a moment of sinister grace and resolved to simply watch what happened next.

Roger walked into the membrane, his momentum wrapping the creature around his face and head. The Accretion's flesh seemed to tremble in delight.

It started with the skin. Upon contact, their skin merged. The process was silent but for the soft, wet sounds of flesh assimilating flesh. A change came over Roger's face, one that hinted at a profound transformation taking place.

Roger looked at me in stunned surprise. The subject's form slid from the glass and thickened, drawing in the pile of bones once more. Roger's eyes remained wide with terror and confusion as the Accretion absorbed his body.

His eyes held my gaze. From the depths of the monster, other eyes emerged, pushing, shoving, in a competition for the newly available sockets. The invading eyes of the Accretion were not content to relinquish their vantage points. They writhed and battled, pressing against each other in a silent contest. Roger's left eye socket now held seven eyes squeezed together. Each eye, with its own story, its own glimpse of the world, now condemned to vie for sight in a body that was no longer its own.

Through all of it, Roger's demeanor shifted from absolute horror into something surprising ... bliss. The transformation concluded as the human form, now entirely subsumed, left the Accretion visibly quivering.

The creature stilled. Left in its wake, the man's clothes and shoes, and his watch, still ticking. Someone screamed loudly in a low, sustained tone. It was then I realized it had been me, my voice hoarse from the exertion.

The chamber became quiet once more, but the image of those vying eyes remained etched into my mind. My own eyes met those of Anton's as he broke the safety glass and pulled the lever, intent on incinerating the beast. Nothing happened. Later, we would find out that someone had intentionally emptied the fuel tanks that fed the flamethrowers. But now, Anton simply laughed mirthlessly.

January 26, 1918

The sight that unfolded before us as we entered the lab chained our feet to the floor. Our former colleague, once as human as we, greeted us with unsettling familiarity. Roger stood in the tank, clad loosely in what he had been wearing when it happened. His reconstituted body reminded me of a broken vase hastily repaired. The pieces fit together, but not quite as they had before.

He bid us a cheerful good morning. The calmness in his eyes contrasted with the panic that clawed at my insides. His smile, meant to be reassuring, only deepened my fear. There was a kindness on his face that had never been present in his former life, a newfound peace. His face, previously pockmarked, was smooth and healthy. A closer look revealed multiple eyes present in his sockets. He was not alone.

As he stepped forward, connected by an umbilical of flesh to the Accretion, I felt a sick detachment. He appeared to be a puppet on a string. Was this Roger? Or was this a familiar mask worn by my subject, meant to calm me?

The day blurred as we spent hours locked in conversation. I

learned more about our subject than we had in the entire time we'd been studying it.

This creature is a living amalgamation of flesh, bones, and the consciousnesses of those it has consumed. It grows by absorbing people it comes into contact with, merging their physical forms and minds into its own mass. The Accretion retains the collective intelligence and memories of its victims, making it not only a physical threat but also a cunning and strategic entity. The process leaves the victims aware within the beast.

I learned our predecessors had done nearly everything imaginable to kill the beast, only to be denied at every turn. Wounds sustained by bullets healed instantly. Poison metabolized with no lasting effects. Viruses did nothing. It appears to be indestructible, immortal, except for the effects of salt and fire.

Roger, and I'm sure it is Roger now, seemed happier than ever before. He said the beast had cured the woes he once felt, both physically and mentally. He was enthusiastic about all the knowledge he now shares with those also absorbed by the Accretion. Included within are our two former counterparts, previously believed to have run off. Roger now speaks German.

Full of excitement, Anton discussed the potential healing qualities we could derive from the specimen and the various fields of science that could experience significant growth. Anton has since fled the facility. I cannot say that I hold it against him. He has his reasons.

Roger spoke of liberation, of a union that transcended human woes—a utopian ideal birthed from radical ethical questions. His new multicolored eyes, windows to the souls within, pleaded with a sincerity that moved me.

His proposition was apocalyptic, or revolutionary, depending on your point of view. Envision a world united in a single, all-knowing consciousness. The thought alone was enough to fracture what remained of my rational mind. Yet, there he stood, speaking languages and equipped with knowledge alien to his former self, proof of the unimaginable intelligence the Accretion wielded.

The hours slipped by unnoticed, my human needs forgotten. I'm still in the lab now, writing these words. Here where age-old shadows, longer and more sentient than night should allow, dance just beyond the reach of electric light. Roger's promise of a painless existence, a collective nirvana, was a siren call to the weary and broken.

Roger's last request was a blade through my resolve, however. He implored us to bring his family to him, to the Accretion, so they could join him within. The thought of his two children, a little boy and girl, being subjected to such a fate sparked a fierce protectiveness within me.

Evening found me alone in the lab, Anton having retreated into the night. The darkness outside mirrored the combat within me, a reflection of the ethical abyss into which we had plunged. Here, in this fortress of science perverted by unnatural ambition, I am forced to confront the ultimate question: What are we willing to sacrifice on the altar of knowledge?

February 3, 1918

My hands tremble as I commit these words, more out of habit than necessity, to paper. They speak to the irreversible path I have chosen. Days, perhaps lifetimes, have blurred since the Accretion's true nature unfolded before us—a revelation both monstrous and, in a perverse manner, divine. With a heart laden, I pen these last words. It's my son's eyes that guide me in these final entries. The laboratory door stands open.

Having been called, I stood before the War Department, animated by only a flicker of purpose. Their plans to release the Accretion on an unsuspecting village pierced the fog that had shadowed my thoughts.

I have grown to respect the Accretion for its potential. By gathering learned men from across the academic spectrum, we could store the world's collective discoveries for all time. The Accretion could serve as a record of everything humanity has ever learned and accomplished, a living Library of Alexandria.

Marching back to my lab, I expected the Accretion to be already crated up and moved into position for release. As much as I hoped to be rid of this responsibility, I noticed a newly seeded passion for denying the War Department their weapon. Unsure of what I meant to do, my pace increased. The dread of losing such a vital resource had replaced any former desire to kill the beast.

Erik, my son, embodies curiosity's purest form, a trait that Castle Aisling's hidden shadows seemed only to stoke. I had previously set boundaries, of course, specifically forbidding entry to the laboratory's sanctum where our research casts the longest shadows. Yet, hindsight whispers bitter truths: It had been a foregone conclusion that Erik would take up Roger's invitation to visit the lab. I hadn't chastised my son or warned him away. It was as if I had invited what happened next.

Upon entering the lab and discovering Erik within the confines of the glass tank, my world as I had known it shattered into unrecognizable shards. There he stood, his small hands clawing at the transparent barrier, his face pressed against the glass. His gaze, once filled with the innocence of youth, had turned into a distant, vacant stare. And when his eyes met mine, it was not the singular, warm gaze of my son. Instead, a multitude of eyes, each a lens into an intellect, swallowed whole.

It felt like my brain split in two, half of it simply slipping away. As one part broke, another seemed to mend. Witnessing my son's transformation has catalyzed a profound metamorphosis within me. I am operating on something primal now.

Erik described it as living in the things he learned in Sunday School, like feeling the all-encompassing embrace of God. My son, ever beautiful and kind, wanted to share this with all his classmates back home. He wanted to bring in his grandparents. He wanted me. And he wanted his mommy.

My son cemented my resolve. His words imbued me with a serene compliance, setting the final act into motion—irrevocable and transcendent. My boy's mother, my wife, Jessica, is now delivered, baptized in the flesh. We will be forever us.

My objective becomes quenched iron. Should the War Department crave a test, I shall deliver.

I am to traverse the thresholds of the known, embarking into the vast, uncharted embrace of unity, my own baptism. I enlist with a song in my heart.

Our exploration will begin with our unfurling into an eternal quest to learn the depths of the human spirit. Thus, we shall endure, immortalized as the chronicler of souls, the soldier poet, etched into the annals of eternity. We will see humanity from multiple firsthand experiences and gather more to us in a never-ending study on what it means to be human—starting with how they experience terror.

About the Author

Jamie Sonderman was once named Best Filmmaker in Detroit by *Real Detroit Magazine*. He's an award-winning filmmaker who has captured the attention of Hollywood, which used his sci-fi series, InZer0, as a guidebook for utilizing Detroit's hidden, dilapidated, and industrial locations.

One of Jamie's most cherished secrets was the passage he built in his parents' house, leading from the bedroom closet into the attic. This hidden refuge served as a personal sanctuary for years before it was finally revealed. The theme of discovering and cherishing hidden spaces permeates Jamie's work, inviting readers to look beyond the obvious and find the magic in the unseen.

Currently, Jamie is working on a series of novels set in the world of "The Vision Serpent," a series that promises to take readers on a journey through hidden realms and secret places. Connect with Jamie on Facebook and discover more about the hidden worlds he creates.

Dear Nessie

by Bonnie Elizabeth

Dear Nessie,

I know you won't ever read this, since you're not land based and paper disintegrates in water, but it's you I want to share my thoughts with.

Do you remember that time when I was five, running away from home, in the boat, thinking I would row myself across the loch—as if I could—and you rose up and pushed the little thing back to shore when I tired? I looked in your eyes, and I saw both your compassion and your wonder at what a child was doing in your loch in the middle of the night.

I was ill-prepared for the rain that had begun. I remember my hands were so cold, my fingers could barely clasp the oars of my father's rowing boat. The fog had come in, as it so often did when you appear—you like hiding, don't you?—and made it even colder. My parents, had they another boat, would never have found me hidden in the loch's fog before I died of hypothermia that night. Not that they noticed I'd even gone.

No searchlights shone on the water, and only the light from your eyes allowed me to see anything. I maintain I saw only kindness in them. The love of a mother for a child. Not that I had seen such a thing before. My own mother was as cold as the depths of your loch.

I fell in love with you that day. The love of a child for his mother. A love that would change and grow over the years.

Today, I graduated with a degree in paleobiology. Can you imagine? And it's all thanks to you, Nessie.

Yours,
Robert Brodie

Dear Nessie,

I'm working on my graduate degree here in the Gobi, looking for more aquatic dinosaurs. That's the area I'm focusing on, you know. Thanks to you. I want to know who you might have known in your younger years. Are there others of your kind in the loch?

It's spring, before the heat really hits, and yet sweat still stings my eyes practically before the sun has come up. While I've kept on the sunscreen and covered everything that can be covered, I fear my skin is so red it's going to peel off any second. The problems of being a fair-skinned Scotsman, I suppose. It's hard to imagine that this was once a sea instead of a desert.

Have you rescued any other children in the loch, Nessie? Or was I special that one night?

I met a woman here. I had thought we could get together, but she laughed at my story of meeting you—said it was a child's dream. Just like my family says. But I know that we met. And that I fell in love with you. A child needs a mother, and you were that for me.

If I go back and take out that rowing boat, will you still be there for me, Nessie?

Yours,
Robert

Dear Nessie,

Thank you for showing up for me today. I needed it. Most of the town is at my da's local, sharing memories of him. Probably got lots of them in there, given how much time and money he spent in the place. I'm old enough to go inside now, but those scarred wooden doors that perpetually need paint don't welcome me. They remind me of being beaten whenever Ma sent me down to fetch him.

The dim light inside the local puts me in mind of how dark a heart can be. Ma never stood for me when he'd be drunk and angry. She'd let me, the messenger, take the beating, and then she'd coo and grovel at him, make him comfortable at home where she wanted him, ignoring my wounds or the blood that sometimes dripped out of my nose.

There, I've said it. He wasn't always as bad as he was the night I ran away and you and I met, but he was never good. Those are my memories, Nessie.

I took a boat out tonight, a small one. Not the same one I took as a child. That one had rotted away and fallen apart before I was ten. Perhaps that's why I hadn't met you again as a child. This one is a rental, so I have it for a few days. They'd think I was crazy if I asked for it just for a night. Who goes out in a rowing boat in the loch at night in the winter?

All the same, Nessie, I rowed out to the same place I had as a child. This time, I wore a heavier jacket and gloves. I had rainwear because, although the skies were merely cloudy, that could change in a moment.

Perhaps feeling that I was there, you came. You rose from the water and looked into my eyes and I into yours. I think you knew I needed you. How can we have such a connection? You, the monster, and me, the man? How can I love you with every cell in my body in a way that I can't feel for my own parents?

I worry that I see you and no other like you. No one has ever seen another, only you. There have to be others of your kind down there in the depths. I hope you are not lonely. I hate to think of you alone.

Part of me longs to be other than human, to swim down to the depths with you and become part of a family there. I know you wouldn't let me. You'd lift me up and carry me to the shore, or so I like to think. Maybe it's a fancy.

But you came to me. In the light fog, in the dark, on a night when the lights still shone from Da's local out across the loch, the music wafting across the water along the breeze. So different from the first time we met.

I wish I could send you these letters, to tell you my thoughts, that you are in them every day. I won't be going back to the Gobi. I finished my part of the research. I'm now a professor down south, far away from home, but at least it's just England and not someplace where the sun will curl my skin.

I'll miss you.

Robert

From an article by Dr. Robert Brodie:

While many people still believe the Loch Ness Monster could have been a Plesiosaurus, it's unlikely from the movement of the neck that the creature actually could have been a throwback. It's not impossible that Nessie, as she is affectionately called, could have been an evolutionary descendant whose neck does move in such a manner.

While most scientists believe that if there ever was a Loch Ness Monster, she is long gone, though there remain sightings around the loch. Most academics claim that these sightings are the ravings of men and women who have had too much to drink in the nearby taverns.

The Loch Ness Monster is not the only sea monster that people have claimed to see. Given the commonality of such sightings, it makes one wonder what exactly is out there, beneath the lakes of the world.

Dear Nessie,

I hope you don't mind that I wrote about you. I had to publish something, and the article was a big hit at a popular magazine. It wasn't as scientific as my other papers, but it definitely raised my profile.

I can't say that I didn't enjoy writing about you, bringing you closer. You are a mystery to me, even though I know that my sighting wasn't that of a drunken man or a dreaming boy. My students know I'm a fan of you, and several leave articles and links to YouTube about you, to be sure I see them.

The more I study aquatic dinosaurs, the more I wonder about your life in the loch and what you are. You don't fit, Nessie. Are you an alien being that was dropped here on Earth and found a home in the cold waters of Loch Ness? Is that why you've lived here for so long?

It frustrates me to have no way to explain you to the world. You are more my mother than the woman who bore me ever was. You are my family in a strange way. You sent me on a path to this career. I have traveled to places I'd have never dreamed of going thanks to you.

My life feels complete, although I have never married. I have yet to meet a woman who doesn't look at me from the side of her eye when I ask if she believes that you live in Loch Ness. They laugh or think I'm testing them. Not a one admits to believing you exist.

Until there is someone who can believe in us—in you as my family—I won't marry. I hope you don't mind that I have made this stance. I hope you don't have dreams of my own children rowing out on the loch to see you. But there are things I have to share with a wife. You are one of them. At least a belief. A willingness to join me one night on the loch, perhaps in a rowing boat so you can bless our union.

Yours, as always,
Robert

Dear Nessie,

My mother invited me home for the holidays. She said it was important, so I came. She's been battling cancer. She told me that she realized she hadn't ever stood up for me with my father. It was a fine moment. Her sister was there with her, watching her carefully. It was only later, as they were drinking together, that I overheard my aunt tell my mom that she did a good job. My mom laughed and said she should have been an actress.

I wished we still had a rowing boat. I bundled up in my heaviest coat, leaving behind the smell of the Scotch, some of which must have spilled on the floor, and walked outside. I headed down toward the docks to look out over the water. If we'd had a rowing boat, I would have gone out, despite the snowflakes that flickered around my face.

Colorful lights came from the tavern just up the hill, the one where they toasted my da at his funeral. That night you comforted me when no one else did. Huddled in my coat, I walked along the shoreline and then out onto one of the wooden jetties.

The loch was black, and there was little light. The wind that whipped over the waters made me shiver despite my warm clothing. Living in the South has made me soft. I wouldn't have been able to stand the cold night when I rowed out onto the water as a child.

There I stood, shivering and watching, barely aware that tears flowed down my face until the chill made them nearly freeze against my cheeks. I used my scarf to wipe them away. I like to imagine I heard the faintest *plink* as they fell into the loch, though the gusts of wind would have made that impossible.

You rose up near the dock and watched me. I wonder if it was my tears—that somehow you knew they belonged to me. What a connection we have, Nessie! Each time I have need of you, you come and stare at me with such compassion in your eyes.

I reached out a gloved hand to touch you this time.

Your breath was warm against my glove, and we stood like that for nearly a minute.

Then lights from a car flashed, and you quickly sank beneath the loch once again, and I was a man alone, holding his hand over the waters, perhaps offering a blessing.

If I could bless you, Nessie, I would.

Yours,
Robert

Dearest Nessie,

I am home again, not for a holiday or even a funeral. I'm just here to visit you. I met someone. Someone willing to believe that you are real. I brought her here to see you.

We rented a rowing boat, such a romantic thing to do, and, after a late dinner, we put on our warm clothing, though the day had been pleasant enough, and rowed out on the loch.

Gentle waves lapped around our little boat. She was quiet as I told her about you. About your kindness to me, and how you had helped me during my most difficult times. I said your eyes were kind and your breath was warm. I had touched you, once, at Christmas three years ago.

We sat out there in the night for hours, waiting.

You didn't want to meet her.

I don't know if she's hurt or if she believes I'm a liar. I know she still thinks you exist, and she's right to do so.

I worry you didn't come because you don't approve of this woman. She is certainly not the sort one would expect for a professor's wife. Her da does maintenance on the Tube. She works in a transit office. Not exactly my class, if you must know. But she believed.

She's leaving tomorrow. I'm staying here. I want to try to speak with you again, without her here. I told her I'd be home soon. I hope she's still there. Maybe if I see you, I'll understand your message.

Yours,
Robert

Dear Nessie,

You showed yourself for me alone last night. I think I know what that means. As always, you looked sadly at me. You let me touch your nose again. This time my hands were bare. Your skin was slightly wrinkled, but surprisingly soft. I expected heavier scales, I guess. But perhaps you are more akin to a seal than a fish.

I don't know what that means for my studies, for my articles. I have to consider if many of the aquatic dinosaurs were like that. It changes so much.

And then there's my relationship with the woman I wanted you to meet. That will change too.

The way we looked at each other told me she wasn't right for me. You didn't approve. Of course, my biological mother didn't approve either. My future wife isn't much for drinking, which didn't go over well with my mom. She thought this young woman was judging her.

As if I hadn't done that my entire life. Ah, Nessie, at least I can trust your judgment and I know things would never work out with her.

Yours,
Robert

From South London University News:

University professor Dr. Robert Brodie has been relieved of duties due to mental health concerns. Several students have reported increasingly erratic behavior on his part, and the university has made the difficult decision to let him go.

From Dr. Robert Brodie's blog:

Descendants of plesiosaurs live in the world's oceans. Note that Loch Ness, where the famous Nessie appears, is particularly deep and cold. Descendants of other plesiosaurs would naturally live in the deepest, coldest parts of the oceans, surfacing only rarely.

Most of you, dear readers, are skeptical of my sightings of Nessie, and I understand why you might be so. However, my sightings have informed my research and my studies proving the veracity of my claims. How many other Sainsbury's store assistants can discuss plesiosaurs the way I can?

From The London Independent:

Robert Brodie was arrested for indecent exposure. The former professor of paleobiology has seen his fortunes sink over the years after what university officials once called "increasingly erratic behavior."

While working as a convenience store assistant, Brodie began a blog about the Loch Ness Monster, claiming that she was his mother. He leaped into the Thames, believing he could somehow swim home to Scotland to be with her.

He is being evaluated at a local hospital for mental health issues.

From the internet:

Search for: "Robert Brodie blog" "Loch Ness Monster"
No such files found.

Dear Aunt Mairi,

I'm not sure I ought to return to Scotland for the holidays this year. I am sure you and Ma will have a lovely time without me.

While my fortunes have taken a turn for the better, I still do not have the seniority to take time off for the holidays, not long enough to spend any time in Scotland. Besides, I know that Ma has no real desire to see me, else she would be the one that had written to me.

I continue with my therapy and my medications, and I have not had any further desires to swim home. I assure you, if I do return, it will be by train and by auto.

Robbie

Dear Aunt Mairi,

I was so glad you could make it to the wedding. I am sorry Ma could not come down with you. We'll try to come visit sometime soon, but I recently have found a position as a clerical worker for one of London's finest banks, and, as Elizabeth is a secretary for the local Council, it is difficult to arrange for time off.

Robbie

Dear Aunt Mairi,

    I'm sorry Elizabeth and I had to cut our visit short. Unfortunately, Elizabeth was not pleased with Ma's negative reaction to the news that we are not planning on having children and is holding Ma's actions against her—and, apparently, against me as well. Elizabeth feels as if I've tried to trick her into becoming a mother, though she is past prime childbearing years. I've tried to tell her I had no idea Ma felt so strongly about grandchildren. I thought that at her age—and ours—that Ma had settled for not having any.

    Further, having seen Ma, Elizabeth has concerns about the turns my mental health may take as I age. Not that I can blame her after our last visit, though I do thank you for attempting to speak for me.

    We are currently in counseling, but I am uncertain that it is going the way I hoped it would.

    Robbie

Dear Nessie,

    I am coming home. Alone. Elizabeth has filed for divorce, which may not be a surprise to you. It was not to me.

    You're the only one who has always been there for me. It's taken me all this time to come to terms with the fact that I need to be near you. I've found a placement as a cashier at the local bank.

    I hope to see you soon.

    Yours,

    Robert

Dear Nessie,

    Coming home was the right thing. Ma is in care right now. She can no longer be left alone at the house. I live there now. I have a girl who comes in twice a week to clean. She's lovely. Too young for me, of course, but it's nice to listen to her tell us about the town gossip.

    She knew Ma, of course, and worked for her for a time. Said she saw her getting worse and worse. Said her own ma worried about me as a child, given how cold mine own could be. They all knew my da was a bit too fond of the drink.

Makes me wonder why the only one who stepped up for me was the monster in the loch.

Perhaps tonight I will visit you, Nessie.

Yours,
Robert

Dear Nessie,

The loch called to me, so I took a rowing boat out last night. The stars were bright, and there were few clouds. How rare that is. I wore a light jacket and was quite warm. I'm not sure if it's just my blood thickening from being home or if there's another reason.

You were there, for me, as always, rising out of the water to give me your look. One of compassion, perhaps even joy that I was there. My heart lightened. I know where I'm supposed to be, Nessie. Here with you.

It's true that I've fallen on hard times. I can't say that I love being a cashier. I'm no longer young. Last year, on my birthday, I became older than my father was when he died. I feel the age in my joints and my bones. I have no real desire to live as long as Ma.

Aunt Mairi is living with her daughter over near Glasgow. I rarely see her. She's moved Ma into care closer to her as Ma complained I never visited, though I went once a week. Now, she can complain about how Mairi never visits.

I left you alone for years, yet you never complained, dear Nessie. You and I have always understood each other. Perhaps if I had understood the woman who birthed me in the same way, we both would have been happier.

Yours,
Robert

Dear Nessie,

It's happened. I worried for years about inheriting the cancer that plagued my father. I've not felt quite well in some time.

Liver cancer is not a good way to go.

I don't know what else to tell you.

Yours,

Robert

Dear Nessie,

Robert asked me to finish the journal. He couldn't write the last as he isn't here to do so.

I rowed him out to the loch. I didn't believe you'd be there, because I don't believe in you. At least I didn't.

But then you rose out of the water.

Robert stood up, and though he near tipped the boat over, something steadied us. I think it was you.

The two of you looked at each other with such sweetness it brought tears to my eyes. I near forgot that I was out in the freezing water of the loch on a cool autumn night and that a man was standing up in a rowing boat which could capsize and kill us both in seconds. You made me not care.

I'm sorry for the blots on the paper. I don't even know who I'm apologizing to. It's not as if you'll read this. If you know, you already know.

Though I doubt anyone else will find this journal, if you do, just know that those two shared a love. Mother and child, perhaps. Or more. Soulmates.

Robert Brodie wasn't insane. He knew you, Nessie. I saw it.

And when the two of you stared into each other's eyes, it was as if you knew what he needed. You lowered your head to him, and he reached up his arms and latched them around your long neck. You carefully lifted him from the boat and then backed away before you sank beneath the surface, taking him home.

I can't write any more.

Just know that I am glad someone loved Dr. Brodie that much.

Sincerely,

Jean McClure, housekeeper and friend of Dr. Brodie (and perhaps of Nessie)

About the Author

Speculative fiction writer Bonnie Elizabeth draws on her varied work background to create unusual characters. Those characters explore the way things could be, using her mantra, Connection Is Magic. She is currently writing her next paranormal novel, and you can find all of Bonnie's writing and her newsletter at https://bonnieelizabeth.com/.

On the Trail of the Swamp Soggon
by Mark Leslie

Transcript from the *On the Trail Of* vlog by Charles "Quester" O'Reilly. August 9, 2011. 11:43 AM

[Video opens with a close-up of Charles O'REILLY, white male, early thirties. An array of freckles that covers his face might normally be his most prominent feature if not for the huge, toothy grin he sports as he apes for the camera. The image jostles as he raises his right hand into the frame of the image, offering the universal peace symbol.]

O'REILLY: Hey, everybody. Quester here at Halifax Stanfield International Airport.

[The video frame pans quickly across a blurry background that suggests the inside of an airport.]

Or YHZ. That's right, I said "zee," even though the preference for most Canadians is to pronounce the final letter of the alphabet as "zed." But apparently that's something they waive for IATA airport codes. Perhaps we can blame the popular Rush song "YYZ," which is the code for Toronto's Pearson Airport, for that one. As you know, I'm here to investigate the mysterious disappearance of nearly half the population of a town of about one hundred people two years ago and how it might relate to a creature known as the

Swamp Soggon, and, of course, to the Scarecrows of Necum Teuch.

[The video drops to show O'Reilly's legs and the floor. Some incomprehensible dialogue in the background is audible.]

Okay, peeps, I'll be back. I've got to put this down to go through Canada customs. Talk at y'all later. OTTO out!

Transcript from the *On the Trail Of* vlog by Charles "Quester" O'Reilly. August 9, 2011. 12:34 PM

[Video opens on a fast-moving, forested landscape as seen through the window of a vehicle moving along a highway. The visual rotates to inside the vehicle and the face of Charles O'REILLY.]

O'REILLY: Quester here again, everyone. I'm now in a taxi leaving Halifax airport and on my way to the village of Necum Teuch, on the trail of the Swamp Soggon. The local legends tell of a woman by the name of Angella Geddes who put this remote village on the map with the hordes of realistic-looking scarecrow people that grace her property on the edge of the highway through town. Geddes claims to have created these scarecrow villagers—who can be seen standing near her home, in the garden, as well as in the nearby swamp—as a nod to a most mysterious creature that lives in that swamp. Described by Geddes herself in her 1996 book The Scarecrows of Necum Teuch, the creature is an "ugly, selfish" monster who got angry and turned almost everyone in town into scarecrows.

Though Geddes died in 2006, new scarecrows continue to appear randomly on and near her now-vacant family property. Nobody has ever claimed responsibility for continuing the woman's tradition of constructing scarecrows, and yet someone or something is causing them to multiply slowly.

The most well-known documentation of the disappearance of townsfolk comes from the blog of software engineer and multimillionaire Wilson Kendrick. This well-respected founder of Daisan Software retired young and moved to this small village, allegedly in search of a long-lost love of his life. But in the fall of 2009, Kendrick, along with more than three dozen other local villagers, disappeared overnight. They simply vanished, leaving their vehicles, their homes, and all their belongings behind.

The only evidence of foul play that night came via the rambling of a local maintenance man named Dale Lowe who claimed responsibility for the arson of several dozen scarecrows scattered through a handful of adjacent lots. The fire also completely leveled the home where Kendrick lived. Investigators never found any human remains in any of the charred ruins. Lowe claimed the missing villagers had been turned into scarecrows, and since he had burned them all, nothing—and no bodies—were left.

Apart from the psychotic ramblings of young Dale Lowe, the only other evidence that something truly remarkable and mysterious took place that night was Wilson Kendrick's last blog entry, written in the early morning hours of October 30, 2009. While municipal, provincial, and federal investigations into this mass disappearance have been launched, none have ever seriously explored the possibility that it relates to the mysterious creature that Angella Geddes tried to warn the world about—the Swamp Soggon.

But Quester has got you covered, people. Quester and the On the Trail Of vlog will keep you in the loop during every step of this ongoing quest to find the truth. OTTO out!

Complete text from the blog of Wilson Kendrick

Title: A Murder of Scarecrows
Time stamp: 1:32 AM October 30, 2009

I'm uncertain of what is happening to the villagers of the small town of Necum Teuch, where I've lived since March, but as a man of science, I can assure you that it has nothing to do with the alleged

Swamp Soggon or its army of scarecrows that the locals enjoy yattering on about endlessly.

While it makes for a most intriguing tale that is alluring to tourists, I have yet to bear witness to evidence of any such creature. But it is entirely possible that the swamp itself lies at the heart of this most disturbing occurrence.

About an hour ago, I woke to discover numerous local townsfolk frozen stiff while standing or even sitting, still clutching items they held as if their bodies had succumbed to rigor mortis instantly at the point of death rather than hours later.

My hypothesis is that these sudden and bizarre deaths are a result from the ingestion of a deadly airborne neurotoxin carried in from the nearby sea on the evening's soupy thick fog. Tetrodotoxin is one such poison found in aquatic creatures and is known to affect the nervous system and cause paralysis. The side effects of this toxin are likely what led to the local lore of some monster turning people into scarecrow-like statues.

I am sharing this post on the chance that I do not survive the evening. For all I know, I may have already ingested the contagion and will suffer the same fate as so many others already have.

But I am not going down without a fight. Dale—a local maintenance man I have befriended—and I are going to douse the most recent victims of this poison in gasoline and burn them, in the hopes that this macabre infection remains limited to this isolated region of the country.

If I do not survive the night, then perhaps it is fitting for me to remember that I am a distant descendant of Vince Coleman, the train dispatcher who, on December 6, 1917, sacrificed his life to stay behind and telegraph an urgent warning that would save the lives of the 700 passengers of an incoming passenger train from the Halifax Explosion that had killed nearly 1,800 people.

This is, after all, the least I can do.

Transcript from the *On the Trail Of* vlog by Charles "Quester" O'Reilly. August 9, 2011. 7:21 PM

[Video shows O'REILLY sitting in a chair, the arms of which are covered in lacy doilies. Across from him, in a matching armchair, sits a handsome, burly man with blond hair who appears to be in his mid-twenties. The second man is clearly confused and nervous.]

O'REILLY: Hi, everyone. It's Quester again. And let me tell you, it's been a long day. Nobody in this town has been willing to speak with me. But I have found someone who is not only coming on camera, but who was a firsthand witness to what happened on the fateful night of the mass disappearance of October 2009. Allow me to introduce you to Dale Lowe.

LOWE: *[Cautiously waves to the camera.]* Uh, hello. Everyone.

O'REILLY: Now, Dale, you've been a resident of Necum Teuch your entire life, correct?

LOWE: *[Looks at the camera hesitantly, then back at O'REILLY]* Should I look at you, or at the camera?

O'REILLY: Whatever you prefer. Now, Dale, as I understand it, you were the last person to see Wilson Kendrick alive in 2009. Is that correct?

LOWE: Which do you prefer? I can—I can do either. I just need to know what you prefer.

O'REILLY: *[Raises his hand with his first and second fingers held in a V shape at eye level, pointing toward himself.]* Right here, Dale. Look right here.

LOWE: Yes, I was the last person to speak with Mr. Kendrick when he was alive. But he was dead by the time I got to him.

O'REILLY: What happened that night, Dale?

LOWE: He called me when he saw the scarecrows appear. I warned him about the Swamp Soggon. I warned him. I told him to get out of there. But he wouldn't leave. He wouldn't get out. So I told him he should start a fire. Fire would keep him safe. The Swamp Soggon was afraid of fire and would stay away if he could start a fire.

O'REILLY: Did he listen to you, Dale?

LOWE: No. No, no, no. He didn't listen to me. That's why I went over there. To help him. With the fire. But it was too late when I arrived.

O'REILLY: What was too late, Dale?

LOWE: Mr. Kendrick had already been turned into a scarecrow when I got there.

O'REILLY: So what did you do?

LOWE: I did what I had to do. I doused him, and the others, in gasoline. And I set them on fire.

O'REILY: And then what did you do?

LOWE: I set Mr. Kendrick's house on fire. I knew that was the only thing that would keep the Swamp Soggon away. A huge fire. And Mr. Kendrick's two-story house would be perfect.

O'REILLY: Dale, can you please explain the details of—

[Fists banging on a door and gruff voices can be heard off camera]

Can you please explain the—

[More banging and indistinguishable yelling is heard.]

LOWE: *[Getting up from the chair]* Coming, Mother. I'm coming.

O'REILLY: No! Dale! Sit down! Please. Sit down and tell me—

[LOWE disappears off camera, muttering about being in trouble for locking the door. Both a male and female voice are heard frantically speaking overtop one another. O'REILLY stands from the chair, his hands out as if trying to calm down whoever is off camera.]

MR. LOWE: *[off camera]* Turn that camera off right now. This interview with my son is over.

O'REILLY: Mr. Lowe, please don't stop this. Dale is sharing something truly important for the world to know.

MRS. LOWE: *[off camera]* Why can't you people just leave my poor Dale alone?

O'REILLY: Please. This is important. I'm on the trail of the Swamp Soggon!

[MR. LOWE steps into the camera frame, completely blocking the view of the rest of the room.]

MR. LOWE: Take your camera and get the hell off our property. Right now!

[A hand reaches for the device. Partially blurred from a man's palm, the camera is lifted, then the view quickly rotates in a dizzying manner as if the camera was thrown. The last decipherable voice picked up from the camera is faint but clear.]

LOWE: Don't go there, Mr. O'Reilly. Don't go into the woods. Not after dark. The Swamp Soggon will get you.

Transcript from the *On the Trail Of* vlog by Charles "Quester" O'Reilly. August 9, 2011. 7:30 PM

[Video opens on a close-up of O'REILLY looking down at the camera

from above. He seems to be moving quickly. There is a hairline crack running across the middle of the frame.]

O'REILLY: Hi, everybody. Quester here. A little shaken, but still in one piece. Well, that didn't turn out like I'd expected. I'd waited all day for Dale's parents to leave so I could interview him. And we didn't get a chance to get into any of it before they arrived. I had to hustle out of there, and I'm just so glad my phone wasn't destroyed.

You see, friends, that's what you get for not backing down, for wanting to uncover the truth about the monsters that are out there going bump in the night. But your old pal Quester will not be deterred by a little manhandling and idle threats. No way. The truth is out there. And I'll go to the ends of the earth to find it for you.

[O'REILLY looks up and around as he continues to walk before facing the camera again.]

Right now, I'm on my way to the Kendrick residence where I'll try to find evidence of the Swamp Soggon, and maybe even capture it on video. OTTO out!

Transcript from the *On the Trail Of* vlog by Charles "Quester" O'Reilly. August 9, 2011. 8:13 PM

[Video pans the remains of the footings of a house that has burned down. Voice of O'REILLY is heard from off screen.]

O'REILLY: Quester here. I'm now walking about the old, burned ruins of the Kendrick residence. As you can see, there's nothing left. Just some charred debris of wood and brick are left standing. This lot has remained vacant since Kendrick's disappearance and assumed death back in 2009. And there's no indication that any new landscaping or build is going to take place here. Now that I'm on these grounds, I plan on venturing closer to the edge of the field that leads to the nearby swamp and wait for sundown. I'll come back live to you from there, my friends. Because this is your trusted Quester, on the trail of the Swamp Soggon. OTTO out!

Transcript from the *On the Trail Of* vlog by Charles "Quester" O'Reilly. August 9, 2011. 9:04 PM

[O'REILLY sits on the edge of a fallen tree trunk, visible in the darkness due to a single light shining on him from near the camera lens. In one hand he holds a long thick object, the shape of a baseball bat. His other hand constantly flails through the air, slapping at different parts of his body. The constant whir of crickets is heard, overpowered occasionally by the buzz of mosquitoes flying close to the camera.]

O'REILLY: I'm still out here on the old Kendrick property, about one hundred yards away from where the house used to stand, which I showed you earlier. I'm on the edge of the forest and swamp area. The sun set a little over half an hour ago, and it's completely dark.

I'm not sure what's bothering me more—the damn mosquitoes or that putrid smell of the swamp. Those familiar with legends of Bigfoot know that witnesses often smell the creature well before they see him. And the smell they have described seems an awful lot like the stench coming from this swamp. None of the legends I've read or heard about regarding the Swamp Soggon involve any sort of smell, but I can only imagine what anything that lives in this horrid swamp might actually smell like. Oh, the things I do for you, dear viewer.

[Off camera, the howl of some nocturnal creature is heard in the distance.]

O'REILLY: Did you hear that? I think it's a coyote, or maybe a wolf. Perhaps even a fox. But I'm pretty sure it has nothing to do with what we're looking for tonight. No, what we seek—

[An audible clicking is heard from off camera, and the sound of crickets ceases completely. O'REILLY turns to look somewhere off camera. Another clicking sound is heard, and his head whips around to the other side.]

O'REILLY: Now that is something I can't explain. Did you hear it? Some odd clicking. It's coming from the woods on my right and on my left. Like some giant insect or something. And the crickets have stopped their night song entirely. There it is again. That clicking.

[The clicking sound gets louder, and then seems to multiply, as if coming from hundreds of locations. O'REILLY's head swivels back and forth, trying to pinpoint the sound.]

O'REILLY: Such a unique sound. It's the frequency and pitch of a cicada, but instead of the shrill buzzing, it's more like a clicking. Like there's some invisible horde of old ladies madly knitting just out of sight in these trees. It's getting closer too. I suspect we're about to see the creature soon. That's right, dear viewer, here I am risking life and limb to get you footage of the elusive Swamp Soggon. I'm holding this torch in my hand, which I'm prepared to light to ward it off if the monster gets too close. But I'm waiting to see it come forward first. And I'm sure the Soggon won't appear if I start the fire too quickly.

[The loud cracking of a branch is heard, as if something large has stepped on it. O'REILLY jumps from his perch, waving the unlit torch in the air in front of him.]

O'REILLY: Oh, no. It … it's not what I expected. It's not an it. It's a they. They're here now.

[He looks in all directions: up, down, back, and forth.]

Oh my god. There are so many, so many … My friends, there is no single large lumbering creature here. The Swamp Soggon is not a creature like Bigfoot. It—they—are something entirely different.

They act and move in a giant coordinated pack. They're magnificent. Like nothing I've ever see—

[Something black flies into the camera, and it rotates about, briefly showing the flailing arms of O'REILLY as he is overcome by what appears to be an army of dark shadows that latch onto him. His screams are drowned out by an increasing fury of maddening clicking sounds before the video stops.]

Selected comments posted on the *On the Trail Of* vlog by Charles "Quester" O'Reilly

8/9/11 09:30:12: Great FX, OTTO! You really outdid yourself with this video!

8/9/11 09:45:45: I hope you're safe, OTTO. That looked really scary.

8/14/11 02:11:30: Fake. I've watched this, like, 100x & you can totally tell its just dudes in costume.

8/19/11 12:14:11: Has anyone heard from OTTO? I've been waiting for a follow-up post ... #prayingforOTTO

8/19/11 12:15:23: Swamp Soggin got 'em, I bet. Haha #stayouttatheswamp

8/23/11 08:22:22: O'Reilly, this is Dirk Denniger from *The National Enquiring Examiner*. I've been trying to reach you for two weeks now. Why aren't you answering your phone? Please contact me ASAP!

About the Author

Mark Leslie has always been afraid of strange creatures in the woods, ghostly tales, and the monster under his bed. He has channeled many of his fears into his writing that includes the horror story collection *One Hand Screaming*, his nonfiction books, which include *Haunted Hospitals*, *Tomes of Terror*, and *Spooky Sudbury*, and his humorous urban fantasy series that include *A Canadian Werewolf in New York*, *Fear and Longing in Los Angeles*, and *Only Monsters in the Building*. When he is not cowering beneath the covers, wandering awestruck through libraries, bookstores, or craft beer establishments, Mark can be found online at www.markleslie.ca.

Hunting the Headline
by Sara Itka

Author's Note: Don't try any of the following at home, unless you are a certified Florida Man.

FLORIDA MAN STEALS ALLIGATOR FROM MINIATURE GOLF COURSE

By Barry Merrow | UPDATED April 15 | Fox35 Orlando

KISSIMMEE, Fla. A 32-year-old man, native to the Delray Beach area, admits to stealing an alligator from its enclosure while vacationing in Kissimmee. Police say they were patrolling Irlo Bronson Memorial Highway around 3:15 AM on Sunday morning when they saw the man, later identified as Carl Moorsen, leaving Congo River Golf carrying a three-foot alligator in a Mickey Mouse beach towel. Officers say when they approached Moorsen, he swung the alligator at them by its tail. Police eventually disarmed Moorsen of the alligator and restrained him.

When questioned, Moorsen claimed he planned to drive the alligator home to eat the iguanas in his yard.

Moorsen faces charges of animal cruelty, possession or injury of an alligator, unarmed burglary, and resisting arrest.

The alligator was examined by a Gatorland veterinarian and pronounced unharmed. It was returned to Congo River Golf.

Notes:

- Weapons of choice: shotgun, machete, bottle, golf club, alligator?

Rough green rustles against my strappy sandals, itching like a nest of fire ants hosting a barbecue. I kneel by the water's edge, staying light on my feet to leap back at the slightest ripple. Hunting isn't for the faint of heart, but Mama raised her boy smart. I'm researching a story, not making tomorrow's headline.

I wipe my forehead with my bandanna. I'd wrestle a gator for some cloud cover against the merciless Florida sun boring through my sunscreen like a woodpecker on a palm. My scalp sizzles through my Marlins cap, but I doubt my sweat will even get me a B.

Why I'm going for my MA in journalism is a mystery to my parents. Like they didn't teach me "truth is more precious than gold." The only mystery to me is why I chose Lynn University over FAU, and how I got stuck with Professor Sea Bass.

Mae Sebasse is the associate director of the communications media graduate program, meaning she's not too high to not care, but high enough I wish she didn't. She consistently arrives five minutes late to her Research in Journalism class. She knows we call her Sea Bass, because she's never given anyone higher than a C. I think she's proud of that reputation.

A high-pitched yelp startles me, and I whip my head up. A young woman in shorts and a tank walks along the opposite bank. Another yelp, and I make eye contact with the fluffball she has on a leash. A Pomeranian. On a leash. By a lake.

I shake my head. "You, my guy, are gonna end up a snack."

Transplants. Haven't figured out yet every body of water has an indeterminate number of alligators. Even worse is when they let their infants play by the shore. Can't they read? The sign says "no fishing."

"Uh, buddy?"

I look up at a middle-aged man, backlit by the sun as he gets out of his golf cart. Scruffy beard. Khaki shorts. Golf bag over one shoulder. Eyes slightly out of focus. Could it be?

I pull my journal from my shorts pocket, opening it to the latest paper-clipped *Sun Sentinel* headline: FLORIDA MAN THROWS GATOR INTO WENDY'S DRIVE-THROUGH WINDOW.

"Look, bud." The man's shadow falls on my journal. "Do you have a reservation?"

I look up again. "A what?"

"A reservation." The man stares, eyes blank as his tone. "For tee time. You have to make a reservation to play."

Ah, I understand the confusion. "Oh, it's fine. I'm not playing." Golf is for those with too much time to kill, or who need to recreationally hit something with a club. I'm here tracking the most elusive story yet—and I once saw Bigfoot behind an Office Depot. I stand, stepping away from the water's edge. "My name's Jackson Perch." I give the fellow my hand. "I'm researching suspicious activity in the area."

The man shakes my hand. "Well, I'm sorry, Mr. Perch, but if you're not playing, I'm going to need you to step off the green. We don't want to disrupt folk's sport."

I glance around the empty artificial hills, artificial sandpits dug into the natural sand. It's 2:00 PM on a Wednesday in mid-April. Even the iguanas have gone to find AC.

I huff a laugh. "There's no one here."

He shrugs. "Rules are rules. There are paths if you want to walk around, but if you're not playing, you need to step off the green."

"Come on, man." I haven't been this frustrated since Sea Bass failed my exposé on my HOA closing our pool house to turn it into a meth lab. "I'm not causing any trouble. Just having a look around."

"I'm sorry, mister. It's basic golf etiquette."

"No one's playing! You've gotta be kidding me!"

"Look, I don't appreciate your tone." He takes out his phone. "Do you need me to call the cops to sort you out?"

"Hey, man." I step back, minding the water's edge. "No need to get your shorts all bunched." I put my journal back in my pocket. "I'm leaving, okay?"

Shaking my head, I storm off the green. I was doing honest

research! How am I supposed to find signs of Florida Man with losers like *that* up in my face? I'm ashamed for thinking he might be an actual, wild Florida Man. This is all because Sea Bass insisted I need more "field experience." Like *she's* spent a day outside of central air.

Trudging past a canal, I flip off a plastic goose and the cormorant on its back. I'm going back to the papers. I don't care if it's a "secondary source," at least sunsentinel.com won't kick me off their site.

FLORIDA MAN BITES CASHIER IN MACHETE FIGHT, CLAIMS SELF-DEFENSE

By Felicia Diaz | UPDATED April 20 | ABC25 WPBF News

BOCA RATON, Fla. Arthur Johnson testified he acted in self-defense during a confrontation with his ex-boyfriend, Collin Davis, at a Shell gas station on Powerline Road.

Davis had been on shift at the station's Food Mart, when Johnson was caught on a security camera entering with a machete. He approached the counter and threatened Davis with the machete. Davis disarmed Johnson, taking control of the weapon. Johnson is seen on the footage leaping over the counter and biting Davis's face.

A patron of the store called police, who took both men into custody. Davis was given medical treatment and was released after evaluation of the footage. Johnson faces two charges of assault and battery, but pleads self-defense, since Davis had the machete at the time of the bite. Johnson claims he "feared for his life."

The Palm Beach County Sheriff's Office has yet to release an official statement.

Notes:

- Defenses: biting, resisting arrest, road rage, public indecency, unpredictability?

I slam the rusted door of my Chevy Silverado and leave it parked at the pump. The bell chimes as I enter the 7-Eleven and get in line behind the two types of people: a woman wearing only a bathing suit cover-up, and a man wearing a sweatshirt in ninety degrees. A father herds two small children by the Slurpee machines in the corner. Damn, I hoped it would be empty this hour of the afternoon. After last week's strike out at the golf course, I need a lead. Yesterday's Florida Man was a *Tampa Bay Times* headline: FLORIDA MAN BEATS DOG AT GAS STATION. I don't have time to drive to the west coast and back before class, so this location will have to do. This 7-Eleven was the site of FLORIDA MAN RAMS CAR INTO BROWARD GAS STATION five years ago, so it's due for another sighting. Lightning doesn't strike the same place twice, but this is the lightning capital of America.

I'm desperate. Professor Sea Bass officially threatened to fail me, and if my final doesn't wow her, I'm as dead as a manatee under a motorboat. But she's the one who lectures about the power of "sensationalism." Well, all the local headlines to make it national have been about Florida Man, and mine's gonna hit the biggest. EXCLUSIVE: INTERVIEW WITH FLORIDA MAN, by Jackson Perch.

Who said writing's no career for a man? Take *that*, Dad.

The guy in front of me grabs his Big Gulp and shoves his wallet in his pocket. I pull out my journal just as the family gets in line behind me. Great. Just what I need, impatient kids.

Nodding to the cashier in a Gator orange T-shirt, I step to the counter. "Hi, my name is Jackson Perch. I'm a journalist." A journalism grad student, but details. "Could I ask you a few questions?"

The man chews his gum at me.

"Right." I smile. "First question, has anyone attempted to rob you, perhaps with a machete?"

He steps back, eyes wide. "Whoa—"

I wave my hands. "Don't mean to alarm you. Just a matter of professional curiosity." And academic desperation.

A high-pitched voice from behind me cuts through my words. "Aba, my Slurpee is melting!"

"It's going to do that," the father murmurs to his daughter. "Do you need a paper napkin for your henteleh?"

The cashier runs a hand through his locs and frowns at me. "Hey, man, I don't know." He waves a hand at the family. "There's a line …"

I scowl. That's why I hoped to find the place empty. People will take any excuse to avoid talking to the press. You'd think they'd jump at the chance to help a Good Samaritan and get their name in the papers, but no. They'll complain about the damn iguanas and raccoons in their yards, but when faced with a true infestation plaguing our community, their lips seal like a clam.

"I just need a statement," I plead. "A simple yes or no? Give me something, my guy."

"No." He shrugs. "No dude's ever pulled a knife on me. We good? You buying anything or what?"

I sigh and stash my journal. Maybe I should give up and become a vlogger. "Yeah." Reaching past a fidgeting child, I yank a Slim Jim off the rack and throw it on the counter. At least I'll leave with *something*.

**FLORIDA MAN BREAKS STANDOFF
WHEN SWAT OFFERS PIZZA**

By Robin Kevinsen | UPDATED April 29 | Pensacola News Journal

Pensacola, Fla. A Florida man accused of threatening his family via text message was taken into custody after his wife called 911. When police showed up at the house of 47-year-old Charles Thompkins, the man had barricaded the door and refused to come out.

Shortly after, the wife called 911 again to report Thompkins had taken her daughters out of school. When questioned, Thompkins admitted to having the girls, ages 11 and 9, with him in the house.

After a five-hour confrontation, Thompkins agreed to come out with the girls after being promised a <u>freshly baked pizza</u>. Police took Thompkins into custody. He is charged with kidnapping, threatening violence, and nonviolent resist of arrest. Both daughters were returned safely to their mother.

There has been no official statement whether Thompkins received the <u>pizza</u>.

Notes:

- Diet: hamburgers, beer, pizza, iguana, opossum, crystal meth?

"Yeah, I'll take a Bud Light."

The waiter types my order into the computer. "Anything else?"

"Nah. Got lunch." I hold up a brown Publix bag.

Her dyed green hair tips swish as she nods and looks up from the computer. "ID?"

"Really?" I laugh. "Do I look under twenty-one to you?"

She holds out her hand, unamused. "It's policy."

I roll my eyes but get out my wallet and pass the card over the bar.

She takes it, gaze flicking over and back to me. "Sir, this is a medical marijuana card."

"So? It's a state-issued photo ID."

Sighing, she hands it back. "I'll get your beer."

"Wait!" I hold out a hand. "I'm writing an article. Can I ask you a few questions?"

She hesitates. "I'm really not sure—"

"It'll just be a moment," I plead. "I'm just wondering if you've had any suspicious activity recently?"

"Uh …"

"Anything you can think of." I gestured around. "This is a Publix café. You've got to see some weird go down. Any instances of pizza being used as a bribe or weapon? Any strange men harassing employees? Perhaps on drugs?"

The waiter steps back from the counter. "I'm going to get your beer, sir."

"Oh, come on!" I call, but she's already weaving her way past the taps to the very back.

Man, this is my fifth Publix. Good thing they're not far apart. Why will no one answer my questions? My outline was due yesterday, and I'm still lacking primary sources.

Scowling, I open my journal, flipping past FLORIDA MAN BREAKS INTO NEIGHBOR'S HOUSE, MAKES HIMSELF MARGARITA and FLORIDA MAN ROBS DOLLAR TREE 12 TIMES OVER 3 YEARS to my pages of painstakingly gathered notes.

Florida Man

- *<u>Parasitic</u> life-form*
  - *Ghost? Alien? Spores? Virus? Swamp gas?*
  - *Hosts attract hostility from wildlife. Asymptomatic carriers?*

I mutter a curse, then dart a glance around the café. No one's looking. Good. I deserve a good curse about the lack of a conclusive method of Florida Man contagion without offending anyone's sensibilities. This is where Professor Sea Bass will stop reading my article. "Speculation piece" are her favorite words to slap on my papers.

- *Spreads from host to host*
  - *Host must show <u>predisposition</u> to Florida Man behaviors*
    - *This predisposition can come through <u>substance use</u>*
    - *Many hosts have <u>natural</u> predisposition*
  - *Hosts must be a <u>resident</u> of the state of Florida*
    - *Though not <u>true</u> Florida, panhandle still counts*
    - *Hosts can be transplants, if <u>full time</u>. No snowbirds. Florida Man wants <u>committed</u> hosts*

At least this part is researched. No, I don't have any firsthand accounts, though not for lack of trying.

- *Recorded sightings: 78,924+ rising daily*

How can there be over seventy-five thousand documented sightings, yet nobody I talk to has seen one? Florida Man is by far *the* most documented cryptid in existence, with Bigfoot having under three thousand by comparison. One might argue, as I will in my article, this is due to Bigfoot preferring remote wilderness, whereas Florida Man finds his hosts mostly in suburban locales, which could lead to the disparity in evidence. But as I will also argue, I have personally seen Bigfoot behind an Office Depot.

- *Earliest Recorded:* The Alachua Advocate, *Wednesday May 30, 1883: EATING AN OPOSSUM IN HIS SLEEP and KILLED HIS SWEETHEART ("Where Did the 'Florida Man' Meme Come from?" Made By History,* The Washington Post, *14 Sept. 2022).*

According to the same article, the population of Florida grew over nine times between 1860 and 1930, following the first tourist marketing of the untamed wilderness to the industrialized North. In creating the ideal climate, it only makes sense for Florida Man to evolve during that time. See, Professor, I *can* research.

- *Named January 26, 2013, by Twitter cryptozoologist @_FloridaMan*
  - *codified January 31 by subreddit r/FloridaMan.*

Sea Bass will say those aren't "journalistic sources," but I dare her to find a source more reliable than Reddit.

A glass bottle clinks on the counter next to my journal.

"Sorry for the delay, sir." A different waiter pulls up my order on the computer, deft fingers tattooed with Bible verses. "I can take your payment right here."

I sigh and get out my wallet. Pretty sure I ordered tap, but I'm also sure I ordered it from a petite Asian girl with green hair. Whatever. Bottle's cheaper.

The waiter takes my card, quirking a smile. "I hear you were asking some interesting questions. Looking for something special?"

"Yes!" Finally! *Someone* willing to talk.

He nods. "Don't worry, I got you, dude." He leans over, handing me back my card. "I know a guy who can get you what you need."

I put my wallet back in my pocket, unable to stop my leg from bouncing in excitement. "You mean a lead?"

"Oh, yeah. It'll lead you all sorts of places." He winks. "Be under the pier at midnight in two days. Bring cash or crypto."

I wrinkle my brow. My account barely has the padding to cover this Bud Light, but if it'll get me a primary source for my article, I'll find the money. I guess I shouldn't expect people to talk without incentive.

I smile at the waiter and take my beer. "Thanks, my guy. You've been the most helpful source so far!"

He smiles back. "Anytime, dude."

There's a spring in my step as I leave the Publix. Shopping really is a pleasure.

FLORIDA MAN SUFFERS 41 WOUNDS IN RABID OTTER ATTACK

By Eton Cohen | UPDATED May 1 | CBS12 WPEC

JUPITER, Fla. 73-year-old Florida native, John McNemon, received emergency treatment for multiple injuries after an attack by a rabid river otter.

McNemon tells WPTV he was feeding leftover McDonald's to the ducks in the local canal when they suddenly fled. He turned to see a river otter walking along the bank. McNemon threw the remaining chicken nuggets to the otter, but it leaped on him, biting and scratching. The attack continued for several minutes until a neighbor called the police. The Jupiter Police Department pulled the otter off McNemon and trapped it in a recycling bin.

The otter was taken by Palm Beach County Animal Care & Control, and the Florida Department of Health confirmed a positive test for rabies. McNemon was ushered to the Jupiter Medical Center, where he received gamma globulin, the rabies vaccine, and antibiotics.

Notes:

- Weaknesses: sharks, trains, alligator snapping turtles, traffic laws, crocodiles, rabies?

I hate sand. It's nature's glitter made of powdered glass. And it's everywhere. It's the worst part of living in Florida, besides hot-enough-to-boil-a-lobster summers and tourists. And all three are at the beach.

It's not so bad at night, though, when the tourists and retirees are in bed, and even the sun's gone lights-out. My only company is a group dumping a bucket of baby turtles. Natives, at least.

But there ain't no cure for sand.

I pass my phone's flashlight over the grayish-brown ground, watching my step for broken glass, shells, hypodermic needles, and man-o'-war. Avoiding a patch of kelp, I pick my way to where the pier steps out into the water like a flock of wooden ibis. The moon's long set, so I wouldn't see the Publix waiter's contact in the shadows.

What am I doing? This seems shady, meeting a stranger under a pier at midnight. I'm not sure the live cams see this low, or if they have night vision. Are there even cops around? Oh, there's one, hauling a cuffed man into the back of an unmarked car in a lot by a hedge of sea grapes. He seems busy.

Good thing I'm packing. I run a hand over my stomach to the concealed holster of my 9mm Star BM. Mama raised her boy smart enough to not meet a stranger under the Deerfield Pier at midnight unarmed.

My flashlight dances over denim as I trip over a half-buried leg. I hop-stumble a step, kicking sand. Catching my balance, I whip around.

Sitting on a raggedy blanket is a middle-aged man, jeaned legs outstretched, a beanie tucked around graying curls. He squints in the flashlight, brows raised.

Is this my contact?

"Hey, sorry about that." I smile, though he probably can't see me. "I'm supposed to be meeting someone here …?"

The man chuckles dryly, taking a drag of a cigarette. "Sorry, sonny." He jerks a thumb over his shoulder at the cop car. "Your friendo just got nabbed."

I blink in shock. That was my contact? "Why was he arrested?"

Shaking his head, the man huffs another laugh. "I assume for doing whatever you're here to meet him for."

"What?" I wrinkle my brow. "I didn't think information about Florida Man was illegal." Professor Sea Bass would've mentioned that when I submitted my outline two days late, rather than her usual insistence I "find something worthwhile to spend my time on, or, better yet, turn to fiction, since it's clearly my calling."

The man throws his head back. "Information on Florida Man? Why didn't you say so?"

I start. "What? Do you know something?" Maybe this night won't be a bust!

His lips creep up into a smile around the butt of his cigarette. "You're really looking for Florida Man?"

I sigh. "I'm trying."

"I hope not *here*."

"Why not?"

He shakes his head. "Oh, I shouldn't say."

My pulse races. This could be it. "No, please!"

He squints. "Got any cash?"

My heart sinks. I came expecting to pay, but I hoped this guy would be different.

"I have ten bucks and a scratch off?"

He holds his hand out, and I relinquish the entire contents of my broke-ass wallet.

"Well, this is what I can tell you, sonny." The man points towards the dimly lit street. "Florida Man stays away from the beach. All the amber lights? Great for sea turtles, keeps the babies from getting lost on their way to the sea. But Florida Man? Well, he can't see by amber. Hurts his eyes, y'know?"

Nodding, I pull out my journal. It makes sense. Florida Man often infects those abusing crystal meth, which can damage eyesight.

- *Weaknesses: sharks, trains, alligator snapping turtles, traffic laws, crocodiles, rabies?* <u>amber light</u>

I finish the note and look at the man. "So if not the beach, where would Florida Man go? Have you ever seen one?"

"Oh, yes." He nods. "Many in my time."

My mouth drops.

He laughs again. "If you're serious, sonny, you gotta get down and dirty, right? Venture into the beating heart of Florida itself."

"Where's that?" I breathe.

"Isn't it obvious?" Stubbing out his cigarette in the sand, he leans back on his blanket. "The Everglades."

Of course. If Florida Man arrived in the 1880s to seek out the untamed wilderness, it's only natural the commercialization of the coasts chased him inland. He ventures into the suburbs but doesn't live there. That's why sightings are newsworthy.

My phone's flashlight times out, plunging us into darkness. Fumbling over my screen, I tap the light back on. It shines out over the waves, glinting off jagged spines cutting the water.

I step back, hand brushing the pistol under my shirt. "You seeing this?"

The man lets out a low whistle. "You got the worst luck with rendezvous."

I back away another step, not daring to take my gaze off the alligator lumbering toward us, nine feet of black scales coming to a pointed snout. Oh, that's no gator. I can't tell if its bottom teeth are showing, but Mama always says if you're close enough to tell a gator from a croc by its teeth, you're too darn close.

"I'd start running, sonny." The man had somehow pulled up his blanket and was already several paces up the beach.

I gulp, scrambling up the sand. Tearing my eyes from the crocodile, I run in a straight line—the zigzag doesn't work. Very little works against being chased by a crocodile. Not bothering to watch my step for bits of broken glass, shells, hypodermic needles, or jellyfish, I pour on speed. The croc falls behind at the hedge of sea grapes, but I don't stop at the street. I run the three blocks to the parking garage, hurl myself into my truck, and lock the doors.

Breathing heavily, I lean against the steering wheel. More reason Florida Man isn't at the beach, with that sort of wildlife moving in. Though crocs are in the Glades too.

Maybe Professor Sea Bass is right. A real journalist can't find sensationalism if he can't find sense. But this is the most concrete lead I've had this semester, and the first draft of my article is due next week. If I don't get this break, this whole search—every disapproving shake of Sea Bass's head, every sniping word from my father—will end in nothing. I can't fail this class. I *will* find Florida Man, whatever it takes.

FLORIDA MAN EATING CHEESECAKE IN HIS UNDERWEAR ATTACKED BY SHARK IN THE EVERGLADES

By Carlos Davids-Rodríguez | UPDATED May 7 | Miami Herald

COLLIER COUNTY, Fla. Video surfaced of a Florida man, wearing only briefs, being attacked by a shark while knee-deep in the water of Everglades National Park.

Sunshine Lowell, the park ranger who reportedly took the video, told the *Miami Herald* she was patrolling in a boat when she found the man. He is seen on the video claiming to be fine, just enjoying his cheesecake. Lowell is then heard coaxing the man onto the safety of her boat.

The video then shows a shark leaping from the water to bite the man's arm. The shark seems to knock the man down, at which point Lowell steers the boat closer and pulls the man aboard.

Paramedics transferred the unidentified man to a local hospital for treatment of injuries and possible drug use.

According to Marjorie Friedman of public affairs for Everglades and Dry Tortugas National Parks, the shark was likely a bull shark.

While uncommon, shark attacks can occur in the Everglades, and Friedman urges all visitors to take caution around wildlife and water.

There has been no statement whether the shark got the cheesecake.

Notes:

- Habitat: golf course, gas station, Publix, beach, Everglades? water?

My oar slices murky water like a spoonbill, urging my hibiscus-red kayak through a patch of duckweed. The wetlands buzz with mosquitoes, dragonflies, and bellows of gators. The air hangs thick enough to drink, smelling of rot tinged with smoke. Somewhere, the Glades burn. But here, the skies are clear, not a hint of a cloud in sight. Meaning it's hot as Hell's bikini bottom.

But it'll be worth it. I can feel Florida Man close—just like my deadline. The semester ends this week, and Professor Sea Bass made it clear I'm not getting an extension on my final. I have the main points written out, and an all-nighter should finish it, *if* I can find Florida Man. If not, my star interview's a Corona short of a Sunrise.

The bag of key-lime saltwater taffy I brought has melted together, so I tear off a piece to chase the smoke from my tongue. A ripple disturbs the surface by my kayak, and I retract my oar. Water moccasin? Too big. Python? A sleek black shape bursts from the water, hopping onto an arch of mangrove roots. It tosses a fish into its beak, opening glossy wings to either side. An anhinga. I shake my head and plunge my oar back into the river. Damn snakebirds.

There's a whole kettle of them in the mangroves, black males guarding brown-headed females, with a few cormorants in the mix. A spot of orange catches my eye, a scrap of paper woven into a nest.

Ducking under the golden web of a banana spider, I float close enough to get my hand pecked by an angry anhinga. I swear as blood runs down my wrist into the water. Devil birds. Since I've already bled for it, I rip the paper from the nest. I push away before Mama Bird decides to build her nest with my skin.

Shaking off the blood, I hold the paper to a sunray, rubbing my thumb over the orange background to the pink lotto flamingo. The last two Powerball numbers are still in the nest with the rest of the ticket, but I don't need them to be a winner. No lotto ticket ends up this deep in the Glades without the help of a true Florida Man. This is the sign I've been looking for. Watch Sea Bass scoff now!

A dark ripple creeps through the water. I freeze—another snakebird? Snake? Or…

Eyes break the surface, followed by tan spines and a leathery snout—round. I gulp, swallowing my taffy. Maybe I can paddle away?

I turn to dip my oar into the gator-less side of my kayak—only it's not gator-less. Another swamp puppy peers from the murk, and by the distance between eyes and nostrils, it's larger. Both are bigger than my kayak and made of stronger stuff.

Don't I have the luck of half a Powerball ticket. The gators might *not* attack, but they'll snap my oar before I get it in the water. I'm as stuck as a slug on a hot sidewalk.

The first gator opens its mouth, revealing a pink maw of jagged teeth. Maybe I can distract it with food? Moving slowly, I rest my oar in its holder and open my backpack, pulling out a Ziploc with two tuna sandwiches. I flinch at the stereo of hisses as the gators scent the fish. Withdrawing one, I hold it out. I yank my hand clear as jaws snap. My heart races like the Daytona 500. That's one sandwich gone.

Carefully, I Frisbee-toss the other. Gator One follows it into the mangroves. Which leaves me with Gator Two, no more sandwiches, and limited time before Gator One returns for seconds. Ruffling through my backpack for *anything*, I grab the bag of key-lime taffy.

Gator Two opens its maw in a hiss. What the hell.

Balling the wad of melted taffy, I channel my inner José Fernández and pitch it into the gator's mouth. Its jaws snap, jamming the wad into its teeth with a literal ton of pressure. And they don't open again.

Alligators have some of the strongest jaws in the animal kingdom—on the close.

Leaving Gator Two struggling under the elasticity of saltwater taffy—brackish-water taffy now—I grab my oar and ske-paddle.

Bye, alligator, I will not see you later.

Breathing through the haze of adrenaline, I let out a laugh. I can't believe that worked! That was wild, newsworthy. A headline for sure—

Oh.

A chill races along my skin, pricking the sweat like static. Finally, a conclusive method of Florida Man contagion, and it tastes like orange blossoms and ozone. My eyes unfocus, but my perspective is clearer than ever.

Florida Man was inside me all along.

FLORIDA MAN FENDS OFF ALLIGATOR ATTACK WITH SALTWATER TAFFY

By Jackson Perch | SUBMITTED May 9 | Lynn University

About the Author

Sara Itka is a born and raised South Floridian, meaning she believes "Fall" is when a hurricane comes and blows leaves off the trees. She has never wrestled an alligator, but she did have a pet iguana, and she has seen Bigfoot behind an Office Depot. When she isn't working through her seemingly infinite "to be read" list, she can usually be found procrastinating working on her seemingly infinite "to be written" list. Her favorite procrastination methods include procrasti-linguistics, procrasti-brewing-tea, procrasti-making-YouTube-playlists-for-projects, and procrasti-dancing-to-the-playlists. If you want to help her procrastinate, find her at saraitka.com.

Working the Salt Mine

by Sam Knight

New Mexico Territory, 1850

Working overhead more a chore than expected. Et as much dirt as hauled, but vein widening. Good quartz. Good gold must be near. Concerned working too high and collapsing tunnel. No timber for miles. Will press on and keep watch.

Swoop Smith, squatting on his heels and leaning back against the craggy tunnel wall, wiped sweat and gritty dirt from his eyes. He took a deep breath of stale air, then blew more dirt off the pages of his journal before dipping his quill again and finishing notating by the dim lamplight.

He finished chewing his hardtack, closed the journal, and headed to the mouth of the tunnel, where he dropped the book for someone to find if anything should happen to him. Hot as it was in the tunnel, it was hotter out here this time of day.

The small tunnel had taken all summer to carve out with shovel and pickax. Extending nearly forty feet into the side of the rocky hill, it was little wider than his own shoulders in most places. He had difficulty swinging the pick in the tight space, but now that he'd found good color, he was loath to waste effort on widening it.

His calloused hands protested as he took up the axe, but they obeyed, and he struck the stone above his head again and again, fighting the cramped space. The metal head of the pick sang between blows against the quartz, filling the tunnel with wailing sounds. A glancing blow tossed a shower of sparks at his face, and a piece of hot rock hit his eye.

"Goddamn!" Swoop dropped the axe and put his hands to his face. He knew better than to rub; he had scratched his eyes before, so instead he just pressed. His eye watered, but the rock didn't come out.

Hand covering his injury, Swoop headed out, leaving his tools and lantern behind. The glow of day wasn't far away, and he had no problem feeling his way back.

Squinting his good eye against the bright sun of the arid desert, he headed for his makeshift camp: a bedroll and supplies piled up in a lean-to, just outside the mine entrance. His sudden appearance from the mine startled his horses, and they both reared and pulled against their tethers. He ignored them as he fumbled with a waterskin and poured tepid water into his eye.

He looked up into the blue sky, blinking rapidly, trying to clear his vision and hoping he hadn't done any permanent damage.

The horses were still acting up. "Settle down." His voice was strong yet calm. He took a drink before pouring more over his eye.

A boulder shifted up on the hill behind him, and loose rocks rolled down and fell around his feet.

Swoop stumbled away from the hill, afraid of being hit by falling rock. His vision, fouled with water, failed him as he watched for signs of a landslide, fearing his tunnel collapsing. He wiped his eyes, trying to see through the blur. His heart jumped as he realized he likely hadn't spooked the horses.

"Who's there?" He suspected a cougar, but he made no sudden movements. He didn't want to get shot going for his rifle if it was a man.

No reply came.

He waited for his eyes to clear. He'd thought someone had been poking around his camp the last couple of days, but he'd seen no sign other than a few things out of place. A white man would have revealed himself or stolen everything by now, so he suspected an

Indian. The local tribes were Hopi and Navajo, and the Navajo were not known for being friendly.

The horses were finally settling down, and Swoop's eyes cleared enough he was sure there was no one on the hill. He looked one more time. There was no one there. That convinced him it was either an animal or an Indian. He would like to think it was just a rockslide, but the horses wouldn't have reacted that way if nothing had been there.

He took another swig from his waterskin and casually tossed it back, doing his best to seem unconcerned. He hoped if he didn't appear threatening, he could make it back into the mine and grab his rifle.

As he turned for the tunnel, something on the ground caught his eye. A track.

So, he had a visitor after all. The track seemed odd, but he didn't want to stop to investigate until he had a rifle in his hand.

The tunnel was pitch-black compared to the full daylight, and Swoop had a more difficult time working his way in than he'd had coming out. Even when he made it back to the area illuminated by his lantern, his sight was too dim to see well. He grabbed his rifle from where it leaned against the wall and headed back out.

He slowed, assessing the situation, when he could see out of the mine. The horses were calm now, but they both kept their ears cocked toward the area where the rocks had fallen. Swoop slowly stepped into the daylight, keeping watch for any movement.

Making his way to the track he had seen, he kneeled to get a good look at it. It was nearly the length of his own footprint, but it had three toes that splayed twice as wide as his boot. It put Swoop in mind of a giant turkey track.

Standing, he looked around for more tracks but didn't see any. A flying bird would put into account his not finding tracks before too. An Indian legend of the Thunderbird came to his mind, and Swoop was sure a bird with a foot that size could carry off children. No wonder the horses had been nervous.

No longer worried about getting shot by another human, Swoop checked his supplies. As before, things mostly looked like he had left them, and he probably wouldn't have noticed anything had been touched, except this time something was missing: his salt.

The whole pouch had been dug out of his food pack and taken. And everything else had been put back.

A chill ran down Swoop's spine. Animals didn't put things back.

Swoop moved away from his supplies as a feeling of unease settled over him. He glanced at the horses. They were calm, but still focused on the hillside above.

Rifle in hand, Swoop went to them and stroked each gently across the nose as he looked back up the hill where they watched. With his eyes, Swoop followed the cut on the hill left by the gravel that had fallen, and he spotted the boulder that had shifted. Next to the boulder lay a small, worn leather pouch. His salt.

He hefted his rifle to his shoulder and looked for the best way up the hill, finally deciding to circle to the right before coming back across to avoid the loose scree. Keeping watch for any sign of movement above, Swoop had little trouble reaching his pouch, but as he reached down to pick it up, he froze.

Prickles ran up and down his skin, and his knees trembled with fear as he realized his pouch was still clutched in ... a hand?

The slender, four-fingered hand was the same dusty color and mottled texture of the loose rocks and dirt around it, camouflaging it very well.

As his eyes traced the contours of the hand, he found the forearm and followed the thin shape up, past an elbow, and to the body. And then the head.

Swoop's mouth went dry, and he found he couldn't swallow as he realized the large rock next to his foot had closed eyes and nostril slits.

Now that he could see it, the body was obvious. It looked like a small, willowy man with the head of a lizard.

As he examined the form, he saw the real boulder had crushed a leg. He could see the dark blood soaking into the dirt around the edge of the large rock.

The creature wasn't moving, but Swoop took no chances. He raised his rifle and aimed for the middle of the skull. As his finger tightened on the trigger, he realized the beast wore something around its neck.

He lowered the rifle and peered closer. A collar? Could this creature belong to someone? The material was obviously fabricated. It was an intricate weave of grasses that formed a repeating, diamond-shaped pattern.

One eye blinked.

Swoop jumped and tripped backward.

The creature woke up and tried to scramble away, but its trapped leg held it pinned. Hissing, it began flopping and twisting, coiling about itself inhumanly, trying to free its leg.

Horrified, Swoop continued backing away. He had seen snakes twist like that, curling and knotting themselves to escape when a boot or a shovel had come down upon their head.

The lizard-thing stopped writhing and froze, staring at Swoop, unblinking. A small, forked tongue, black as any serpent's, darted in and out from between inflexible lips. Slowly, the tongue extended out, tasting the air, moving about like a tiny two-fingered arm feeling around for something.

Golden, slitted eyes turned and focused on the salt pouch.

The creature slowly unwound itself, gaze flicking between the pouch and Swoop. When it was untangled, it reached out and picked up the pouch with its four-fingered hand. It brought the pouch close to its face and peered inside, then, using two hands, it pulled the strings and sealed it tightly.

Looking up to Swoop, the lizard man deliberately tossed the pouch to him and waited, watching.

Swoop feared he might vomit. This thing was no creature, no animal. It had intelligence. Had he believed in demons and devils, he would have known this to be one, but Swoop was a man of the earth, and he knew flesh and blood when he saw it.

He bent down and picked up the salt pouch.

The other watched him intently.

When Swoop made no other motion, the reptilian creature slowly closed its eyes and let out a soft hiss, laying its head on the ground. The four-fingered hands curled into fists, and it pulled its arms in close to its body.

Not knowing what to do, Swoop sat and watched. Returning the salt left no doubt in his mind this creature was intelligent. If this were a dog or a horse, he would put it out of its misery. If it were a man, he would help it. But it was neither.

Swoop decided and stood. The golden eyes opened and watched him. Swoop laid his rifle and the salt pouch down and held his hands wide, fingers spread, hoping the creature would recognize he intended no harm.

He approached slowly, trying not to make any threatening moves.

The lizard man watched but remained still.

Swoop came within reach of the spindly arms and hesitated, ready to spring back, but no swiping came at him. He kneeled close to the pinned leg and heard a nervous hiss, but there was still no movement.

The boulder couldn't weigh more than a couple hundred pounds, and the leg was pinned under the edge, so Swoop thought he would have little trouble moving it. He just had to figure out how to do it without hurting the leg more.

He stepped back to where he could meet the lizard man's eyes and made gestures he hoped would be understood as he was leaving but would be back.

The slitted eyes closed without any sign of acknowledgment or recognition.

Swoop returned with a shovel, an axe, a waterskin, and some jerky. He sat in front of the lizard man and uncorked his waterskin as the creature watched him. He took a drink, re-corked the skin, and placed it where the thin reptilian arms could reach it. Swoop then took a bite of jerky and made a show of chewing it up before adding the rest of it on top of the waterskin.

The golden eyes flicked back and forth between Swoop and his offering, but the creature still did not move.

Not knowing how to reassure a lizard, Swoop got up, grabbed his shovel, and set about freeing the creature's leg. He worked slowly and methodically, being careful not to touch the injured leg or allow the boulder to put more pressure on it. He dug enough room to place a rock as a fulcrum and then began using his shovel handle as a lever. When he was ready, he tried to caution the lizard man to prepare, but he still got no response.

He waved his hand to get its attention, and it focused on him again. He held up a finger and said, "One." He held up another and said, "Two." With the third finger and the word "Three," Swoop mimed grunting and pushing the rock off the leg.

The reptilian eyes didn't blink.

Swoop and the creature looked at each other for a moment before the creature tiredly closed its eyes again.

Swoop went back to the boulder. He levered his shovel handle and counted out loud. "One. Two. Three!" He pushed down on the handle, and the boulder rocked off the lizard man's leg.

The lizard man scrambled away with lightning speed, startling Swoop as the boulder rolled over and began lumbering down the hill. Swoop forgot about the lizard man as he realized his horses might be in danger.

"Hiya!" Swoop yelled to get the horses' attention. "Hiya!" If they didn't pull off their tethers, he hoped they would at least be able to move out of the way.

He needn't have worried. The rock fell past his mine entrance, hit the ground, and stopped where it landed. The horses were shaken, but they would be fine.

Swoop remembered the lizard man and turned quickly, worried that he had left his back unguarded from attack.

The creature was between him and his rifle. It would have been on all fours but for the injured back leg that hung limply. No longer drowsy, it was completely alert, and it was injured.

Knowing that an injured animal, or man for that matter, was dangerous, Swoop squatted where he was and waited.

The lizard man just watched him.

After a moment, Swoop realized the water and jerky were within his reach, so he slowly picked them up and repeated his earlier show of taking a drink and eating. Mouth full, he gently tossed the waterskin toward the lizard man, following it with the jerky. Chewing, he waited.

The forked tongue flickered toward the items, writhing in the air, as though it had a life of its own and wanted the food even though the rest of the body refused to move. Finally, the golden eyes dropped from Swoop to the waterskin, and the creature slowly crept forward to reach it.

Swoop was careful not to move as he watched the lizard man sit down. Inhuman hands easily uncorked the waterskin and poured liquid into the gaping reptilian maw. Needle-sharp teeth glinted in the sunlight as the water splashed across them. The lizard man capped the skin and tossed it back to Swoop. It picked up the last of the jerky and put it in its mouth. It didn't chew as Swoop had. Instead, it worked its long tongue in and out of its mouth as it extended and contracted its neck.

Swoop thought he could see the lump of food moving down as the lizard man showed the smooth, pale scales of its throat.

They sat and watched each other for a long time. Swoop was sure there were thoughts in that oblong scaly head, but he was equally sure they were nothing like his, and likely never would be. He doubted the two of them could ever comprehend each other.

The lizard man cocked its head sideways and looked at Swoop's rifle.

Swoop felt his belly knot. Would that thing know how to use his rifle? Would it use the rifle if it knew how?

Long, thin brown fingers reached out toward the rifle, and Swoop tensed, not knowing if he should run toward the creature or away, but knowing he wouldn't be able to get up from his sitting position fast enough.

The fingers stopped short of the rifle and picked up the salt pouch. Golden eyes turned back to Swoop. The lizard man made some quick, complicated gestures, then, in a move that would have broken a man's back, lowered its head and put its chin on the ground.

It rose back up and tossed the pouch to Swoop.

Swoop caught it out of the air. When he looked back, the lizard man was gone.

Think me heat-mad, but I swear on the Good Book true. The visitor be neither man nor beast. Demon, perhaps, but not of ol' Nick. A man-like lizard what can ken.

Swoop put away the journal, not sure what else to write. He didn't believe it himself, yet he hadn't slept the last few nights. His dreams were haunted by lightning-quick snakes and lizards that stared at him with intelligent eyes. He'd considered leaving, but he knew he was so close to the gold that he couldn't bring himself to go.

He continued working the growing vein, making progress inches at a time in the lamplit gloom. He'd dug out enough gold to make up for all the supplies he had bought to get this far, but he was nowhere close to being a rich man.

On the fourth day after he had seen the lizard man, an occurrence he was nearly ready to chalk up to hallucinations from being alone in the heat for too long, he came out of the cave to find his supplies had been gone through again. This time, it was a mess.

"Damn it!" He started toward the pile of supplies.

A hissing sound stopped him in his tracks.

Swoop turned to find the lizard man standing upright on the injured leg. Scabs covered the scaly skin, but the leg appeared strong.

The horses seemed to notice it for the first time and began whinnying and shying away.

It hissed again, looking Swoop in the eye, before it slowly sank into what might be considered a sitting position. It cocked its head and waited.

Swoop imitated it and sank down to sit facing it.

The lizard man held out one of its slender-fingered hands and revealed it had the salt pouch. It leaned forward in its impossible way and touched its chin to the ground. Sitting back up, it tossed the pouch to Swoop.

Swoop opened the pouch and looked inside. All the salt appeared to be there.

More hissing and complex hand gestures from the lizard man were followed by the presentation of another pouch, this one woven from grass, the same as the collar it wore. It tossed the second pouch to Swoop.

Swoop caught it out of the air, surprised by its weight. He pulled at the drawstrings to reveal the contents. Shaking the nugget out into his hand, Swoop could hardly believe his eyes. Gold. Enough to buy a farm.

He felt a stupid grin involuntarily crawling across his face and did his best to suppress it. He looked up at the lizard man.

The slender creature pointed to the salt, then to the gold, then made a gesture of tapping a fist against the flat of its other hand.

"You want to trade?"

The lizard man repeated the motion and waited.

Swoop picked up the salt and tossed it back to the lizard man. He tapped a fist against the palm of his hand. "Trade."

The lizard man hissed in a way Swoop assumed was satisfaction. It rose and turned to leave.

"Wait." Swoop stood.

The smaller figure turned and looked back, cocking its head.

"Trade more." Swoop made the fist-motion again and followed it with a sweeping gesture.

The lizard man did not appear to understand, so Swoop motioned it to come closer. It stayed where it was.

Swoop tried to explain. He sat his gold nugget next to the boulder that had fallen from the hill when he had leveraged it off the lizard man's leg. With hand motions, he tried to show that the nugget was little and the boulder was big. Then he pointed to the salt pouch and to the gold and tried to gesture that he could trade much more salt for much more gold.

When the lizard man's eyes widened, Swoop knew it had finally understood.

Pointing to the sun, Swoop motioned it moving across the sky and counted. "One." He swept his arm across the sky again. "Two." He continued until he reached seven days. Then he made the trade sign again and pointed to the salt and the gold and motioned for much bigger.

The lizard man watched it all with intent interest and then matched Swoop's hand sign. *Trade.*

Town is three days away. Hate to leave the mine for so long. Will barely make it back in seven days but have to try. If the man-lizard reckons same as me, it will be worth it.

When Swoop cashed the gold nugget in at the bank, he couldn't keep the grin off his face. He stabled his horses and headed for the hotel and a hot bath. He'd never had so much money in his life. It was hard to keep his mouth shut, to not brag, not get drunk and spend the evening with the ladies, but there would be plenty of time for all that later.

After a good night's sleep, he bought a wagon and another horse, as neither of his were accustomed to being hitched. He didn't sell either of his horses, thinking perhaps he would buy a ranch, and he might need them.

He restocked his supplies at the general store, buying all the salt they would sell him. The proprietor had two and a half fifty-pound kegs but refused to let some crazy fool buy all the town's supply, so Swoop settled for one and a half kegs.

Swoop was on his way back to his mine before lunch.

Return leg felt like to be forever but made it back in time for the morrow. Mine appears untouched. If trade works, won't matter. Didn't bother unloading, except salt. Can't sleep. What if I mistook?

Swoop awoke at first light, surprised he had slept at all.

He set up the salt kegs in the place he had traded with the lizard man before and got ready to settle in and wait. The last thing he expected was the sound of a hammer on a revolver being cocked behind him.

"Hands where I can see them." The voice was full of arrogant self-confidence.

Swoop didn't own a revolver, only his rifle. And he had left it in the wagon so he wouldn't present a threat to the lizard man. He held his hands out to his sides and turned around slowly.

The bearded face was unfamiliar, as were two of the three faces of the other men behind him. The last man, though, was the teller at the bank where Swoop had cashed in the gold nugget. All of them held guns at the ready.

"Told you boys he'd have a mine out here somewhere," the first man said over his shoulder without taking his eyes off Swoop. "A man don't buy a wagon and horse with a gold nugget unless he's going back for a lot more." He jerked his head to the side. "Thomas, go get the horses. He's the only one here."

"Sure thing, Marvin." A gaunt-faced man nodded, holstered his gun, and headed around the hill.

"William, you and Pearl check the camp out. See if he's got anything else worth a spit." The other two men headed for Swoop's wagon.

Marvin waved his revolver toward the mine entrance. "Show me where the good stuff is, and you might just come out of this alive."

Swoop turned and looked back at the mine entrance. "We'll need a lantern out of the wagon. It's too dark to see in there without one."

"Pearl! Grab a lantern!" Marvin pointed at the mine again. "Get moving."

Beyond the hill, a horse screamed, and the sound of hooves grew loud.

Marvin turned to look, and Swoop went for the man's gun. Swoop was too slow, and Marvin was ready. The bearded man smashed the flat of the gun's grip across Swoop's face, breaking his nose and blinding him with pain. Swoop fell to his knees.

"You try that again, and I'll kill you on the spot!" Marvin kicked him, knocking him down.

As his vision cleared, Swoop saw the men's four horses galloping past in a panic.

"Thomas!" Marvin called out, but there was no answer. "William! Pearl! Go check on Thomas!"

A strangled cry sounded from the wagon. Swoop looked just in time to see a brown flash of movement disappear behind some brush. William, standing next to the wagon, wavered on his feet for a moment, holding his throat, then fell face-first into the dirt.

Pearl screamed and waved his gun wildly. "What the hell was that? Marvin! Something is out here!"

Marvin fired a shot at the brush Swoop had seen the lizard man vanish into.

"It killed William!" Pearl's voice was high and shaky.

"Indians!" Marvin yelled as he turned, scanning the hill above them. "Get down!"

"That weren't no goddamned Indian! It weren't no—!" Pearl fell silent.

Swoop, holding his bloody nose, looked back for Pearl, but the man was gone.

Marvin whipped the tip of his revolver back and forth, pointing where Pearl had been. "What the hell …?"

Swoop blinked as a slender brown figure appeared behind Marvin. With a move so fast Swoop couldn't follow, the lizard man raked its claws across Marvin's throat then ran behind some rocks.

Marvin spun to face an attacker that was no longer there, his mouth working, but no sound coming out. He dropped his gun and put both hands to his neck. His eyes met Swoop's, pleading, as he fell to his knees.

Swoop moved out of the way as Marvin's body fell to the ground.

Using one of the salt kegs to steady himself, Swoop stood up and wiped blood from his broken nose.

The lizard man hesitantly walked out from behind a pile of rocks, scabs still evident on its leg. It cocked its head and looked at Swoop.

Swoop held his arms wide, fingers spread, and then sat back down.

The lizard man sat down and looked at him expectantly.

Reaching for the closest keg, Swoop opened it and pulled out a handful of salt. He let the white grains fall between his fingers and back into the keg.

The lizard man's tongue snaked out, groping at the air, tasting for the salt.

Swoop replaced the lid and pushed the keg toward the lizard man. He then pushed the second keg forward and made the fist-palm sign for trade.

The lizard man hissed, and movement behind Swoop startled

him. He turned to see five lizard men walking forward, each carrying two heavy bags made of animal skin.

It was disconcerting to be surrounded by the lizard men, but after what he had seen them do to Marvin and his men, Swoop knew if they had intended him harm, he couldn't have stopped them.

They set the bags in front of Swoop. A lizard man opened a bag, reached in, and lifted out a handful of gold nuggets, allowing them to slip through its four-fingered hand and back into the bag.

Trade, the lizard man sitting across from Swoop signaled.

Trade, Swoop signaled back.

Excitement among the other lizard men became immediately evident as they moved around the salt kegs with uncanny speed, hissing at each other.

More trade? the first lizard man signaled to Swoop.

More trade, he answered.

The lizard man drew a sun in the dirt and began marking days. Another symbol soon became clear as the moon, and Swoop realized the lizard man was asking for a trade in the spring.

In the spring, more trade. Salt. Gold, Swoop answered.

The lizard man seemed pleased. It stood up and hissed. One of the other lizard men brought over a small pouch and left again. The lizard man with the scabs on its leg began gesturing again, and Swoop was hard-pressed to follow.

It gestured to the other lizard men and the bodies of Marvin, Pearl, and William. Swoop noticed for the first time that Thomas's body had been dragged over from wherever he was killed.

The lizard man tossed Swoop a pouch. Inside was the largest uncut diamond he had ever seen.

Trade, motioned the lizard man. *More trade in the spring. Salt. Gold. Diamond. Men. Bring more men.*

A storm brewed in the distance, darkening the distant edges of the green pastures that rolled in the wind for as far as Swoop's eyes could see. He sat on the porch of the main house, watching his children chasing each other, listening to them laugh, and smiled.

Opening his journal, he dipped his quill and began writing. *Instructions for Working the Salt Mine.*

About the Author

Sam Knight is the owner/publisher of Knight Writing Press and author of six children's books, four novels, and more than ninety short stories, including three coauthored with Kevin J. Anderson. Though he has written in many cool worlds, such as Planet of the Apes, Wayward Pines, and Jeff Sturgeon's Last Cities of Earth, among his family, Sam will probably always be known for Chunky Monkey Pupu.

Once upon a time, Sam was known to quote books the way some people quote movies, but now he claims having a family has made him forgetful—as a survival adaptation.

Best Foot Forward
by Aaron Fors

From: nessieisthebestie@cryptid.com
Subject: Sellout trash

Dear Mr. Harry Walker,

    I have enjoyed several of your episodes debunking obvious hoaxes: crop circles, free-energy machines, the chupacabra, etc., but I find it highly improbable that in all of your supposedly "rigorous" and credible research on Nessie, you were not convinced based on the weight of the evidence, credible eyewitnesses, photographs, seismic and geological data—on and on it goes. So I have just one question: Who bought you off?

    Your episode of *Beating Around the Bush*: "Nessie or Nope? Reviewing the evidence" does a great disservice to credible researchers and serious cryptid hunters by painting us all as raving lunatics and obsessive nutjobs.

    To that end, this email serves as a notice to cease and desist all negative claims about the Loch Ness Monster. I further demand that you retract your episode on Nessie, the noble lady of the Loch, posthaste, or I will sue you to the ends of the flat earth. I bet you'll deny that next.

    Yours in court, jerkwad,
    Bethany Adelante

From: truthwarrrier96@freedomeagle.com
Subject: you lie

Get wrecked government shill. The truth is out their. Disclosure is mear weeks away. The sheer arrogance to think your little podcast could hold back the rising tide will be your undoing.
    Phil Waters III

From: joyfuljosie32@trojaninc.com
Subject: I'm so sorry about all the hate mail

Dear host of *Beating Around the Bush*,
    I know how much hate mail you receive, and I just wanted to let you know, you deserve it. And ten times more. I hope you die. In fact, I'm going to find where you live and—

Sigh.
    I stopped reading after that. Par for the course. Everyone has their golden calf. Turns out people really don't like it when you butcher theirs. Which I kind of do for a living.
    People ask why I didn't go for a YouTube channel instead of a podcast, but I've been told I have a face for radio on more than one occasion. Also it'd be difficult to fit enough of me into the frame even if anyone wanted to see that. I live a simple life in a small home in rural Oregon at the edge of the great Pacific wilderness. Big cities make me nervous—too many people, too cramped, too fast-paced; I've always been most comfortable near nature. I don't even like going into town to restock on supplies, so I try to load up the truck with enough to last me at least a whole month.
    Sitting down at my oak writing desk, mug of coffee in hand, I began writing my monthly letter home by hand. I grew up with a big extended

family—parents, grandparents, great-grandparents, and mediocre aunts, uncles, and cousins—all on the same patch of rural land. It was hard living so far away from them now. I don't make it home much. The podcast is becoming too popular, and visiting is always a logistical nightmare health-wise; my family is immunocompromised, sort of.

Dear family,

Life is good here in the big city. My work is becoming very popular. I am officially the 970th most popular podcast in science communication! (Don't ask the ranking overall.) City dwellers don't much seem to share our love of science and learning. Joe Rogan did, however, invite me on his show after my last episode on climate change, but I will, of course, have to decline. He insists on recording video.

I really think we're getting through to them. The hate mail has stopped, so tell Uncle Jer to stop worrying. I will send this letter with Breadbrain right away. I hope he doesn't have any trouble finding you. Last time he almost got lost flying around the logger's camps.

I'll be dropping off some supplies, including textbooks for the little ones and as many Nutty Buddy Bars as I can fit in the crate for Uncle Jer. So please tell him to stay away from trick-or-treating this year. You know how he gets around Halloween. I promise they can tell it's not a costume. This isn't the sixties. Everyone and their toddler has a smartphone with HD video. Reports are still coming out from his last walkabout in Peoria. (Tie him up if you have to, Xochitl, I swear.) Dropping the crate in the usual place. I'll do my best on my side, but be thorough with the decontamination, Xo.

I love you all with every hair. Hug a tree and sing a song for me.

PS Don't read this part out loud, Xo. I'm including a smartphone with satellite internet and episodes of my podcast loaded up, in case you and the little ones want to hear what I'm up to. Bottom of the crate, hidden in a computer science book. Don't let Gram Grams see it.

I wrote easily in the scrawling pictographic script of my people. Of course, I was the only one to do it on paper, such a fragile and wasteful medium for carrying information, but I was out of bark, and Breadbrain, as a small carrier pigeon, couldn't carry stone. The words were lifeless and lacked all nuance. I only had the three main smell pigments on hand, and my signature smell, of course. The smell for good, the smell for bad, the smell for neutral, and the smell for me. Many of the newer words like "climate change" and "HD" required so many complex scents to compose, I'd be at it for hours without an elaborate typing set up like Gram Grams had, anyway.

That gave me an idea, however. I tore open one sacrificial package of Nutty Buddies, crushed one between my thumb and forefinger, and smeared some of the essential fats in an arcing accent line over the symbols for "food" and "crate." I hoped that would convince Uncle Jer to control his impulses. So there—five scents.

Only Xochitl, my youngest sister, could read the nearly scentless letter filled with human words. It made me feel illiterate and like I was forgetting so much in my self-imposed isolation, but I was determined to make it in the big city and carve out a new life for my family. If this was the price, so be it.

Stuffing the letter in a small birchwood canister and tying it to Breadbrain's left leg, I sent him off with a snuggle and the birdsong for home, for family. The People of the Forest.

That night I came home from the long miles of off-roading into the forest to drop off a massive wooden crate, sweaty and smelling like a Sasquatch.

I got in the shower, rubbed the coarse, scratchy fur growing all along my body, and pulled out the enormous tub of "depilatory cream for sensitive skin." I was already halfway through it, but some areas were too sensitive for it, and that's where the razor came in.

Later, sitting at my desk wrapped in thick towels and smelling like burnt hair, I found two dozen more emails, charming examples of the finest humanity offered.

The hate mail didn't bother me ... much. Most of it came from people with genuine mental illness who saw grand conspiracies and nefarious enemies wherever they turned. They were just trying to make sense of it all, and I struck them as an easy target, but they were no real threat. They usually couldn't make it through an email cogently, and, while it was cruel to think, I knew no one would ever believe them, even if they were right.

From: artemisseeking@mail.reed.edu
Subject: Clcalmish

I know. Meet me at 2:30 PM at Purrington's cat café. Be there or be exposed.

No. No, no, no. The denial echoed in my head, along with much less polite things that didn't translate well and would get my podcast flagged NSFW if I were to record them. My thoughts were suffused with the overpowering smell for "bad": fire and rotting meat, with a hint of gunpowder, a modern addition to the word.

All languages shifted and changed with time, lest they become irrelevant and go extinct. Is that what was going to happen to my people? They were so close already; only a few hundred small families remained, peppering the forests of the Americas with their ginger fur, sweet songs, and gentle tending of the migratory food forests thousands of miles wide—though less every year—and tens of thousands of years old.

Was this how it ended? *Clcalmish.* That one word was all it took. This wasn't a Sasquatch word, of course. It was the Salish word for my people and meant roughly "People of the Forest." But the word hadn't been in use for more than four hundred years. Not since Gram Grams had been young. No human alive should know it.

Ignore it. I would just ignore it. How much could they know? What could they possibly do?

A dot-edu address, at Reed College no less. The most prestigious university in the Pacific Northwest prided itself on promoting "intellectual curiosity." Right now, I hated intellectual curiosity.

I presumed the name was a reference to the Greek goddess of the hunt, but a quick search for an Artemis at Reed College yielded a female graduate student in mycology and anthropology. That explained some. An overachiever by human standards, but of course she wouldn't have the knowledge of the forest of a yearling still growing in their first coat. How did she know that word? How did she find out about me? Surely no Salish alive was old enough to remember their people trading with my own.

No matter. I would find her and eat her.

Sigh.

I'd been amongst humans for too long. Not good to feed into stereotypes. My people were largely vegetarian. We would eat the dead of the forest when the meat wasn't diseased, but it was a rare part of the diet.

But intimidate someone into silence? Surely I could do that. I was short for my species, but I was still approaching eight feet.

So what, now I was some bruiser who intimidated smart women into silence? *Ugh.* Wasn't my purpose here to try to educate humanity? Yes. To hide my people in plain sight, discredit attempts to find them, and buy some time, but also to shift the balance on issues that impacted us all. Climate change, sustainable practices, and all the sciences humans seemed slow to advance. Medicine for starters. No wonder they were so shortsighted when they only lived a hundred years at best. Besides, she'd probably just tase me and have me arrested. That'd be some headline:

Bigfoot Discovered Hosting Science Communication Podcast in the Backwoods of Oregon after Assaulting Doctoral Candidate Listener at Cat Café. Clearly Hates Women in STEM and Cats.

Still, I felt a plan forming in my mind. My people were not the brutes that had spread across the globe by force, outbreeding and outeating all other forms of life. We were the slow-moving, quick-thinking People of the Forest. We outthought and outlasted enemies.

Wearing my 3XL hoodie with my show's logo on the front, a wide-brimmed hat, and an N95 mask—Covid had been amazing for my anonymity; even after things returned to normal, it had become commonplace to see masked faces out and about—I took care of my monthly supply run first, in case things went south and I had to make a run for it.

I arrived outside Portland's only cat café at 1:45 to case the joint. The mid-October rain was the perfect excuse to pull out my umbrella and obscure my face further. Small miracles.

The smell of cat was overpowering, only intensified by the rain. Circling the parking lot on foot, I came to a messy purple Volkswagen that smelled like books, forest, energy drinks, and the desperation of student loans—yes, it was a smell distinct from all others. I had found my hunter, and she was already here. Was she staking me out? What if she was watching me right now? A chill ran down my spine, but then I was always cold without my fur; it was an important part of my people's thermoregulation. The chill would have raised the hairs at the back of my neck, too, but the depilatory cream had taken care of those. The costs of modern living.

Following the scent trail inside, I was greeted at the door by a herd of frenzied cats running into my legs and eagerly singing me the songs of their people, instantly evaporating all hopes of making a stealthy entrance. Cat café. My hunter knew. It had been a trap, after all.

All cats carried the instinctual memory of my people. We had started domesticating them some million years ago or more, as the story goes, when they still had fangs that hung outside their mouths. Later, the new people domesticated dogs, all the while claiming our cats were "not domesticated." Rude.

Long story short, cats loved us, and we loved cats.

Panicked, my eyes searched the café frantically. There, in the corner. She locked her eyes on me, her mouth drawn into a wide grin like a hunter's bow. That smile of hers looked like she had caught a canary and was holding it caged behind her teeth. Moss-green eyes glimmered, every bit as feline as the ones looking up at me from the floor. Bright red hair curled around her face like redwood bark, reminiscent of my people's own fur. I felt a flush of shame as I realized I lacked all traces of it save for a mop on my head serving as hair, hidden beneath my wide-brimmed sun hat.

I had come this far. Closing my umbrella and removing my hat, I strolled over without lifting my feet, gently wading through the tide pool of writhing cats, and sat across from her, feeling ridiculous as the tiny chair creaked beneath my weight.

We sat in silence. Finally, losing the standoff, I cleared my throat and spoke.

"Look, I don't know what you think you've discovered, but I promise you if there were a species of giant, non-human, bipedal primates traipsing around the Americas, we'd all know about it. You're obviously very bright. Think about your promising career. Once rumors you're into this kind of stuff start, they have a way of following you forever."

"Was that a threat?"

Her soft voice came out smooth as a river, completely unperturbed, as if I had just offered her a mint.

"... Yes?" I was terrible at this.

She just looked at me. Looked *through* me. Then she sniffed. "Oh my god. It's true. I can't believe it's true, but just look at you! What are you—eight feet tall? And that deep voice!"

"Shh! Please. Keep it down." I looked around the café. The only humans looking at us seemed more annoyed that their cats were swarming our table than suspicious of me, but how long could my disguise hold up to serious inspection? I pulled my mask further up on my face.

"Listen, is it money you want? Surely you have interests other than wasting your life chasing Bigfoot and fairies. *Beating Around the Bush* receives several small grants as an educational nonprofit. It's not a lot, if extortion is what you had in mind, but maybe you have some other research you need help funding?"

"A bribe? Boy, you are desperate. Did you really never plan for this? Surely you knew someone would catch on, eventually. What if someone really bad-news caught on, like the FBI, CIA, some other three-letter agency? Wouldn't it be easier to just hide than make a podcast claiming you didn't exist?"

"Humoring you, my podcast examines the evidence for a whole host of supernatural and mythological phenomena. Why would you think I was a Sasquatch rather than a ghost, or Nessie, for Pete's sake?"

"Oh, I didn't. I knew you were covering them up, but I didn't know you *were* one, not for sure, until you showed up. But you have a pattern. The rest was all clearly filler, but every four months like clockwork you'd have a Sasquatch or a Bigfoot or a Yeti episode, and I noticed you'd carefully lead people away from certain areas or into others. It felt like I was looking at a map. Then the way you dismissed the Patterson/Gimlin video from '67, I was like, come on."

"Yes, yes, a very convincing fur suit."

"Bah! Yeah, same year they made *Planet of the Apes*, they had suits *that good* but just chose not to use them for the film? I guess those good ol' boys faked the moon landing too?"

"Damn it, Uncle Jer." I groaned involuntarily.

"What was that?"

"Never mind. Look, let's say you are right. You're a woman of science, studying other cultures ... Well, you study this one, and you risk destroying it. Trust me. Is that really what you want?"

"Me? No. Gods, no, and look, I'm sorry for saying I would expose you. I actually thought you were just some government spook hiding evidence of Sasquatch to justify continued deforestation."

"So, what do you want then?"

"I want to help."

"I'm sorry?"

"I said I want to help."

"Help us? Why?"

"My great-great-something-something-grandfather told a story. He was a fur trapper, mauled by a bear; dying, he came across a Salish village, where he met my however-many-greats-grandmother, but he was too wounded for their medicine. So, they took him to a village of wise giants who healed him with powerful magic."

"Just science," I mumbled. I remembered the story. That would have been one of the last contacts my people had with humankind. When the Europeans came and brought their new bacteria and viruses with them, disease decimated my people. The new people knew nothing of immunology back then.

"Just science, eh? Well, that's what I figured. When I started my studies, the stories all seemed to be uncannily similar around the continent, abruptly ending right around the time European settlers showed up. But if the stories are to be believed, and if you've really been living off the land for all this time without being discovered, then, well, look, you obviously know something we don't, and if we're going to save this planet, maybe we could learn from you. No offense, but for a people called Bigfoot you have a very small carbon footprint."

"So now you want to follow in our footsteps?"

"Funny, too. But yes. You've got a good thing going here. People listen to you, but I think you're thinking too small. With a few tweaks, we could change the world, really do some good. Maybe save a forest or two? So long as they don't know you exist, the narrative that there's no other way to live is justified."

"Whoa, whoa, whoa, I'm not putting my family in danger."

"Easy, Harry. I'm not talking about coming out of the forest just yet, but we need a long-term plan, right? What exactly are you going to do when there *are* no forests? Call it a skin condition?"

"That was one thought. What do you propose?"

One Year Later

Next week on The Joe Rogan Experience, *the cohosts of the number two podcast in the nation—the enigmatic Harry Walker in his first public appearance, and the face in front of the voice, Artemis Beltz— talk about their revolutionary conservation efforts and political lobbying that led to the groundbreaking climate change compliance act: Bipartisan Initiative Guiding Future Orientation of Technology, which has already earmarked millions of acres of coniferous and rainforest as protected land, and mandated the investment of billions of dollars into researching sustainable agricultural and energy infrastructures.*

Dear Grandson,
 Please come home soon. We have missed you, but we are so proud of

you. I have heard your show. Xochitl and the little ones are not so sneaky as they think. Your grandmother is still hip and with it.

Uncle Jer has been using the phone. He has discovered dating apps. He's your problem now. Also, he wants a guitar. He told someone he plays the guitar. He does not play the guitar.

I have also heard that you have a partner now? What do they smell like? What color is their fur? Are you bringing them home? Eagerly awaiting your reply, more Nutty Buddies, the quietest guitar you can find, and your presence. The younglings are reaching puberty. The forest smells of teenagers. Pity me.

Gram Grams

Gram Grams had written it herself, in her own hand, and it must have held a thousand, thousand smells. The nuance and detail made me think I was home again when I closed my eyes. I would be soon enough.

Dear family,

I'm coming home to visit soon. I am bringing Artemis. Her fur is red, she smells like—Artemis's smell is rubbed on the paper here—no direct translation, but roughly, ripening berries and bark in the rain. Xochitl should receive a shipment of vaccines a couple weeks before we come home for the holidays. If you are making her a sweater, however small you are thinking of making it, please cut it in half. Trust me.

I love you all with every hair.

PS I'm letting it grow out, but I'll still be a little stubbly when you see me. So I could use a sweater too. You know, if it's not too much trouble.

About the Author

Aaron Fors loves telling stories, first as an actor and filmmaker—his passion and day job since he was eight—and now as an author of sci-fi, fantasy, and whatever hyper-fixation he can't get out of his head this time. He lives in Los Angeles with his beloved partner and her many unused skeins of yarn. He is also the servant of two beings masquerading as cats: an ungrateful gremlin that swallowed a defective kazoo in her formative years, and the fluffy reincarnation of someone who died on a hunger strike. When he's not writing, there won't be any books from him. Find him online @aaronfors or AaronFors.com.

Surviving
by Janessa Keeling

1

You check Zillow for any affordable houses. It's a hopeless task, but you do it three times a day. After that, you sit on the edge of your bed and alternate between staring at the dripping water stains that run down the curling wallpaper and a postcard from your mom that you've taped on the wall.

> Let me live in a house by the side of the road
> Where the race of men go by—
> The men who are good and the men who are bad,
> As good and as bad as I.
> I would not sit in the scorner's seat
> Nor hurl the cynic's ban—
> Let me live in a house by the side of the road
> And be a friend to man.[1]

Screaming and blaring car horns bleed through the cracked glass of your apartment window. You really should send your landlord another reminder about that.

Grabbing your phone, you see the time.

---

1. Sam Walter Foss, "The House By the Side of the Road," 1897.

You've spent too long pretending to be a vegetable, and now there's no time to sit in the café next to your work, indulging in a cup of coffee. The baristas joke with you, and in doing so, remind you that you're a person. You submit a to-go order from your phone.

You throw on yesterday's clothes because they aren't too dirty, and no one is going to notice. You move through the crowds professionally, artfully stepping around deep cracks and potholes, and cross the street without anyone slamming on their brakes.

In the coffee shop, there is a long line of people you recognize from work. You move to the order-ahead counter. Your drink isn't there. You still have five minutes. The baristas turn out drink after drink. But your name is never called. You have two minutes.

It's hard getting their attention. You ask about your drink. They put your drink out eight minutes ago. Someone must have taken it. They offer to make you another. You don't have time.

2

You get to your cubicle, sweaty and a little out of breath, one minute before you're supposed to be on your first call. You log in and put on your company-issued headphones. They cut into the top of your head just like they did on your first day.

Your phone rings. You begin the countdown to your government-mandated fifteen-minute lunch.

After four hours, you drag yourself to the break room, grab one of the eco-friendly cups that makes the coffee taste worse, and try to fill it.

There's no more coffee.

The person who empties the pot is supposed to start a new one. You swallow your rage as you start a new pot.

As the water heats, you scan the posters lining the walls for your favorite one.

> Two roads diverged in a yellow wood,
> And sorry I could not travel both
> And be one traveler, long I stood
> And looked down one as far as I could

To where it bent in the undergrowth;
Then took the other, as just as fair,
And having perhaps the better claim,
Because it was grassy and wanted wear.[2]

The coffee machine beeps. You only have a few minutes of your lunch left. You pour yourself a cup and head to your desk.

You have two minutes, so you check your emails.

Zillow has sent you houses.

There is a cute one bedroom, one bathroom on five acres of land in the middle of nowhere. Just hit the market.

The house's mortgage is less than half your apartment rent with double the space. Your company has been offering to let people telework. You submit an offer.

3

You pull up to your new house and park. The fancy pictures they used were old. The paint is cracked and faded. There are symbols spray-painted around the doors and windows. Over the car's engine, the cicadas fill the glade with their annoying buzzing.

It's perfect.

As you get closer, you notice strings lined with bells, running along the outside of the house and across the windows and doors. The deck is loaded with them, crisscrossing everywhere. You lift your knees high to keep from tripping.

You're reminded that country people believe in superstitious nonsense.

The inside is as the pictures promised: a cottage nestled in the woods. Your cottage now. On five acres of your land. The cicadas aren't so annoying with the front door closed.

There's a note on the counter weighed down by a pack of beer.

Rules for Survival: "No, you didn't."

Well, not really a rule, more a motto. Because of all the unspeakable horrors. They operate under some kind of observer effect.

---

2. Robert Frost, "The Road Not Taken," 1915.

Can't hurt you if you don't acknowledge them. We hope. Who can say if the last guy who went missing did everything right, and they just decided the rules didn't apply anymore.

Here's how they play the game. And how you can play to survive:

- *Leave the strings and bells alone.*
- *Don't sing or whistle; it attracts them.*
- *Do not go out at night, especially during storms.*
- *If you go into the woods, don't leave the path.*
- *You will see things in the woods. Do not look at them.*
- *If you feel like something is following you, pretend you didn't notice.*
- *If you see a friend beckoning to you from the woods—no, you didn't.*
- *If you see something out of the corner of your eye—no, you didn't.*
- *If you hear something crawling around on the roof—no, you didn't.*

Left a shotgun and a box of shells in the bedroom closet. Oh, the water heater sometimes short-circuits. The breaker box is next to the back door.

You crumple the note and put the beer in the fridge. The former owners were probably scared by bears or a mountain lion. Even though they told you about the shotgun, you're surprised that it's there.

4

You cut down the strings and bells. They're an unsightly tripping hazard, and you have boxes to move.

Then you head to the store for some paint and food.

When you get back, you paint over the ugly symbols around the windows and doors. You hum a song to drown out the screeching cicadas. Your phone rings. It's your mom. You put it on speaker. She talks to you about family and things. You tell her about the house. She's thrilled for you. She says she wants to come out.

You say no. You don't have a place for her to sleep. She insists. She'll be there in a week.

You smile because you want to see her. She has to go; something is burning.

You open the windows and doors because you've never been able to do that in the city. You're finally home. The woods call you to explore. So, you grab your backpack, fill your water bottle, and head out.

No matter how far you walk, the cicadas keep up their high-pitched clacking. You come to a fork. A sign tells you to go right. That gently rolling path bends out of sight. The left-hand path ends in a clearing.

You go left.

The clearing is littered with antlers, as if all the forest deer come here to shed their racks. It's impressive. Some have more than a dozen points. The trees look sick. Maybe the deer have stripped the bark.

The cicadas go silent.

There is a predator.

You turn back. Fifteen paces from the clearing, you hear it—stalking you—and you remember the note. Even though you want to look, you don't.

> Like one, that on a lonesome road
> Doth walk in fear and dread,
> And having once turned round, walks on,
> And turns no more his head;
> Because he knows, a frightful fiend
> Doth close behind him tread.[3]

You see it out of the corner of your eye—and you pretend you didn't. Even though you definitely see some kind of red monkey creature with limbs that are too long. It's looking right at you. It wants you to look at it.

---

3. Samuel Taylor Coleridge, "The Rime of the Ancient Mariner," 1798.

Your mom calls your name, and you can't help but turn.

She steps out of the woods and beckons you with a smile.

With shaking hands, you pull out your phone and call your mom. She answers. You tell her you'll call her back in a bit.

The thing standing in the forest smiles wider. Too wide for a human face. A fear you didn't know you carried rises in you.

Uncanny Valley: A primal evolutionary response embedded in the human brain that teaches us to be afraid of things that look human.

Your mom can tell something is wrong. She's said your name a dozen times, and each time she says it, the edge of hysteria is closer. You hang up. Because you have to move.

The thing that looks like your mom turns and walks into the forest. Calling your name in the same tones your real mom just used. The thing sounds panicked and scared. You do not follow. You turn and force yourself to walk. You do not run.

You hear it the trees above you.

You do not look up. Dead leaves rain down around you, and it takes everything you have not to look up.

You walk as if nothing is wrong. Your vision tunnels and your legs shake. You drink the air in gulps, reminding yourself that you can panic in the safety of your house. Your knees feel like they may give out.

The path leading out of the clearing comes into sight. You know that if you don't go now, you aren't going to make it. You drop the backpack and sprint.

Quick footsteps crunch the gravel not three feet behind you.

You burst into your yard and stumble, but you do not look back; you push yourself forward. When you make it to the porch, you turn. Nothing. You brace yourself on the wooden railing and stare into the empty forest.

The cicadas start their high-pitched whine.

5

You shake yourself and figure the sign in the forest was warning you away from a toxic area, and you breathed in something that caused hallucinations. You head into the house through the still-open kitchen door.

As you stand in front of the sink, you can see its blurry reflection in the open window. It plays with your hair.

You remember the note.

Don't let them see you react. The observer effect will keep you safe. Can't hurt you if you don't acknowledge them.

You will not run. You will not turn around. You say in a voice half broken with fear, "Alexa, play my favorites."

And you will sing along. Because if you can convince this thing that you don't believe it's there, it might leave. As you cook and sing, the thing touches you less and less, and you really start to believe it will not hurt you. Hell, you dance because these are your favorite songs.

Then once you're sure it's gone, you calmly lock all your windows, shut all the curtains, turn off all the lights, and crawl, trembling, into your bedroom closet.

Your food burns in the oven, but you don't care because you have a shotgun the previous owners left you. You didn't understand at the time, but now you get it. You also understand why the house was so cheap.

As you're sitting in the closet, you hear something in there with you.

Its long fingers scrape across your scalp.

It says your name.

You will not react.

But it won't matter.

About the Author

Janessa Keeling is currently attending Arcadia University for a master's in creative writing. When not writing, Janessa likes to watch her chickens and work on DIY projects that she'll never finish.

Nessie's Morning Cup of Coffee

by Angelique Fawns

Brad's Coffee
Tall Brazilian Medium Roast
Double Cream, One Sugar

Nessie lurked in her hunting position just below the surface of the peaty loch. The pink-and-red sky heralded the rising of the Scottish sun. Her head was foggy, and irritation itched up the length of her scaly back. She wanted a cup of coffee. Careful not to create a ripple, she yawned.

Nessie saw three humans on the pebbly beach from her vantage point. A family. Even through the inches of silty water, she could smell the richness of the drinks in the adults' hands. Their brew was smoky and steaming, the chicory notes of a Colombian brew wafting from the cups.

She salivated, the liquid squirting between her fangs. Every morning presented the same challenge. How could she get people to put down their drinks *and* be sufficiently distracted so she could loop her long tongue into her hot addiction?

Nessie stalked the entire loch, but Dores Beach was the best hunting ground, with a fair amount of tourists visiting daily.

The child—Nessie guessed he had less than a decade of years—picked up a rock. "Wanna see me skip this stone, Dad?"

The father put his drink down on a flat piece of driftwood next to the shoreline. Nessie curled her lips in anticipation. An internal conflict raged in her ancient brain. This was a dangerous addiction, and she cursed the day she first sampled the human beverage:

Henry's Coffee
Large Americano
Black

The fisherman had caught a massive northern pike and spilled his cup directly over her head. But it was, oh, so good. Even diluted, the drink had been the most extraordinary thing she'd ever tasted.

She focused on the father as he picked up his own pebble from the beach. "These chunks are probably too round."

Nessie watched him examine the stone with a frisson of excitement. The jolt of anticipation before the actual jolt of caffeine. She could smell the cream mixed with his coffee, dribbles of it adhering to the side of the paper cup. The tip of her tail flicked infinitesimally. She preferred it black, like the first one she ever drank, but she'd take it any way she could get it.

The boy danced on the spot. "I challenge you to a skipping competition!" He cocked his arm back, ready to heave his stone.

Linda's Coffee
Grande Vanilla Latte
Soy, No Foam
Lavender Shot

The adult female spit out a mouthful of her vanilla-scented latte. "Guys! I thought we were up at this ungodly hour to look for the Loch Ness Monster. You'll scare her away by throwing rocks."

The kid paused, tossing the rock between his hands. "Ma! You know that's just a legend, right? I wanna skip stones."

The boy lobbed his rock, and Nessie's eyes widened with horror as the boulder rippled through the water on a collision course with the top of her head. What were the chances the child's aim would be so perfect? She squinted, preparing for impact. At least it was a chunk of shale, the softest rock in Loch Ness. Her eye caught the bits of quartz and calcite glinting in the sun, trapped in the clay and mud. The fine-grained sedimentary rock was formed at the same time as she was born, about four million years ago.

Nessie winced when the stone clonked her on the head and remained, nestled on her skull. Another scar to the thousands tattooing her thick hide.

"Good try!" The man threw his rock. He angled the piece of granite correctly, and it skipped three times before disappearing into the murk. "I win."

Nessie's heart pounded. The son's rock was still on her head! She needed to distract these people and steal their coffee, but they couldn't see her. A shudder ran through her. Being caught would be disastrous. She'd be put in a cage and never have coffee again.

The son, his face crestfallen, shrugged. "Let's go get breakfast."

The father was reaching for his drink on the driftwood ...

Nessie dug her talons into the sand. No, she didn't want to lose that cup! Who knew when her next opportunity would be? Hot crankiness burned her gut. The stone on her head wasn't helping the situation. Nessie's dark-green eyes brightened to turquoise. Or was it? Tensing her neck muscles, she catapulted the rock off her head in one explosive movement.

The rock burst through the water several hundred feet from her position, and the family gasped.

The kid, his voice high-pitched with enthusiasm, said, "The Loch Ness Monster! Get your camera out, Mom, we're going to be famous."

The three humans ran down the shore toward the ripples left by the shale.

Nessie floated silently upward and let her nose breach the surface. Like light, odors filtered through the water. Oh, the purity and intensity of the coffee left on the driftwood! Her nostrils flared as she sucked in the smell. She'd been wrong underwater. This was a Brazilian brew. She took another deep breath, letting her exceptionally long tongue flick out and probe the top of the cup.

With an expert lick, she removed the lid, rolled the edges of her tongue and slurped.

Endorphins raced through her brain, and she closed her eyes as the liquid traveled along her taste buds and into her mouth. The sweet nuttiness of the drink was delicious. She swallowed, and the caffeine hit was immediate. Excellent. Satisfying.

With a happy sigh, Nessie sank back into the water, leaving the empty cup askew on the driftwood.

She was ready to start her day.

About the Author

Angelique Fawns is a journalist and speculative fiction writer. She began her career writing articles about naked cave dwellers in Tenerife, Canary Islands. After selling her first story to EQMM, she fell in love with weird fiction, which is *actually* stranger than nonfiction. You can find her lurking at @angeliquefawns on X, blogging about upcoming calls at www.fawns.ca, or gazing into the abyss, hoping it stares back at her. She has had more than sixty stories published. Find some in *Mystery Tribune*, *Amazing Stories*, and *Space and Time*. She was the lucky recipient of the 2024 Eric Flint Scholarship to Superstars Writing Seminar.

The Leeds Devil
by Jeff Thompson

Rosalyn,
 I hope this letter finds you well. I would have called, but Jack never left me your number. Your father was a good man, and I miss our hunting trips together. I need your help with a recent project in Atlantic County, New Jersey. I have contact details below and don't want to put too much down here. It's—well, let's just say it's an extravagant hunt. Please call me as soon as you get this. I hope your address didn't change.

Kenny's hand was quick with the letters, some of them with smeared ink, and Rosalyn couldn't help but imagine his large, outdoorsman's frame scrunched behind a small, schoolboy writing desk, likely with his tongue sticking out the side of his mouth in concentration. His hair was flecked with gray, even though he was only a decade older than she was. She nearly laughed at the image. She remembered his eyes vividly: sharp as the hawk he used for hunting expeditions, and bright with intelligence. No doubt he still wore the beard, slightly scraggly from too much time outside and not enough warm showers to civilize it. She guessed other women would have found him attractive. He wasn't her type.

She wondered why he was reaching out to her. People called her a medium, a psychic, a crazy person, and several other less appropriate terms. It all amounted to the same thing, regardless of what others believed. She communicated with the dead. She reached out and touched energies that were no longer available to most people. She could exert her will and force those energies to leave a place. Sometimes she could help them move on to whatever the next place was. None of it was something that could help Kenny. A woods guide and hunter like him had very little use for a Sensitive.

Kenny had been close with her father and would no doubt want to share some of their old stories with her. She sighed out her frustration as her stomach tumbled like circus acrobats. She didn't like thinking about her father, and she especially didn't want to talk about him. Thinking too much about someone who passed, or feeding too much of her emotions into it, brought a very real possibility of summoning that energy. She didn't want that. Some part of her abilities told her clearly that her father had not moved on, and it wasn't worth the pain of remembering, of being reminded he was no longer alive. It was much easier to pretend he was out on another adventure somewhere.

At the bottom of the letter was an address carefully written in block letters and a phone number. Glancing at her watch, she decided now was as good a time as any. She dialed the numbers, shaking only for a moment with a tremor of nerves. She hadn't thought of her father or his old hunting guide for a long time. Had Kenny even been at the funeral? She'd barely made it herself, so she couldn't really blame him. As a general rule, she avoided funerals—so much energy flying around quickly became overwhelming.

The phone rang twice.

"Hello?"

"Hey, Kenny, it's Rosalyn Amori. I got your letter." She tried to be friendly without seeming too brief. Too often, others misunderstood her brevity for irritation or rudeness. It was neither. She just didn't like talking to people.

"Roz! How have you been, girl?" Kenny said. She could hear the smile and warmth in his voice. It felt like a hug forced too soon.

"What's up, Kenny? Your letter made it seem like there was something pretty important. I'd rather we skip straight to that and catch up after. No offense," she added to take the edge from her words. Her old girlfriend, Roxy, had once suggested she add little comments like that to show she wasn't trying to be rude.

"Just like Jack. God, that's what I love about you, girl!" He was quiet for a moment, and when Rosalyn didn't respond, he continued, clearing his throat and lowering his voice. "Have you ever been up near Pine Barrens?"

"I'm not much for the forest life. And I'm not a hunter, at least not like you are."

The fact was, Rosalyn was a hunter of sorts, and they both knew it. She had gone after poltergeists and enraged energies more than half a dozen times. Removing them from family homes was a specialty of hers, and she took pride in her effectiveness at locating them.

Sometimes people assumed she was a fraud. Strange things start to happen inside a home, and a few days later, a young woman shows up and offers to remove the evil entity for a nominal fee? Yeah, it sounded like classic snake oil, and she knew it. That was why she would offer free readings to everyone once the darkness had been exorcized from the home. Thankfully, it wasn't like movies or church exorcisms, with holy water and Bible theatrics. No, it was the literal removal of something from a location, which usually only took a great deal of concentration and her own energy, two things she had in abundance due to a nervous nature and a proclivity for avoiding people. Mixing that with meeting strangers and explaining that she could help them with their ghost problem had been a real challenge at first. She'd gotten over it, but it was still a challenge sometimes.

Kenny continued, and she realized she'd missed the start of what he was saying.

"—only a few days at most. I don't think there is any real Jersey Devil"—she almost saw him making quotes with his fingers—"but this guy is paying serious money, and frankly, he's having serious problems up here with his livestock. I was hoping you would come up and poke around, maybe see if there is any devil business, or whatever you want to call it, going on."

Rosalyn's annoyance flared. "You're calling me about the Jersey Devil? A monster that was almost certainly simply a vicious rumor started hundreds of years ago when two farmers had a feud?"

"You *have* heard of it then? That's great, Roz—"

She cut him off. "Cryptids aren't real, Kenny. Stop wasting your time. Stop wasting my time. Probably wolves or a cougar or something."

"No, it's not. The biggest thing here is the occasional black bear, but this thing isn't a bear," Kenny said, his tone friendly and undeterred by her flare-up.

"Wolves," Rosalyn said stubbornly.

"Coyotes, maybe, but listen, Roz, you don't even know what's going on out here. And I sure as hell have *never* seen stuff like this. Please just come out here. I'll pay for the plane or bus or whatever you need. I need an Amori on this one, and your old man isn't around for it anymore."

"Don't tempt me. I can send him your way, you know."

"I *do* know, Roz! You were maybe ten years old when you came up and started telling me how my grandma was so disappointed by my tattoo," Kenny said, nervous laughter caressing his tone.

"I remember that. She was so mad," Rosalyn said as a smile tickled her lips. She took a slow breath. "Travel and time expenses paid. Friend or not, I have work to do and bills to pay."

"Fair!" Kenny said at once. "And regardless if we find something or not, I will still pay you."

"Obviously. I'll see you soon," Rosalyn said and hung up.

Three days later, she walked down a muddy path through a thick, overgrown forest trail with a waterproof poncho and new set of rubber hunting boots, all provided by Kenny when he picked her up at the airport. They were on what Kenny called a "game trail," but it looked like a regular hiking trail to Rosalyn. Trees stretched high into the overcast sky, silent sentinels to their passage.

Rosalyn's breath misted out with each laborious step. The small backpack Kenny had prepared for her dug uncomfortably into her shoulders. Rosalyn hadn't been camping since before her father died, and she hadn't been the biggest fan to begin with. Kenny, on the other hand, nearly lived in the woods year-round. He not only made his living that way, but he also seemed to genuinely enjoy the entire wet, cold, uncomfortable experience.

He showed little sign that he was carrying a fifty-pound pack slung across his shoulders. A rifle was nestled with the barrel pointed down across one side, and a large revolver dangled from his hip.

"Are those for the occasional bears or the nonexistent wolves?" Rosalyn asked.

Kenny glanced back and followed her eyes. He nodded soberly. "These are for whatever has been out here killing Mr. Nauser's livestock. And since I don't really know what it is, I figured I would bring everything."

"Where's your hawk?" Rosalyn asked, disappointed that she had not seen Kenny's feathered companion when they first parked and started down the trail.

"Kansas? He went up to birdie heaven a few years back," Kenny said.

"Did he now?" Rosalyn asked.

She opened herself to the surrounding area and immediately felt a pinprick of energy above them. She looked up and saw a shadow of Kansas the hawk as he hovered on some ethereal wind. She connected briefly and knew the hawk would stay by Kenny's side for another year or more. Kenny had raised the bird since it hatched, and they had a special bond.

"Haven't had the heart to look for another one just yet. I know I need to. My falconry license will expire in another year if I don't start training. Just not ready yet," Kenny explained.

"You said something was happening to the livestock? Something has been eating them?"

"No, not eating," Kenny said, his voice quieter. "My guess is it's people. That's why I brought you along, to see if you could, you know, do your thing and find something."

"Yes, I'll just 'do my thing' and magically know where the bad people are," Rosalyn said sarcastically. "What's been happening to the livestock, though?" She was certain she didn't actually want to know at this point.

"Something's been killing them. There was a blood trail last time. That's how I found the bodies. Whatever, or whoever, had somehow taken a sixty-pound goat to this tree and impaled the poor thing on one of the upper branches. It was ... wrong," Kenny finished, clearly unsatisfied with the inadequacy of the word.

"Sounds like a wacko running around up here," Rosalyn said, suddenly very aware of every heavy drop of rain that fell to the forest floor and how it sounded ominously like footsteps. She looked around, but the large poncho hood obstructed a good amount of her vision. She allowed her energy to seep out around them, blanketing a circle of twenty or so feet. She would feel the presence of something, human or otherwise, which might give them the warning needed if they were suddenly attacked.

They continued deeper into the forest, silent with their thoughts. Rosalyn kept the circle of energy around them. Kenny stopped walking, and her eyes shot open. He looked off into the distance, his hawkish glare intense and mildly predatory.

"Do you see it?" he whispered.

Rosalyn's pulse tripled with a sharp intake of breath. Her eyes frantically roved through the forest, hoping to identify what Kenny had seen. Panic rose thick in her throat, a tightening bile that clouded out all reason.

"Where?" she breathed.

"Just ahead, on the trail," Kenny whispered back while remaining completely still. His hand didn't drift toward the gun on his hip or the rifle on his back.

She leaned around him cautiously, eyes slashing wide cuts, looking for movement along the trail.

A shadow moved, and her breath caught. Three rapid heartbeats and the shadow moved again, silent as the moon on a cloudless night. Details emerged, and she nearly toppled over as a deer walked carefully across the trail.

"Ken, you ass!" Rosalyn said, slapping at his arm.

"What?" Kenny asked, genuinely confused as the deer bounded away into the trees from the sudden commotion.

"I thought you actually saw something!"

"I did. It was the deer. How long has it been since you've seen one? I thought you would be excited," Kenny said. He did a good job of keeping any sort of smile from his shaggy beard, but laughter danced in his eyes.

"How much farther is the tree where you found the goat? I want to be out of here before dark."

Kenny looked surprised. "I figured you knew we were camping here tonight. That's why I brought all this gear. You thought we were trekking this all in for a day trip?"

"I don't know," Rosalyn responded defensively. "Wait, why are we staying overnight? Are you planning on hunting this thing after dark?"

"No, hunting after dark isn't really a thing out here. I mean it is, if you are after a coyote or maybe a fox, but most people don't hire a guide to go after that sort of game."

"Why are we staying the night, then?" Rosalyn asked, annoyed.

"I thought that was when, well, you know ..." Kenny said, somewhat embarrassed and clearly uncomfortable.

Rosalyn ate up the silence, her penetrating gaze holding him in place.

"That was when I figured you could do your thing. Call up ghosts or whatever and figure out what is going on. Jack always said that it was stronger at night for you to summon things."

"I'm supposed to call up a ghost of a *goat* and ask what happened?"

"I mean, can you?" Kenny asked.

Rosalyn growled in frustration and stomped past him down the path. "I guess we'll find out tonight. How much farther to the campsite?"

An hour later and the rain had turned into the subtle promise of snow. Flakes drifted down lazily, and the cold bit with real teeth. Kenny wanted to take her to the tree where the goat was killed, but Rosalyn declined. Instead, they found a small clearing and made camp in short order. Kenny worked to start the fire and set up two separate tents. He was methodical, and Rosalyn felt guilty for not helping him. At one point she offered, but he waved her away and explained he was used to it with his guide work.

Night came faster than Rosalyn expected, and with it, the sudden drop in temperature. She sat on a mini camping stool, hands outstretched to the fire, an occasional shiver spidering its way along her neck and thighs.

"Sorry, it wasn't supposed to be this cold tonight. I'll keep the fire going all night," Kenny said as he finished his bag of soup.

Rosalyn had eaten most of hers earlier and given the rest to him, worried about what soup from a bag might do to her stomach and not having the slightest interest in finding out at 2:30 in the morning.

The fire was nice. Flames danced vividly back and forth, occasionally cracking the logs with a sudden pop. Kenny gathered more than enough wood and stacked it in a neat pile nearby, each log closest to the fire taking its turn to dry out before it was cast into the flames. The stars came out with a twinkling glory. The snow stopped, and the night echoed with silence.

"Years ago, your father, me, and Kyle were out on a hunt," Kenny started.

"I don't really want to hear old war stories, Ken. Sorry," Rosalyn said without meeting his gaze.

"Yeah, that makes sense. This one, though, you do have to hear. It goes along with something I have been meaning to give you for too many years now. I'll keep it brief. I promise." He paused as if waiting for disagreement or complaint.

Rosalyn remained silent, her eyes glued to the flames, though thoughts of monsters and wackos in the forest kept a quiet march in the back of her mind.

"Your dad, he fell out of a tree stand and got hurt pretty bad. Kyle and I thought maybe he wouldn't make it. Kyle was always fast. And he sure as hell was faster than me, so he went running back to get help. I stayed with your dad."

"I remember that. Nasty scar up his back and shoulder," Rosalyn said.

"Yeah, he was lucky, honestly. Anyway, he thought he was going to die. Hell, *I* thought he was going to die. He asked me to write some things down for him, in case he did, you know, die. I wanted to mail this to you a thousand times, but I told myself I couldn't risk it getting lost, so I hung on to it until I saw you again. Months turned into years and, well, I'm sorry it took so long. Anyway, here is the letter."

Kenny handed over a worn, folded piece of paper. He looked embarrassed, and tears glazed heavily along the edge of his eyes, reflecting the firelight like tiny diamonds.

Rosalyn took the letter and unfolded it. The light of the fire jumped and swayed, making it hard to read at times.

Rosalyn,

I am beyond grateful to have known you your entire life. The pride I feel in watching your every accomplishment cannot be overstated. You are my entire reason for waking up, and I strive each day to become a better man and father, deserving of your love and respect. My only regret will be that I won't be there for you on the hard days or celebrating all the great ones. And you will have great ones. I hope the joy and love you feel with each of our memories together will forever overshadow any sadness that comes from this day.

All my love, always,
Dad

The last word was written in her father's shaky hand with brown smudges that Rosalyn guessed was blood. She sat in silence for a long time. Kenny said nothing. They both allowed the fire to roll through their memories and emotions, and the night wore on.

Kenny rose to his feet and stretched. He threw another two logs on the fire, and his tone turned more serious.

"Do you need anything before I call it a night?"

Rosalyn remembered why they were there. A small smile cut the edge of her lip. "Did you bring the bell?"

Kenny's forehead furrowed. "I didn't know you needed one."

"I do, Kenny. Especially if I'm summoning goats. Goats only come to the ring of a bell." She held his gaze for a long minute before breaking into laughter.

"Okay, Roz. Good one. I'm going to bed now, but holler if you come up with something."

Rosalyn smiled and returned her gaze to the fire. Before long, Kenny's not-so-subtle snoring filled the night.

"I suppose it's time to see who's about," Rosalyn sighed to herself.

She extended her senses out, allowing her mind's eye to see and feel everything around her. She heard distant footsteps. Not really hearing them, of course, more like the echo of a memory. Impossible to describe, but tangible and solid as the trees that stood silent vigil around their tiny campsite.

"What's your name?" Rosalyn asked the energy as it came closer into their camp. Wisps of details jumped out. A brown suit. A busy waiting room. Earthy medicinal smells she could not identify. He healed people, Rosalyn realized.

"I was called the Black Doctor of the Pines," the specter responded, materializing in her mind's eye, sitting across from her. His onyx features shimmered and solidified. A prominent, straight nose that flared at the end, thick lips, and deep intelligence behind shadowed eyes.

"And what was your real name?" Rosalyn asked.

"James Still."

As the name touched her mind, she felt a resilience there. A vivid interest for knowledge and the drive to help those in need. *I am in need*, she thought fiercely, hoping he could feel the truth of it.

Communicating with an energy differed from traditional conversation. Fewer words and more pictures with whispers of meaning. Rosalyn assimilated pictures and flashes of words into a cohesive idea. "Do you know of a monster in these woods? A creature that kills things?"

"All things die. But none with so much fear and pain as those killed by the creature."

"So it *is* real," Rosalyn said, more to herself than the apparition. She had not expected that. "Can you show me what it looks like?"

"It is an unnatural twisting of nature. We called it the Leeds Devil for 'twas their family that sired it. Flee, child, before it takes you."

"You once saved people, I can feel it. Could you walk away when others needed you?" Rosalyn asked, both physically and with images sent through her mind's eye.

"I tried to walk away but could not. It eventually took my health, if not my life."

"So you understand why I cannot leave. Help me understand what it is. Help me know it so I can stop it from killing the livestock."

"It doesn't just kill livestock. It wears their skin, changes it ..." the spirit lamented. Cold eyes pierced through her, looking off into the distance. "It comes."

This last part she both physically heard and saw as a tumbling tornado of destruction and death within her mind. An ear-splitting screech rocked through the night air, breaking the ominous silence. She felt the ghost of James Still vanish like smoke around a snuffed candle. The screech called out again, and Rosalyn threw her awareness wide in a frenzied arc to identify where it was coming from. At the same time, she started yelling for Kenny.

The screaming stopped a moment later, and Kenny stood by her side, a rifle in hand, his hawkish gaze searching for any movement.

"Did you see it?" he asked without taking his eyes away from the darkness.

"Only heard it," Rosalyn whispered back.

Kenny visibly relaxed, his shoulders sagging before jumping with silent laughter. "You mean the owl call?"

Rosalyn remained silent, embarrassed and unsure of herself. She tried to collect her thoughts before giving a half nod.

"That screech was just an owl. They are legitimately terrifying in sound, but harmless. Unless you're a mouse," he added with a smile.

Rosalyn's only warning was the sudden black coldness that touched the edge of her awareness. She spun and pointed into the night, lashing out wildly with her awareness.

Kenny spun with her, leveling the rifle toward the unseen intruder.

Heavy steps shook through the darkness as a monster slowly stalked forward. Rosalyn felt the dark energy around the creature. A cloak of malevolence and hatred shrouded it. With each terrifying second, the writhing light revealed more of the grotesque cacophony that was its body. Hooved feet connected strangely to muscular legs. Coarse brown hair crawled halfway up the strong limbs to a torso that was hunched and rippled with primal muscle. A broad neck and shoulders connected with clawed hands made a vile attempt at being vaguely human, all culminating in a face that was elongated like that of a wolf but rounded just toward the nose. Bright red eyes flashed from the firelight, and enormous bat-like wings stretched to their fullest extent, pulling a pitch-blackness in their ten-foot span.

Bang! Bang! Bang!

The sound was so loud and sudden that Rosalyn fell to the ground, her hands crashing over her ears to keep the noise away as Kenny fired round after another into the abomination. She could feel the dark energy around the creature circle and rise like a cobra ready to strike. She pushed out her own energy, forcing everything she had into a tight ball around herself and Kenny.

The darkness lashed forward and struck.

She felt the impact as a physical blow, but she kept the darkness away as Kenny fired his rifle at the physical form.

Another sound broke through the night. It was a guttural, heart-stammering roar that made Rosalyn dizzy. The scream cut through her like shards of glass, embedding fear and terror with every piercing moment.

Kenny cast aside the rifle and emptied the revolver into the Devil.

It did not try to flee, but instead staggered forward and closer into the light.

The damage from Kenny's rifle and revolver were suddenly apparent along the putrid form. Black ichor wept from the many wounds, and the blazing red light from the eyes dimmed. The physical form faltered and finally collapsed before them.

Rosalyn felt the dark energy around the creature coalesce and swirl. She held firm to the barrier she'd raised between the darkness and herself, thankful a moment later when the hateful energy shot forward once more.

Kenny was speaking to her, unaware that the true threat was still very much present.

Rosalyn had learned many years ago how to shield herself and others from negative energies. She closed her eyes and imagined the brightest white light emanating from her in pulsing waves. Whether it was some type of magic or just controlling her own vital energy was irrelevant. The fact remained that it worked. She pushed with everything she had to keep the darkness away from her and Kenny. It tore at them like a ravenous lion, working with a frenzied panic to reach them. She refused to let it in and only faltered when Kenny moved closer to the creature.

"Don't," was all she could manage.

He froze, backed up a step, and reloaded the revolver.

Rosalyn forced her own brilliant light of energy, visible only in her mind, out toward the monster, pushing it away in rapid succession. The darkness recoiled several times, as if crushed by tidal waves. A shuddering breath ran through her as the impossible crashing waves slammed against the dark energy. Another hit, and the energy abruptly fled into the night.

She nearly collapsed at the effort, her head hanging low and her breathing ragged.

"We are okay now," she managed to get out.

Kenny took a few steps forward, his eyes visibly widening as he wandered over to the corpse.

"It had wings. Wings and hooves. It was monstrous, Roz. Tell me you saw it?" he stammered.

"What do you mean, 'had' wings?" Rosalyn asked as she climbed unsteadily to her feet.

Kenny stood before the crumpled form, silence heavy across his shoulders.

She stood next to him and looked down at the ruined body of a young man. He was dirty and unwashed; clearly, he had been living in the woods for some time. His gaunt features stretched over high cheekbones, and his ribs lay just beneath the skin. Bullet wounds littered his chest and stomach, but no blood flowed forth. He was dead.

"It wears their skin. That's what James told me," Rosalyn whispered with realization.

Kenny dropped to his knees and wailed. "I killed him. It was a man, and I killed him!"

The sudden force of his anguish hit Rosalyn. It rang against her like a morning church bell, high and clear, resonating deep inside her chest. Her eyes burned with tears, and she felt the impossible weight of wide-eyed panic wrapping long fingers around her throat. She staggered beneath his sudden avalanche of emotion and immediately walled herself off from it. She pulled her energy back in and pushed away all that he was feeling. Her own fear and sadness lingered like a hangover, muddying her thoughts before cold logic finally took her.

Rosalyn knew Kenny had killed no one. He had only removed the shell that the Leeds Devil inhabited. She hoped he could eventually forgive himself and recognize the peaceful release they had given the stranger. Perhaps not peaceful, but this man was no longer a prisoner to the darkness. They had done something good. She had to believe that.

They burned the body and left that same night. Kenny terminated his contract with Mr. Nauser, admitting he was unable to find the culprit of the senseless livestock killings. He was beside himself with grief.

Before Rosalyn left for the airport, she hugged Kenny and allowed her awareness to seep out into that place between moments where space and time held little meaning. She gently felt for the energies, pulling ever so slightly on a memory of her father, like a child picking carefully at the string of a favorite sweater. They were fishing by a stream. She felt him there. Not just in the memory, but there with her in that place outside of time. His warm presence was like a sunrise, warming her and easing her mind. It would be okay. She and Kenny would be okay.

A week later, the news story broke over the radio.

"The burned remains of missing hiker John Rems were found earlier this week. He was identified by his dental records. The police are still searching for clues but feel this is undoubtedly the result of foul play. More to follow as this story develops.

"In other news, sightings of the infamous Jersey Devil have dropped drastically during a time when the creature is reportedly most active. Don't worry, folks, I'm sure we will see more of it next year."

About the Author

Jeff Thompson's work has appeared in the *Bangalore Review*, *The Write Launch*, and *On the Run Press*. He has self-published two books on Amazon, with a third on the way. Jeff spends every spare moment reading or writing, and he attributes any success to his amazing friends and family.

How to Be Friends with a Human
by Annmarie SanSevero

September 3

Dear Reginald,
    I received my letter from the Cryptid Pen Pal Club, and they said you are my new friend. I was told to introduce myself. I am a Fouke monster from Arkansas. Some people confuse us with Bigfoot, but we're not always looking for attention.
    My introduction letter told me you are a Champy and live in New York. That must be exciting! You're almost as famous as the Loch Ness Monster. Do you get to see many humans on Lake Champlain? Once, some of them wandered into our area of the woods. I had a real hankerin' to talk to them, but my dad said I'm not ready. Between you and me, I think he's afraid of them. Ever since he saw a TV show about people who hunt monsters he's convinced they're coming after our family.
    I really want to have a human friend, but that doesn't mean I'm not excited to be your friend because I am.
    What do you like to do?
    Your Pal,
    Eugene

September 10

Dear Eugene,

We are most unequivocally meant to be friends because I want to be a humanologist and you want to meet humans. I love science. My mother says it is because I'm nosy, but I think it is more that I have an insatiable appetite for learning things. Insatiable is a word I learned. It means you never get sick of it.

Right now, I'm not insatiable about school because all we're doing is reciting the locations of all the secret tunnels under the lake so we can hide when the humans bring their big boats too close. Next year, we get to race to the tunnels, which will be more fun. There are races in each location, and at the end of the year, we see who can reach all of them the fastest. Do you guys get to do anything like that? If I weren't so busy with humanology right now, I'd improve my swim times.

Can you keep a secret? I have already started studying humans. You know what that means, right? I can use my insatiable knowledge to help you get a human friend. But you have to promise to tell me everything you learn about them after you become friends. We'd be partners.

Here's my first tip: Make them scream. I know! It sounds crazy, right? But I was doing a field study on some humans (that's science talk for studying them in the wild), and they were talking about a party they went to, and they all said it was a scream and the best party they'd been to. I think if you make them scream, they will look upon it favorably. In science, this is called a hypothesis.

Also, they said the party was "very cool." Make a note to find out if their parties all have specific temperatures, please.

Try that and then report back your results.

Sincerely,

Reginald

September 30

Dear Reginald,

I tried your tip. It did not go well. Are you sure they said scream was a good thing? I mean, they screamed all right, but they didn't seem happy about it. They threw things at me, except for one human who used his phone to film his friends throwing things at me. I hope my dad doesn't see the video or I will be grounded—or worse, he might make us move again. I would not put that past him because he's getting seriously paranoid.

I have a field report, though! (Is that how you say that?) One human left their wallet behind when they ran away, screaming like a stuck pig. I wanted to take a picture of the stuff for your science, but my dad won't let me touch his phone right now. He's got a human alert on it because he's worried about those hunters from the TV. He's afraid I'll mess up the settings.

So, I'll just list the things for you:

1. $6 in human money
2. A driver's license
3. A picture of one of the other humans. (She was great at screaming.)

Your Pal,
Eugene

October 4

Dear Eugene,

I am sorry that my hypothesis proved incorrect. Science is like that sometimes. I've made a note that screaming is not always favorable. We'll have to test out whether it is only favorable at parties after we get you some Homo sapiens friends. (I learned that is science for "humans.")

Thank you for your great field report. I've done some research on the items you listed, and I believe that a driver's license can tell you where one of the Homo sapiens has their nest. Do you still have the items? If so, look for something called an address. If you find the address, it should lead you to the nest. This is a marvelous opportunity.

My suggestion would be to apologize to the humans for making them scream at the wrong time. In my personal observations, whenever my father apologizes to my mother, he has a higher success rate if he also makes an offering of some kind. I don't have much evidence yet about what would make the best offering to humans, but I have observed that they are always eating when they come to the lake. I would bring the best food offering you can find.

In the meantime, I'm going to do some research on a Homo sapiens party to see if there is always a temperature change and how often screaming is involved.

I am hopeful your offering will be accepted and then you can hang out with them for a while. Think of the scientific advancements we'd make!

I was thinking about you guys' television. That would be a good place for you to get some human information. I wish my parents would let me watch human shows, but they feel I am too obsessed as it is. It is hard getting them to understand my insatiable need for science. Though, I suspect it also has to do with the cost of waterproof televisions. Science is worth the investment, don't you think?

Sincerely,
Reginald

October 10

Dear Reginald,

I went to their nest. No one was there, but I left my offering because I didn't want to waste it. I found the best deer I could. I picked that because it's "deer season." It's my favorite time of year because there are a lot of humans in the woods and we don't have to go to school for safety reasons.

I left a note for the humans at their nest. It said, "Sorry. I was hoping to be friends." I wrote it in big letters with the blood that was leaking from the deer.

I'll go back later today and see if they got my note.

When I got home, my dad was spreading skunk musk everywhere. He said it's a human repellant. I don't want to smell like something that will repel humans, so I am writing to you from my grandmother's nest.

Oh, hold on ... my dad's bringing skunk musk to my grandmother's. This is a good time for me to see if the humans are back at their nest yet. Hopefully, I'll have good news soon.

Your Pal,
Eugene

PS I hope you don't mind me writing *humans* because I can't spell the science words for them.

October 10

Dear Reginald,

I'm writing twice in one day because I have big news and need your advice. I went back to the human nest, but there were a lot of their police there and they were taking pictures of my offering and note. I wasn't sure if that was a good thing or not, so I went home.

What do you know about human police?

Your Pal,
Eugene

October 13

Dear Eugene,

Here's what my research determined about the police. They are there to help people in the Homo sapiens community. Sometimes, if a human goes missing from their nest and their parents need help finding them, the police will put the human's picture on their television and ask people to look for them.

The only confusing thing is sometimes the police do the same thing when they want to catch one of their criminals, which is the other way they help people. I think we'll have to wait and see what happens.

I'll keep researching.
Sincerely,
Reginald

PS Your dad is right about the skunk musk. Homo sapiens hate it, but they will bathe in something called "grease-cutting dish detergent" to get rid of the smell. We don't use dishes, so I don't know where to get some. Do Fouke monsters use dishes?

October 17

Dear Reginald,

So, I am definitely on their television. I don't know how they got the picture of me because they weren't in the nest when I was there. The TV said something about a "door cam." I know about trail cams because at our school we have to memorize where they are. Some of the teenaged Foukes dare each other to cross the cams sometimes. I didn't know doors could have cams too.

I can't tell if the police are hoping to find me because they think I'm lost or because they think I'm a criminal. They called me a "person of interest." Do you know what that means? I liked that they called me a person, but they also said I was in a costume, which hurt my feelings. I don't think my fur looks like a costume, but maybe my mom is right and I don't brush it enough.

Oh, about that dish detergent, we have some somewhere, but it doesn't matter right now because my dad saw me on the news. I can't go out for a week.

Your Pal,
Eugene

October 21

Dear Eugene,

I'm sorry you are grounded. I have some great news for you, though. Did you know that Homo sapiens worship monsters once a year? It's something called "All Hallows' Eve," and everyone dresses up like their favorite monster. I think this is your best chance to get near them. You've already got the perfect attire! Don't brush your fur too much because I think you want it to look like a costume.

You could do some real fieldwork. The Homo sapiens children dress up and go door-to-door asking for offerings. The older ones have parties and hand out the offerings. They like the offering to be candy. I'll try to keep an eye out for some humans on their boats and in the water. They tend to drop things a lot. If I find any candy, I'll send it to you.

See if your dad will let you watch some television while you are grounded so you can learn about the "All Hallows' Eve" gathering.

Sincerely,
Reginald

October 23

Dear Reginald,

My dad has been letting me watch human television. He's actually making me watch the show about the monster hunters so I'll know to stay away from them. They are really good at killing monsters, but I think they only kill monsters that are trying to hurt humans. I would never do that. Do you have any advice on how to show that I won't hurt humans if I run into these hunters?

I saw some of the party things you were talking about on the television. They do a ritual called dancing. It involved a lot of shaking and moving their arms. Though, sometimes they'd just hug each other and move back and forth with the music. I should probably learn how to do the moving and shaking thing too. (Whew! I'm going to be busier than a one-legged man in a butt-kicking contest.)

I've been on the news a little less lately, so I'm hoping Dad will let me out in time for the worship monsters night.

Your Pal,
Eugene

October 25

Dear Eugene,

A boat went by that was having a party. I noted a couple of things. First, the temperature was definitely cool. However, it is October so that could be statistically irrelevant. I've logged it into my research but made a special note about the date. Second, there was some screaming, but mostly when one of them fell into the water. I don't think that will be a factor at every party.

I did something dangerous, but we're friends, so I thought it was worth the risk. Plus, it will further my knowledge of humanology. I poked my head onto their deck to watch. They were all drinking something that made them do more of that dancing ritual you were talking about.

Don't tell anyone, but I stole some of it. You should get a package soon that contains some cans of their special juice. Bring it with you to the party. I think it will help you get accepted.

I've been thinking about the monster hunters you were telling me about. I did some research, and when police are trying to catch someone, they often have the people raise their hands in the air to show they will not do any harm. If you run into any hunters, please do that.

Sincerely,
Reginald

October 31

Dear Reginald,

I have so much to tell you, I don't even know where to start. I WENT TO A HUMAN PARTY! I'll put all my observations in this note. I didn't go to the address where I left the offering because I worried about ending up on television again. Instead, I walked around until I saw a house with a bunch of people going in.

First, thank you for the special juice. You are an amazing scientist. Everyone got very excited and yelled (in a good way, not in a screaming way) when I held the cans up. They all patted me on the back and told me my costume was amazing. I didn't even mind them calling it a costume.

On the temperature thing, the room was pretty warm, so I don't know if a cool party is different.

I did the ritual dancing, and the humans even got in a circle and clapped for me when I danced to a song about monsters mashing.

Then, the scariest thing of all happened. You're not even going to believe it when I tell you. Two people dressed like monster hunters showed up! They walked right up to me and said, "You know, we kill monsters." Everyone was staring at us, smiling, like something fun was about to happen. I wasn't sure if maybe your hypothesis thingy about humans worshiping us that night was wrong and I was about to be sacrificed. At first, I froze up, but then I remembered what you told me, so I held up my hands and said, "I come in peace, humans."

Everyone laughed, and we went back to the dancing thing.

Okay, try not to pass out when I tell you this, but after the party, I rode in a real human car! The hunters saw me walking and offered to give me a ride. They dropped me off near the woods and said they hoped to see me around.

I think I have human friends! But, honestly, you're my best friend and a great scientist.

Your Pal,
Eugene

About the Author

Annmarie SanSevero is a Staten Island native who was transplanted to the South. When she isn't dodging tornadoes or running screaming from bugs of unusual size, she writes fantasy, science fiction, and mystery.

Treading Eggshells
by John K. Patterson

Flaming Cliffs, Mongolia
460 km southwest from Ulaanbaatar

Dr. Dominic Alderidge kept one hand on the Delica's steering wheel and pounded back his last energy drink, driving up to the fossil dig site at the base of the cliff. His standard diet of steamed mutton and dumplings wouldn't be enough for a night like this, and that was normally the best fuel he could get on the edge of the Gobi Desert. He'd been saving the fluorescent green can for an emergency.

Tonight qualified. Someone had shot one of the bears he'd been tracking, and he needed to rescue her cub if he could.

A scattered crew of locals and sunburned grad students chipped away at rocks or navigated the grid of stakes set up over the site, only a few approaching to greet Dominic as he pulled up the 4x4 minivan alongside their pickup trucks. He crushed the now-empty can, grabbing a thermos of hot water for his daily peppermint tea. He'd splurged on a good thermos, so it would still be hot when night fell.

The nearest figure came up to greet him, a Black man in his fifties or sixties with close-cropped white hair. His cargo pants and black shirt had been officially baptized in the dust of the Gobi.

"You're head of operations, I presume?" Dominic asked.

"Correct," the man said as he extended a hand. They shook.

"Kirk Berg, paleoecologist. Your bear is a hundred yards north from the site. I'll take you."

They passed a trio of folding tables where some fossils were collected, many of them encased in plaster and aluminum foil. Bones and teeth were set around a large centerpiece: a clutch of white eggs, still set in reddish sandstone as if prepared for a museum exhibit.

"Thanks for calling me," Dominic said. "Are those dinosaur eggs?"

Berg nodded. "Protoceratops. Like a Triceratops but with no horns, about the size of a German Shepherd. Thousands of eggs! Even more than Andrews found here back in—"

"I'd love to hear more about it later, but we're running out of time."

"Just excited, is all," Berg said with a grin. "At least you were close by. I expected you'd be in the capital, not in the field."

"I've been tracking this bear's mother to the south." By now, Dominic was well acquainted with *Ursus arctos gobiensis*, the Gobi Brown Bear. The subspecies was the only bear adapted for life in the deep desert, not to mention the rarest in the world, with only thirty-one known individuals. Though their population was recovering, each death was a steep step backward.

Dr. Berg leg him to a furry brown shape rising above the dry bushes. The mother.

Dominic tucked his thermos under his arm, bending down to examine the body. Aside from the three bullet holes and accompanying blood, there was nothing out of the ordinary.

Now that this was more than just a phone call, now that the animal lay dead at his feet, his knees wobbled, and his eyes misted over.

One step closer to extinction. But at least you had a child. He made a silent promise to her he'd protect that cub.

"Her cub's still out there?" he asked.

"Yes," Dr. Berg said. "One of our guides had to shoot the mother. Cub took off before we could grab him."

The sun raced to the horizon. Dominic couldn't spare much time, but he could conduct an autopsy in the morning. "How was she acting?" he asked. "You told me over the phone it was self-defense. She was aggressive?"

"Extremely. Snarling and twitching like someone hit her with a cattle prod." He paused, closing his eyes for a moment. "We could tell she was in pain. Maybe poisoned. Got way too close to one of my students. Then *bang.*" Berg used his hands to mimic holding a rifle.

Dominic scratched his beard. "Poisoned? That rules out poachers." Mongolia had few cases of bear poaching, none of which involved poison.

"You're thinking a wild source, then?" Berg asked, wiping his forehead with a handkerchief. "Ate something that didn't agree with her?"

"Could be. Or brain damage, or an infection. But that can wait." The orphaned cub would be only a few months old, defenseless against hungry snow leopards or golden eagles. "You got a tracker?"

"Our shooter volunteered," Dr. Berg said. He waved up a figure in a green windbreaker who had been standing next to the dig site, leaning on a dirt bike painted red and blue. "Baatar's a good man. Best English speaker in the group. Ready when you are."

Nodding, Dominic stepped forward as Baatar came up to meet them. The Mongolian man looked to be in his mid-thirties, about five years younger than Dominic and a few inches taller. He'd cut his hair shorter than most of the other locals helping at the dig site.

Dominic noted the Mosin-Nagant rifle strapped over his back. Baatar looked down at the bear, full of regret.

"I can use my bike," he said with a strong accent. "Faster than horses. Faster than your Delica." He aimed an accusatory finger toward the minivan.

Dominic nodded. "I don't doubt it. But we're going to need the van to transport the cub back, so we'll have to bring both."

"We'll have a cot set up for when you get back," Dr. Berg said.

Within an hour, the setting sun burned the clouds in the kind of spectacular display Dominic lived for. This was the unfiltered wild, out in the arid purity of Mongolia.

It took less than an hour for Baatar to track down the cub, and another ten minutes for Dominic to get the little guy calm enough to place him in a pet carrier, which now rode shotgun next to him. A little anticlimactic for his sense of adventure, but with the rarest bear on Earth, an uneventful rescue was always a cause for relief.

Hardly bigger than a terrier, the tiny bear called for its mother plaintively, but there was little Dominic could do until they got him to the shelter in Ulaanbaatar.

"Hang in there, little guy," he said, gently patting the top of the carrier. "We'll take care of you."

Baatar accompanied him on his bike, heading back toward the fossil dig.

Without warning, Baatar veered off-course.

Frowning, Dominic turned the van to follow him. After ten seconds or so, Baatar stuck out a hand to wave him down and skidded his bike to a halt.

Putting the van in park, Dominic looked through the front of the carrier at the little cub. "Stay here, buddy." He was getting cold, so he grabbed his thermos and took it with him.

"What's wrong?" he asked Baatar.

The man crouched low to the ground. "I wondered," he said quietly, as if to himself. "Yes, here. I'm seeing the mother's path." He stepped forward, rifle slung over his shoulder.

Dominic could see many of the same faint details, having spent time with these bears before. The pattern of dry plants pressed or crushed by a heavy foot, a loose scattering of stones, a fingernail-sized clump of fur on a twig; if you didn't know what to look for, it would be easy to miss. They must have been only a few minutes from the dig site now.

"You saw this from your bike?"

"I saw a hole in the ground—up there." Baatar pointed. "Had a hunch she'd been through here. There might be a clue about what poisoned her."

"Assuming she was poisoned."

He followed Baatar, rocks tripping him up. The desert quickly lost its heat, and Dominic grew nervous. He didn't want to be here for the nighttime winds.

The dry desert plants had concealed a small hole in the ground, about a meter in diameter. Dominic was impressed that Baatar had seen it from his motorbike. They were about twenty meters away from it when Baatar skidded to a halt, falling backward. Dominic helped him back to his feet.

The man shouted something in Mongolian. "We have to leave. I shouldn't have checked! We have to go."

"Baatar? What are you panicked about?"

"*Olgoi-khorkhoi!* Now I know what happened to the mother!"

"*Olgoi*—" Dominic started to repeat the name before it registered. He had heard of it, and though he'd only met Baatar today, he still felt a deep exasperation rise in his gut. The man should have known better. *Olgoi-khorkhoi* loosely translated as "intestine worm," a fabled wormlike creature so deadly, even looking at it could be fatal. The wide-eyed and credulous had even ascribed to it the cheesiest name of all: the Mongolian Death Worm, the final nail in the proverbial coffin for such a creature to ever be taken seriously.

And now Baatar had gone from a grounded, intelligent man to someone fearing a glimpse of the worm. Their effort to secure an endangered cub had hit a snag on local mythology.

"Don't tell me you believe that crap," Dominic said.

"We have not seen it for years," Baatar said, having regained some of his composure. "But I remember my grandmother speaking of it."

"Maybe she ran into a pit viper. Come on, there's no such thing as a Death Worm."

Baatar licked his lips, eyes wild. Good grief, he really believed in it.

Dominic glanced back at the van. The cub wasn't going anywhere. Checking the ground for snakes or insects, he approached the hole.

Baatar snapped out of his fearful gaze, and he rushed forward as if to grab him.

Dominic glared at him, lifting the thermos up. "Get back, all right? Just back up. Look, there's no worms, see?"

He turned around to look at the depression in the ground. Curiosity and confusion were dual chains, fastening him to the spot.

Sure enough, no worms awaited him in the curious meter-deep

void in the ground. But it held something else: a cluster of seven or eight whitish round objects the size of his fist, nestled together in a small chamber. They glistened with a coating of liquid or mucus with dark particles of sand clinging to them, and their surfaces were depressed, appearing to have a soft and leathery texture like reptile eggs.

When Dominic had been nine years old, his family had gone on vacation to Costa Rica to watch sea turtles come ashore to dig their nests. The similarity to a turtle nest was so strong he could practically hear the surf lapping at the shore and feel it sweep between his toes. Mongolia's dry wind screamed like the shorebirds that waited for the turtles to go back to the sea so they could descend like harpies on the countless nests and raid them for easy protein.

But Dominic was thousands of miles from the coast, and any turtle big enough to lay eggs like this had been extinct for millions of years. What was he looking at?

They couldn't be eggs. He would already know of any animal big enough to lay them. Could they be some sort of fungal growth?

He stepped around to the other side of the hole, where a smear of dried mucus crusted the dirt. One of the white objects had been dragged out, and something had taken a bite. He noted the telltale bear prints next to it.

Gobi bears were omnivores and always on the lookout for a little extra protein. But if eating one of these white objects had poisoned the bear, he'd have to treat them with caution. Dr. Berg and his students could look at them.

Dominic fished a penlight out of his pocket and turned it on as the light of dusk diminished.

"Sir!" Baatar said, as if from a hundred miles away. "Don't touch them."

"Not going to. We gotta get Berg out here."

Dominic wrinkled his nose at an unpleasant smell, traces of hydrogen sulfide and rotting meat. Maybe this was some way Mongolian shepherds fermented food, or Chinese poachers had some new method of storing animal organs to be collected later. But the white objects looked too natural for that.

The white sphere's contents had spilled out in something like a red, slimy mass. Admittedly his mental picture was of some large worm, but when he got a closer look at where the bear had bitten it in half, he could see white bone.

Vertebrae? What on God's green Earth ...?

Movement drew his gaze back to the hole. A few of the white orbs twitched or rattled against the others. One orb broke open, and something lashed out at his ankle. He yelped at the sharp pain and kicked out of reflex. He tried to step back, but the loose gravel gave way under his shoe and he fell on his backside.

A red worm had fastened to his sock like a disgusting lamprey. He tried to shake it off, but the thing held on tight, flopping around. He had to keep whatever it was from breaking the skin in case it was venomous, so he risked a firm grip on its slimy body just behind the head. He could see two small eyes, almost vestigial and covered in a thin layer of skin.

Carefully, he worked to pry the mouth off the fabric of his sock. Translucent fangs snagged on the threads until he pulled it away. Keeping a grip behind its head, he jammed the creature sharply against a stone, shattering its head with a wet *smack.*

He'd killed it.

Fangs? On a worm?

The brief observation vanished as an electric spasm of agony shot up his arm, like someone had jammed a taser into his entire nervous system. Dominic couldn't even scream. He fell back, his body locked up and numb. His brain allowed him no more motion, not even to get away from the creature. The dead thing slipped out of his hand.

Was he having a heart attack? No. The creature that could not— *should not*—exist must have been toxic through its skin as well, like a poison dart frog. He heard something metal and heavy hit the ground with a *clunk.* His thermos of hot water for his tea.

"Sir!" Baatar came running to Dominic, giving the dead worm a wide berth.

It took effort to push the words out through his locked teeth. "Don't touch. Toxin ... in skin." Whatever it was, Dominic expected his heart to stop at any moment. Every sound became louder, rattling in his ears. Even his own stilted breathing sounded like nails on a chalkboard.

With careful hands, Baatar grabbed Dominic under his arms and dragged him away from the hole. His foot bumped the metal thermos, and that noise cut into Dominic's mind like a knife.

Wait. The thermos. Hot water could denature toxic proteins. It worked for jellyfish stings, at least. No guarantee of it working here. But he had to try. Maybe he would at least live a little longer.

"Hot water!" he said. Or tried to say. "Thermos! Open it!"

"What, sir?" Baatar said.

"Hot water. On ... hand!" Was the man able to understand him? Dominic's own voice was painful to hear. But Baatar picked up the thermos, came back to stand over him, and unscrewed the lid. Maybe Dominic was speaking more clearly than his own ears implied.

Intense heat spilled over his hand, and Dominic cried out. The flow stopped. "No! Keep pouring! Don't waste it!"

Baatar did so, and as the stream of hot water resumed, Dominic could feel it working. The electric pain ebbed away. He could breathe a little easier. The effort to speak sapped him harder than expected. The world pulled away slowly, then all fell to darkness.

Searing bright light drove through Dominic's retinas. He shut his eyes. Sullen soreness weighed down every cubic inch of his body. But it surprised him that he still *had* a body.

That creature, that impossible worm with vertebrae and fangs, had tried to bite him. Had anything gotten into his bloodstream?

He lay atop taut fabric. A cot. Folding tables loaded with fossils stood next to him. Overhead, spectacular stars filled the sky. A couple of portable lanterns lit up the area. Dr. Berg stood over him, shining a flashlight into his eyes, with Baatar looking over Berg's shoulder.

As if from miles away, he heard the yowls and grunts of a bear cub.

"Your furry little friend is okay," Dr. Berg said. "Baatar here saved your life. We can't tell for sure, but it looks like you got a light dose of that toxin. Seems to hit humans differently than bears."

Baatar leaned forward, a cigarette dangling from his lips. "How's that for a myth?" he said with a sardonic laugh.

Trying to move his head, Dominic got another stab of pain through his temples.

"Easy there," Dr. Berg said. "The toxin is working its way out of your system. I'm guessing the creature wasn't fully awake, and it just reacted to protect itself. Minor abrasions on your ankle, but the teeth didn't break through."

Nodding gingerly, Dominic forced himself to speak through the headache. "Yeah. Looks like they were eggs. Or cocoons."

"My money's on cocoons," Berg said. "I got a look at that nest, too, just a few minutes ago. They kinda reminded me of lungfish. Those can secrete a mucus cocoon, stay underground for years."

Dominic fixed him with a stare. "Did you know about these things?"

Berg shook his head. "We got the one you killed in a plastic bag. Soon as we can find some ethanol, we'll preserve it. Don't worry, I'm not taking credit for the discovery. It's all yours."

Baatar flicked the cigarette away. "This lucky idiot. Only man I know who's survived *Olgoi-khorkhoi*."

"Go easy on him, Baatar. I thought it was a myth too. Just hadn't seen one until now."

Dominic's right arm struggled to reach the edge of the cot. There was a tremor, but he tested his hand by touching his thumb to all his other fingers. "My phone. I need my phone."

Baatar nodded and reached into Dominic's shirt pocket, handing over his phone.

Sitting up, Dominic groaned as his head throbbed.

"Take it easy." Baatar put a hand on his shoulder. "You're not ready to walk. Here." He moved somewhere Dominic couldn't see and returned with a large plastic bag containing what looked like a red intestine, over a foot long. The creature looked even more repulsive up close. The head was half smashed, but unbelievable as it was, the set of jaws remained intact, the sharp teeth straight out of a monster movie. He hadn't been hallucinating. And there were those fading eyes, as if the creature was evolving away from needing sight. Two sensory appendages on the muzzle looked like short versions of catfish whiskers.

Dominic turned on the flashlight on his phone and held it up to the bag, looking at every detail he could. The eyes and teeth, the vertebrae he'd seen on the other creature half-eaten by their dead bear ...

The animal seemed familiar to him. "It's definitely not a worm," Dominic said. Wrong clade. It's a vertebrate."

"I suspected a legless lizard at first," Berg said, "but it doesn't have external ear openings."

"I know a guy who can give us something more specific." He tapped the phone, going into his contacts to find the right name: *Dr. Nolan Douglas, Herpetologist, UW.* One of his colleagues at the University of Washington.

After Baatar helped him take some photos, Dominic painstakingly typed a text, trying to be as specific as possible:

> ID? Burrowing creature at Flaming Cliffs.
> Emerged from cocoon like lungfish. Legless
> lizard? Venomous. Toxin absorbed through skin,
> denatured with hot water. I'll send coordinates
> when we can talk.

He hit the Send button, hoping Nolan would get back to him soon.

"If he can't help us, who do you want me to call?" Baatar's leathery hands folded together, and he sat down in a camping chair with a quiet heaviness.

"Next of kin would be a good idea," Dr. Berg said.

"I'm not dying," Dominic said. "We've still got a bear to take care of."

Baatar nodded. "I'm caring for it too. I orphaned him."

"Don't blame yourself, Bataar," Dominic said. "You saved my life. Thanks for that."

The phone rang. *That was fast,* Dominic thought, accepting the call.

Nolan Douglas's deep voice boomed all the way from Washington. "What is this, Dom? Some kind of prank? I'm flying out to Cameroon in the morning, so this better not be some—"

"No." He coughed. "No, it's real. Here, I'll put you on speaker." He tapped the phone so Baatar and Dr. Berg could hear him. Berg filled Nolan in, Dominic adding details as he could.

Dr. Douglas cleared his throat. "All right. Good news and bad news. Which do you want first?"

"Good first. I've had a rough night." Dominic coughed again.

"Sounds like it." Nolan took a deep breath. "Okay, good news. I know what this is. The small sensory tentacles on the snout give it away."

Nolan spoke a name, but in his torpor, Dominic didn't quite catch it. It sounded like *Sicilian*. "It came from Sicily?" he said, fighting the desire to fall asleep and maybe, just maybe, never wake up.

"No," Nolan said, "the name's phonetically similar. The technical term is *caecilian*. It's a type of amphibian."

At last, his toxin-fatigued brain latched onto the title. "That's the term. Rings a bell, but from way back in college." He heard the weariness in his own voice but willed his body to not give up.

"They're pretty obscure," Nolan said, a tremor of worry straining his words. "Dom, are you okay? Can you get to a hospital where you are?"

"Just tell me," Dominic said, clutching the phone tight. "Are caecilians toxic?"

"Yeah, they can be. That's the bad news. That was discovered only a few years ago. Nasty teeth too. If it bit you, I'd check for anticoagulants in your blood."

"Almost got me. But no. I didn't get bitten. The problem was skin absorption." He glanced at Baatar. "A local guide saved my life with hot water, after I'd grabbed this ... caecilian to get it off me. That's when my hand hurt."

"Another toxic amphibian, then," Nolan said.

Dominic noticed Nolan's voice sounded hollow and somehow farther away. But he clung all the tighter to hope. How warranted was that hope? "These caecilians—are any of them desert-dwellers?"

"No, all of the known species are tropical. Something like that in the Gobi Desert could burrow deep where there's moisture, but it would still need to evolve a water-retentive skin. First time for everything, I guess."

"This thing was in some sort of cocoon. There were others too. I think we should collect them for study. We recently had a flash flood.

Maybe they're emerging to mate." Amphibians were not his specialty, but he knew African bullfrogs would lie dormant in deserts or savannas to wait for the rains.

A brief silence on the other end. Dominic could practically hear the gears turning in Dr. Douglas's head. "Speculation, but we'll go with that. I remember hearing rumors about some kind of Death Worm in the Gobi."

"You said these are obscure," Dominic said. "But there's gotta be something about this thing in the literature, right? Something other than legends, I mean." Dominic could hardly accept the notion that such a creature spent all this time evading discovery, no matter how deep it normally burrowed.

"Nope," Nolan said. "Not a thing, Dom. You've found a new species. I think congratulations are in order. We'll make it official later. Just focus on getting better so you can enjoy it, okay?"

Dominic managed a weak laugh. "I'll give it my very best shot. I'll call back tomorrow." And he promised himself he would be alive tomorrow to make that call. "It's a lot to take in, but at least I can help give a bear cub a new home."

About the Author

John K. Patterson is the creator of the Arrivers and Queensland Crater universes. A self-trained author and artist who takes his monsters way too seriously, he can usually be found haunting the local coffee shop while working on his novels. He lives at the roots of Pikes Peak in Colorado Springs, Colorado.

The Alien Hunter
by John M. Campbell

I sat in the rocking chair on my front porch, watching the fluffy snowflakes drift down to form a velvety blanket over the valley stretched out before me. This was why I'd settled at this location in Colorado when I came to Earth. Finally, I could open the windows in my cabin and shut off the air-conditioning that kept the interior at a temperature most humans regarded as "frosty." The layer of fur I kept hidden under my shirt and jeans was aptly suited for this weather.

"I have something to tell you. I am a Gargo, and I come from the same planet as the chupacabras." I had seriously considered saying this to Judy, the self-described Alien Hunter. We had been sitting on this very porch the morning after we had dispatched a juvenile Chupe by spraying it with four liters of Costco garlic juice using her modified Super Soaker. She was convinced chupacabras were alien vampires who sucked out the blood of their victims, hence the garlic juice. She had it mostly right.

During the fight, the Chupe had stunned her and simultaneously knocked out the holo projector I kept in the crown of my Stetson. Judy saw my real face, but in her dazed state, she thought I suffered from the same disease as Joseph Merrick, the Elephant Man. In her mind, it explained why I wore a mask and lived in isolation in my mountain cabin.

The Chupe had taken off in its flying saucer and "skedaddled back home with its tail between its legs." I'd learned that phrase from the movie cowboys in the old Westerns I used to train the speaking voice of my holo.

That fight with the Chupe cemented my friendship with Judy. She was happy to have rid the Earth of an alien monster intent on hunting and killing our animals. For me, in my role as marshal of this sector, I was happy to get rid of a threat that could expose the aliens who lived in peaceable anonymity among humans. The fact that I contemplated revealing myself to Judy showed how close we had become, but it would have opened a can of Earthworms, as the human expression goes. So, I remained silent.

My phone buzzed, interrupting my musings. An email from Judy had arrived, triggering a flutter of anticipation in my pelvic area. For a human, such an involuntary response would be interpreted as lust. But because a Gargo's heart resided between its legs, the flutter meant one of two things: either I feared the Alien Hunter had discovered my secret, or I was happy to receive news from my friend of her latest hunting expedition. Given these possibilities, I opened the email with some trepidation.

A video was attached. She recorded her videos while driving her RV and transmitted them when she was in range of a cell tower. She was investigating reports of a werewolf sighting on the Canadian border.

Judy: "Hi, Garry."

[She is sitting at the wheel of her RV, wearing a weather-beaten Yankees ball cap. Light and shadow play along the familiar wrinkles of her face. She glances into the camera before returning her gaze to the road.]

Judy: "I just overheard some hunters in a diner talking about seeing a scruffy-looking giant wolf trotting through the forest outside of town. It could be a chupacabra."

[She downshifts as the RV starts up an incline.]

Judy: "My contact at NORAD confirms a series of intermittent radar blips unassociated with known aircraft have been heading in this direction, which correlates with the hunters' story."

The composite material used to make flying saucers absorbed radar waves, making them difficult for the primitive human tracking technology to detect reliably. But if a radar pulse hit at just the right angle, it would penetrate the saucer's skin and reflect off the antigrav engines, causing a blip to register.

Judy: "There have been no cattle mutilations, but that's not too surprising since there's not much grazing land up here. Mostly it's pine forest. I'm not sure what the alien's got in mind, but it can't be good. Talk to you later."

Hearing she still suspected nothing about me, my heart rate slowed. But normally, any new settler would register their intent to immigrate to Earth. If this was indeed an unregistered intrusion, I agreed with Judy: It couldn't be good.

A few days later, Judy's next video arrived.

Judy: "I got lucky. A saucer sighting led me to this meadow."

[She turns the camera around to show a snow-covered area surrounded by pine and fir trees. Bushes stick up randomly through the snow, but there is no sign of a saucer.]

Judy: "I might have to change my mind about crop circles being hoaxes, because I found a snow circle. That unusual shadow is a circular indentation in the snow, half a foot deep and maybe thirty feet wide."

Chupian saucers were that size. And although they possessed a holographic cloaking device, they couldn't hide some physical clues.

Judy: "Within the circle, a couple of bushes were mashed flat. I stepped over the edge to examine them, and damned if I didn't bump into the saucer. It left a bruise on my knee."

[Her voice is breathy as she recalls the incident. She closes her eyes and sighs.]

Judy: "I'm back here beyond the tree line, waiting to see what it does. I'll let you know when something happens."

The video ended. She'd found another Chupe. Now what? Blasting it with garlic juice was enough to chase away the last one, but it might have come back for more. If so, it would be prepared this time. And by Judy bumping into its ship, it probably already knew she was there.

And if the Chupe abducted or harmed her, it could trigger mass paranoia among humans, making it nearly impossible for aliens like me to remain incognito. I had to intercept this Chupe before that happened. But what could I do? Where exactly was she?

I scrolled through my list of phone apps and clicked on the EXIF viewer to open Judy's last video file. I flipped past the time and date, the file attributes, and the audio/video settings until I found what I was searching for: the latitude, longitude, and altitude coordinates of where she recorded the video. While humans didn't have antigrav engines, they still produced some clever technology.

Unlike the Chupes, Gargos are a peaceful, nonconfrontational species. My ancestral gut told me to stay put and keep a low profile. The Chupe would eventually eat its fill and go away. But my heart and head told me Judy was in danger, and I couldn't live with myself if she got hurt or killed. I needed to go after her.

My electrified whip hung coiled on a hook on my cabin wall. It had bristles capable of penetrating most clothing. When activated, contact with one or more bristles would immobilize even the largest perpetrator. I took down my whip and went to the barn. There, I threw tools, ropes, and first aid supplies into my wagon. Then I loaded the wagon and my ATV into my saucer and took off, heading north.

Once I was airborne, I called Judy on Skype. She answered from the RV.

"Garry? I wasn't expecting a call. Is everything all right?"

"I'm fine, Judy. I just finished viewing your video. I was afraid you'd try to confront the alien. I'm glad to see you've reconsidered."

"Yeah, it took off." She peered upward through the windshield. "Did you know flying saucers become visible when they take off?"

In fact, I did know. Activating the antigrav engines pulled full power from their fusion reactors, leaving nothing for the holographic cloaking device. For that very reason, I didn't like flying in the daytime, as I was doing now.

"I'm busy trying to keep it in sight." She peered at the phone's screen and raised her eyebrows. "Where are you calling from?"

I glanced behind me at the gray metallic walls of my saucer. "I rented an RV. I thought I'd come join you—"

She squinted. "Really? That's sweet, but—"

"You can't confront that alien by yourself. It's too dangerous."

She peered up through the windshield again. A shadow passed over her vehicle. "I'll be okay, Garry."

"At least wait for me. I'm not far away. We can go after it together."

She shook her head. "This is something I've got to do alone."

"But why? You'd be risking your life. If this is the same alien you humiliated the last time, it'll be out for vengeance."

"I know that." She glanced at the phone and seemed to decide something. "You remember when I told you I was a catch-and-release hunter? Well, that was only partially true. I release them the first time, but if they continue to harm animals, I eliminate them."

I stared at the screen. "What do you mean, 'eliminate them'?"

She lifted a hand, curled her two shortest fingers, extended her two longest fingers, and pointed them at her chest. "I put a silver bullet through their heart." Her thumb came down.

She spoke in a tone I'd never heard from her before. A shiver ran through my body. What I originally believed to be a mission to rescue Judy was now becoming a mission to prevent the murder of the Chupe, as well.

"Sorry, Garry. I've got to sign off now. The saucer has landed. Take care." The screen went blank.

I banged a gloved fist on the console. I had to get to her before she found the Chupe. But how? Skype didn't include a location in its broadcast stream.

I was approaching the site of her last video. Few roads traversed this dense forest. Maybe I could follow a road until I found her RV.

I clicked on Google Maps to display my position on my phone. I vectored to the nearest road. There! Vehicle tracks in the snow beside the road showed where she'd parked. The tracks turned onto the road heading north.

I skimmed the treetops, keeping the road in sight below. There was no traffic on this remote stretch, and nothing parked on the shoulder. Ahead, an unpaved road meandered off to the east. No vehicle tracks disturbed the snow, so I continued on.

The map showed the road branching. One side led to a village a few miles away. The other side led deeper into the forest. I chose that direction.

With every mile that passed under my saucer, my dread grew. Images flashed into my mind, alternating between Judy's slashed throat bleeding red in the snow and the Chupe's body gushing bright blue blood from a hole in its chest. Any hope of finding her RV in time was fading fast.

My phone buzzed. Another email from Judy: no text, just a video.

[Judy's face is close to the phone.]

Judy: *[whispering]* "I've found it. The Chupacabra is attacking a bear!"

[She rotates the camera to show the scene. Roars and crashes and screams of pain accompany rapid movement through the trees.]

Judy: *[voice trembling]* "I can't just watch anymore. I've got to stop this. But I had to show you what's happening in case I don't make it back."

[The video freezes on the gun in Judy's hand.]

I accessed the video's metadata and copied the coordinates into Google Maps. Taking the direct route to her location, I arrived in seconds.

Below, an unbroken expanse of snow-dusted conifers obscured my view of the ground. I located the nearest road. She must've parked there. Yes. There was her RV, but I couldn't land the saucer on the road. The risk of being spotted was too high.

I shot straight up and found an opening in the trees carved by a stream. I eased the saucer down until it rested on the banks, straddling the water. The holographic camouflage activated. Clipping the whip to my hip, I mounted my ATV, opened the hatch, and drove into the forest.

A minute later, I came to the road. There was the RV. I spotted Judy's path into the forest. Weaving through the trees, I zipped forward, keeping her footprints in sight. Above the hum of the ATV's motor and the hiss of my tires on the snow, I listened for the sounds of a struggle. Only silence reached my ear holes.

Then in the gloom, it appeared: the scene of the battle. Broken trees were bent in every direction. As I came closer, I saw trampled underbrush. Disturbances in the snow revealed great gouges in the pine straw beneath. My eyes picked out the body of a large creature.

I halted the ATV at the edge of the scene, scanning the area for Judy. Where could she possibly be? I dismounted and ventured forward.

The smell of blood mingled with the tang of pine sap and the earthy aroma of decaying pine needle duff. Utter silence reflected the somber mood of the forest at the gruesome death of one of its creatures. The bear lay face down; the snow around it stained scarlet. It must've stood eight feet tall when rising on its hind legs. Its dark red fur was unusual for a bear its size. The sole of a foot was visible—but it didn't have the claws of a bear.

I clenched my fists. It couldn't be. I crept to the body. It had hands, not paws, with defensive wounds on its fingers and palms—and splotches of blue blood. My eyes focused on an axe nearby. Blue stains streaked its wooden handle and stone blade. The Chupe had not escaped unscathed.

I grasped the creature's shoulder and rolled it over to verify my suspicion. The creature's humanlike features confirmed it to be a Sasquatch. Its chest was an empty cavity where its heart and liver had been.

Rage bloomed in my gut over this criminal act. I could relate personally to these peaceful, solitary creatures who once ranged widely throughout the Earth. For centuries, the Chupes, in their bloodlust, had hunted them nearly to extinction. Only rumors of the Yeti in Asia, the Yowie in Australia, and the Sasquatch in North America hinted at survivors of that genocide.

I stood and scanned the area for any sign of Judy or the Chupe. Scattered drops of blue blood on the snow and tree trunks caught my eye. Then I noticed an unnatural gray shape protruding from the surface.

I pulled Judy's handgun out of the snow, a device of crude, boxy construction the size of my gloved hand. It was a distant descendant of the silvery revolvers used by movie cowboys, with their elegant grips made from wood or animal horn. Embossed onto this gun's artificial grip material was a circle that enclosed the letters SIG.

Nearby was the imprint of Judy's body in the snow. However, there were no signs of injury beyond droplets of the Chupe's blood. Footprints showed the direction it had taken her.

I slipped Judy's gun into a jacket pocket and sprinted back to my ATV. I needed to catch up with them before the Chupe reached its ship. I set off at high speed, following the footprints and blood trail. Red blood droplets appeared next to the blue. The Chupe may have bitten her to inject her with a sedative and keep her subdued, but the amount of blood loss did not seem life-threatening.

Within a mile, the trail reached a meadow. In the distance, the Chupe trudged through the snow, carrying Judy's limp body in its arms. Although the jaws and teeth of its snout were wolflike, the spines along its back were definitely not. Nor were the longer rear legs and shorter front legs. Its claws were more like a grizzly's than a wolf's. It wore a shaggy brown thermal suit that insulated it from the cold while keeping its jaws and claws available for use. Blue gashes in the legs and torso of the suit showed where it had sustained injuries.

A bag strapped to its back adjacent to the spines exhibited a red stain. It likely contained the heart and liver of the Sasquatch, which the Chupe would consume at its leisure.

I twisted the handlebar throttle, and my ATV leapt forward. Up ahead, the Chupe halted, and a hole appeared in the air before it, revealing the open hatch of the saucer.

"Put her down, you bloodsucking mole rat!" I yelled at the maximum volume my holo voice could project. To my own ear holes, the Chupian translation was a brain-piercing screech, but it achieved the desired effect.

The Chupe turned. It was a mature adult, not the juvenile we had encountered before. When it saw me charging forward on the ATV, it opened its jaws and issued a squawk of laughter. It stooped down to place Judy's body on the ground.

"What are you doing here, Gargo fish-eater?" my holo unit translated.

I skidded to a stop and dismounted. "I'm here to bring you to justice." I was too far away to use my electrified whip, so I removed Judy's handgun from my pocket and pointed it at the Chupe. "Your crime spree is finished."

It squawked another laugh as it unstrapped the bag and let it slide to the ground. "What have you got there? Your personal garlic juice squirting device? I heard about how you love your human toys."

The Chupe's hind legs tensed as it prepared to charge. I shifted my aim and fired. The bullet hit the bag on the ground beside the Chupe, splattering blood and tissue.

The Chupe flinched away from the gore, but before I could react, it scooped up Judy and held her to its chest as a shield. "You brain-dead excrement eater!" it screeched.

Judy jerked at the sound and raised her head. Her eyes fluttered open.

"Throw away the shooter before you hurt someone—or I do," the Chupe said.

"By my authority as Marshal of the Epsilon Tau sector," I recited, "I am placing you under arrest."

Another squawk from the Chupe. "The only authority you've

got, Gargopuss, is in that shooter. And unless you toss it away, I'm going to kill your human pet here." It edged backward toward the ship, pulling Judy along with it.

I looked at Judy. She returned my gaze, her eyes clear. "Are you all right?" I asked in English.

"I'm fine," she replied. "I've got a trick up my sleeve, and I'm ready to use it." She flicked her head at the Chupe.

I raised my voice and switched to Chupian. "Does the ship's pilot recognize my authority?"

From inside came the voice of the ship's AI. "Affirmative, Marshal."

The Chupe peeked over its shoulder into the saucer hatch.

"I hereby take control of this spacecraft," I said.

"Acknowledged," the AI responded.

"You can't do that." The Chupe's screech rose in pitch. It squeezed Judy tighter against its chest. "Cancel that order, or I'll kill her."

I locked eyes with Judy and tipped my Stetson.

She raised an arm across her chest and pointed it at the Chupe's head. From under her wrist, a spray of garlic juice erupted in its face.

The Chupe recoiled with a squeal, and Judy scrambled away.

It collapsed to the ground, scooping snow onto its snout and eyes to wash away the garlic. I rushed forward and pinned its leg with my knee while pressing the gun to the side of its head. "Don't move. I don't trust this human tech. We don't want it to explode your head accidentally."

Feeling the Chupe's muscles flexing beneath me, I knew I was only moments away from losing control of the situation.

But so did Judy. "I think you could use these." She unzipped her parka to reveal a bundle of zip ties tucked into an inside pocket.

Beneath me, the Chupe's muscles remained tight. "I claim my right to hunt freely," it hissed, "just as my ancestors have done for centuries."

She eyed the Chupe's powerful jaws. "Keep it still, Garry." She looped a tie around its snout and zipped it tight. She applied two more higher up.

"Killing a sapient being is a Class One felony," I said, "and attempted abduction is Class Two. Put your arms behind your back."

The Chupe's red eyes glared at me. I pressed the gun harder against its skull until it complied. Once Judy had cinched its wrists together, I pulled the Chupe to its feet and gave the gun to Judy.

"May I have the rest of those?" I asked her, indicating the zip ties. She handed them over, and I led the Chupe into the ship.

A few minutes later, I came out and picked up the bag containing the Sasquatch's heart and liver. I carried it inside the ship and instructed the AI to turn it over to the authorities as evidence of the Chupe's crime. Then I joined Judy outside.

The ship's hatch closed, and the saucer vanished. Only the dent in the snow and the flattened bushes indicated the saucer still sat there. The AI pilot activated the antigrav engines, and the holographic camouflage blinked off. The ship sat exposed for an instant. Then, without a sound, it launched straight up, creating a momentary blizzard in its wake.

When the saucer disappeared into the clouds and the turbulence abated, Judy turned to me. "What did you do inside with the 'cabra?"

"I shut it in the excrement chamber and zip-tied the door closed. It won't be returning."

Judy tittered. "You locked it in the bathroom? Will it survive in there without access to food and water during the long trip home?"

"It'll be fine." Humans completely misunderstood interstellar travel. The Chupe would be home before I arrived back in Colorado.

"Were you actually talking to that alien? I heard some really strange screeching going on between y'all."

"Yeah, well, smartphones are pretty advanced these days."

She frowned. "What do you mean?"

"I used Google Translate." My holo voice mimicked the laconic intonation of movie cowboys. Sometimes that deadpan delivery was perfect for the circumstances.

She looked doubtful. "What was that voice from inside the saucer?"

"The ship's AI pilot."

She stopped and squinted at me. "You seem to know more about these aliens than you let on."

"This wasn't my first rodeo. Let's just say, as marshal of this sector, I keep an eye on these things for the government. C'mon. I'll give you a ride to your RV."

She silently absorbed this information as we mounted the ATV and got going. Having her arms tighten around my torso reminded me of our first ride together on that crisp fall evening a couple of months ago, heading to the pasture to catch the juvenile Chupe mutilating a cow. I liked having her leaning against my back with her arms wrapped around my middle.

"What'll happen to the chupacabra when it gets home?" Judy asked.

"The authorities will arrest it."

"Really? Why?"

"It tried to abduct you, and it killed a sapient being."

"What did it kill?" Her voice changed in tenor.

"Back in the woods, it killed a Sasquatch." My unemotional holo voice failed to convey my anger over that atrocity.

Judy gasped at the news, showing she shared my outrage. "A Sasquatch?" she murmured. "I thought it was a bear."

I reached down and patted her hand.

"I assumed Sasquatches were hoaxes or folktales," she said. "I never believed they could be real."

"And I failed in my duty to protect it." Again, my voice did not reflect my abject regret.

"If I'd known that when you handed me the gun, I would've killed that monster then and there."

"Believe me, I felt tempted."

We exited the forest onto the road. When we rolled to a stop at Judy's RV, I mustered the courage to speak. Over my shoulder, I asked, "Now this is done, why don't you come stay with me awhile?"

She squeezed my middle again one last time before dismounting and turning to face me. "I told you before. I'm a warm-weather girl." She smiled. "I've had enough of this cold and snow."

"Yeah, I figured. But I thought I'd give it a shot."

"You're welcome in Florida anytime. I'll take you to Disney World."

"Do they have a penguin exhibit? I would enjoy that."

She gave me the melodic laugh I'd hoped for. My pelvic area fluttered.

"We've got to stop meeting this way," she said, moving in for a hug.

I returned it. "I don't know; I kinda enjoy it."

She released me and stepped back. "Every so often, I'll send you a video."

"I'd like that." I touched the brim of my Stetson with a gloved finger and mounted my steed like I'd seen the movie cowboys do before riding off into the sunset.

On the way to my saucer, I floated on a warm sensation like I was riding a cumulus cloud. Humans may not have antigrav engines, but this feeling was pretty close to it.

My mood shifted as I entered my ship. One final job remained. I lifted off and returned to the meadow, setting down where the Chupe's saucer had been. Before exiting, I hitched my wagon to the ATV. The ride to where the Sasquatch lay was much less frantic than my earlier breakneck dash—and much more solemn.

When I arrived, I took out my phone to capture a video record of the crime scene. I would transmit it to my planet as evidence against the Chupe, along with my account of what occurred. After completing that task, I pulled the wagon next to the body of the Sasquatch. The corpse was huge, but I heaved it into the wagon.

I returned to my ship and hauled the Sasquatch on board. The metallic smell of the creature's blood permeated the ship's interior. Although the odor did not evoke the same visceral reaction in me as it would in a human, it was still a reminder of the tragic loss of a magnificent being.

When I arrived home in Colorado, I landed in the patch of prairie grass near my cabin that overlooked the valley. I piped waste heat from the fusion reactor through the skin of the saucer to melt the snow and soil underneath, which allowed me to dig a grave. I placed the creature's head facing east, where it would catch the rays of the rising sun every morning. As a final touch, I covered the grave with the sod of the grass I had set aside earlier for this purpose. In the spring, new shoots would be nourished as the Sasquatch replenished the soil with the minerals its body released.

Perhaps someday, if Judy came to visit, I would show her its final resting place.

About the Author

John M. Campbell is a first-place winner of the Writers of the Future contest, and his story is published in Volume 37 of their annual anthology. He joined other Writers of the Future winners to found Calendar of Fools publishing. A story of his also appears in the 2024 High Caliber Awards anthology of military science fiction novellas. His short stories appear in the online magazine *Compelling Science Fiction* (Issue 12) as well as in various anthologies. For a complete list of his publications, visit his website at JohnMCampbell.com.

John lives and writes in Denver, Colorado.

A History of Hodags in the City
by Darren Lipman

Hodags were first spotted in the 1870s in Kent County, Michigan. Some believe the creature was a hoax; in fact, Eugene Shepard, who claimed to have had one in captivity, admitted his deceit in 1896. One must ask, then, why would he do it? And why would he do it in Rhinelander, Wisconsin, so far from the original sightings?

New evidence suggests that hodags were once human and, by ways unknown, were cursed into beastly form. Persecuted in place after place, they roamed the Midwest until wily Eugene had the perfect idea: make their entire existence a thing of legend and never worry again. Contemporary hodag sightings are rare, and most are written off as practical jokes, but that's precisely what they want you to think. Your willful ignorance is the key to their safety.

Now, a hundred and fifty years after their first sighting, we know the truth.

—Anita Cortez, "A History of Hodags," originally printed in *Otherworldly Occult Facts and Timelines Almanac*, vol. 8, issue 3, page 24

November

Hans Eskell hasn't showered in two days. He's perched in some bushes, dressed in camouflage that's so new, the dirt beneath his knees hasn't stained it. His silenced cell phone hangs heavy in his pocket next to an empty candy bar wrapper. He runs a hand through his slicked-back black hair and narrows his eyes. Rustling, about twelve yards out. It's been a late year for snow, so the ground is covered in leaves and twigs, but he can't see the deer yet.

A few minutes pass in silence, then another bout of rustling, closer this time.

And grunting? He strains to hear. Definitely grunts, like wild boar. But this isn't boar territory.

He sniffs the air. Beneath the pine and earth, is that a hint of lemon? And rust? Maybe his blood sugar is low?

The rustling moves closer. He stands up slowly, not wanting to scare it off, but eager to catch sight of it. There's definitely something there. Dark fur, thick, bristling. Not smooth like a deer's coat. He shifts his weight to see better and brushes some leaves.

It stops grunting. A second later, it bolts away.

What the hell is it?

Hans levels his gun and shoots without thinking.

The bullet pierces the beast, and it squeals, but doesn't fall. It runs out of sight within seconds.

"Shit," he says. "What was that?"

Hans stores his things and walks a dozen steps to find the first splattering of blood on the ground. There's a good enough trail to follow, allowing him to stalk the wounded creature. His mind races to make sense of what he saw, searching the archives of his memory for something that completes the picture. It was too broad to be a boar. And were those spikes along its spine? Hans presses his forefinger into a puddle of blood and rubs it with his thumb. Whatever he'd seen, the blood is real enough.

Twenty minutes of stealthy walking and Hans arrives at the end of the trail. The tree in front of him has a gaping hole between its roots, big enough for a man larger than Hans to crawl inside. He turns his head to listen. There's no grunting, but ... is that mewling?

Hans grabs a slender flashlight from his pocket and flicks it on, sweeping out the hole. It goes on for some ways, practically a cave carved between the roots. He curses himself under his breath—following a wounded creature into its den is the stupidest thing he's ever done—but he can't help himself; he needs to know what he shot. He drops into the tunnel and crouches down, crawling forward into the haze. It smells of dirt and rocks and musk. Heavy musk. It's so deep, not even the flashlight can penetrate its depths. Anything could be back there.

Then he spots it: a small thing, the fluffiest he's ever seen.

Hans coos at it and reaches out, scooping it up in his hands. Its body is stout, and it could use a bath to get the caked-on dirt out of its fur, but it looks healthy enough.

"Now," he says softly, "who'd have left a little thing like you out here?"

He cradles it in the crook of his arm as he crawls out of the cave. His daughters have been asking for a pet for ages—and it is almost December. His wife might take some convincing, but once the girls see it, she won't be able to say no.

Erika Shepard has promised to show me her transformation in exchange for sharing her story. The hodags have lived in mystery for far too long, hiding in plain sight simply to survive. Shepard wants more for herself, for her daughter.

I ask why it has taken her so long to look for her daughter after the young hodag was abducted near November's end. Erika sits silently at first. Her chestnut hair forms a mane around her slender face. Never in a million years would I think that she could be a vicious beast in human form. She isn't beautiful, per se, but inconspicuous. The kind of person pharmaceutical companies hire for their advertisements, people who look so unassuming, nobody will ever recognize them. People who blend in.

Finally, Erika looks up, and I can see tears in her eyes.

"I was in pain, and grieving," she says. "I had just been shot, and I don't think I was even conscious when the hunter came in; I only knew he'd followed me later, when I found his tracks leading to his

car. I had tried to keep Ash next to me, but she must've wandered toward the entrance. She's curious, like any toddler, even if she hasn't learned to transform yet."

I bite the cap of my pen, nodding along with her. "Tell me more about that. Why couldn't she transform?"

"We're born in beast form," she says. "We're not like werewolves—if those even exist; I've never met one. Whatever this affliction is, it's not transmissible. It's part of our bloodline. I don't—I don't know if we were beasts first and then learned to become human, or if we were cursed to be like this. There's family lore, of course, but it changes depending on who you ask."

I notice Ms. Shepard wringing her hands in her lap.

"Are you alright?"

"Yes," she says and nods. Her hair bounces around her face like crackling fire. "I just—my whole family, we've been silent about this for so long, it's strange to talk about it."

"It'll be quite the sensation when the story comes out."

"That's what I'm afraid of."

I find myself in disbelief. She's so sincere. Can she really be a monster?

"So, afterward, after the pain and grief went away—"

Erika shakes her head vigorously. "They never go away."

"Yes, of course. I meant to ask, when did you know your daughter was still out there?"

Her hands curl into fists. "From the very start. You can't deny a mother's intuition."

—Anita Cortez, "A History of Hodags,"
originally printed in *Otherworldly Occult Facts
and Timelines Almanac*, vol. 8, issue 3, page 24

"Girls!" Hans has barely opened the door to his condo beside the river, and he can already smell dinner cooking—hot dogs and french fries. He's home later than expected; he stopped at a pet store on the way to get a crate, a litter box, and some cat food. Hopefully, his preparedness will help stave off some of Sam's resistance.

Within seconds, Jo and Alison come running into the room. Jo recently turned fourteen but hasn't discovered teen angst yet. Alison is a year younger and a head taller, but she already wants to be the "popular girl" in school, constantly fussing over her blonde hair and repainting her nails. Honestly, he's surprised they've come so quickly, but he usually brings them trinkets after his hunting trips, so maybe it's that.

Jo's eyes widen as her gaze catches the crate in his hands.

"Dad ... is that—"

"Kitty!" Alison has never screamed so loud in all her life, and all that popular-girl demeanor vanishes as she throws herself on her knees to press her face against the crate. Inside, the scared kitten pushes itself to the back, its mewling suddenly a hiss.

"Calm down, Ali," Jo says, crossing her arms. "You're scaring it."

"Let him in, girls," Sam says as she comes from the kitchen.

Hans meets her eyes and winces; the look on her face is only a tremor shy of sheer fury, but she won't show her anger in front of the kids.

He closes the door and kicks off his boots before treading onto the carpeting.

"Hans—"

"I'll vacuum later," he says, kneeling and gently placing the crate on the plush white floor. He unlatches it and takes a step back, standing. "Now, girls, let it come out on its own, okay? It'll warm up to you; it just needs time." He glances at Sam again; her brow is furrowed the way that means *We need to talk. Now.* "Hey, would you two go to the car and grab the supplies I bought?"

"Sure, Dad!" Alison rushes to the door, and almost begrudgingly, Jo follows; Alison had wanted a cat, but Jo wanted a dog, after all.

The moment the door closes, Sam folds her arms. "A cat? You brought home a cat—without so much as asking first? I can't believe you!"

"I found it in the woods." Hans winces, realizing this doesn't strengthen his case. "It was crying and hungry. I couldn't just leave it there to die, could I?"

Sam's face softens, but her arms remain rigidly locked across her chest. Finally, she exhales and stoops down to look inside the crate. The kitten walks out of the shadows and brushes against Sam's leg, and Hans knows that clinches it. The first one to make the kitten purr? There's no way Sam can oppose it now.

"Fine," she says after a long moment. "We'll keep it. But first thing Monday, you're taking it to the vet. And give it a bath before dinner."

"And how long did it take you to find her?" I lean forward in anticipation, ready for the story to continue, and I am surprised by what Ms. Shepard says next.

"I haven't." She purses her lips together, brow furrowed as she holds back tears. "That's why I wanted to do this interview, so if anyone knows where my daughter is, they can get her home safely. Before it's too late. Before she—before she hurts anybody."

I want to chuckle. Erika speaks about her daughter like a lost puppy, not a monster with fangs and horns and spikes. I press her to say more.

"Hodags aren't especially known for our sense of smell. I can't just sniff her out."

"But won't she be recognized? I mean, forgive me for being blunt, but aren't hodags easy to spot?"

Erika's laughter is cold, heartless. "A young hodag looks little different than a kitten."

I am dumbstruck, suddenly at my wit's end. Ms. Shepard's story keeps getting wilder and wilder, and for a moment, I fear I am being pranked.

"I want to share your story, help you find your daughter," I say and ask if she feels ready to transform; I don't mention I won't publish without seeing proof. She stiffens in her chair, and I can tell I'm losing her. "Can I get you some water?"

Her shoulders soften. "That would be wonderful, thank you."

I nod with a smile and step out of the room. By the time I return, hardly a minute later, Erika Shepard is gone—and the back of the chair has been slashed straight through. I drop the glass of water, and it shatters around my feet. Around the edges of the gash, there are tufts of chestnut-colored fur.

—Anita Cortez, "A History of Hodags,"
originally printed in *Otherworldly Occult Facts and Timelines Almanac*, vol. 8, issue 3, page 25

January

Sam has taken a special liking to Fluffums, though she detests the name. Alison hadn't allowed them to call it anything but, and soon Fluffums would respond to nothing else.

Sam pets Fluffums on the couch, a paperback romance in her free hand, and turns the page. In the moment of no contact, Fluffums whines. Back goes Sam's hand, but she pauses. There's a lump at the back of Fluffums's neck, and then one below it, and another below that, all along her spine to the start of her tail. Sam lost a dog to cancer in her youth, and the color drains from her face as she recalls the small tumors that had appeared on his body during his last few years. Those were soft and moved beneath her fingers, but these are like ... bone spurs.

It's probably nothing, she thinks to herself, but she can't focus on the novel anymore.

That afternoon, she takes Fluffums to the vet.

"She doesn't appear to be in any pain or discomfort," the vet says, feeling Fluffums along the spine. "It's probably nothing to be worried about, but we can do some scans if you're concerned."

"No," Sam says, remembering a similar remark from her dog's vet all those years ago. "I'll keep an eye on it and come back if things worsen."

A few days later, Fluffums yawns, and—do her teeth look bigger? Sam peels back her lip, and sure enough, the cat's incisors have doubled in size. No, that can't be right. Teeth don't grow like that. Do cats have baby teeth like humans do? Maybe that's it. Sam purses her lips, feeling unsettled, but pushes the feeling aside. She must be imagining it, that's all.

"Feel this," she tells Hans a few days after that. He brings his hand to the cat's head, and his eyes widen when he feels the nubs on either side of Fluffums's skull. "And on her back—and her teeth—" Sam shakes her head. "I don't think she's a cat, Hans."

"You sound crazy," he says, wincing as the words leave his mouth. "But I—but maybe you're right." His eyes glaze over, and she knows he's hiding something.

"What is it?" She crosses her arms, tilts her hips, and plants her feet so firmly she might as well have roots. "What aren't you telling me?"

Hans licks his lips. "Before I found Fluffums, I—I shot something. It was big. I didn't know what it was, but I could've sworn it had horns and spikes and—"

"And I'm the one who sounds crazy?" Sam's eyebrows rise to her forehead. "Just what did you bring home?"

STRANGE SIGHTINGS

Milwaukee Sentinel Journal
    February 14

Valentine's Day is typically a time of love and celebration, but this year, something's amiss. Over the past week, there have been multiple police reports of strange animal sightings. Some claim it had horns and saber-like teeth, while others said it had spikes along its back. Animal control officers have found no evidence of any actual creature and have told reporters it's most likely a few different animals being lumped together, though they didn't say which animals those might be. In the meantime, police want people to remain cautious walking after dark and to remain vigilant while outside, especially with young children.

March

"It's not a cat." Sam's hands are on her hips while she faces her daughters on the couch. Fluffums is locked in her crate nearby, mewling softly; she isn't used to being confined like this.

"I don't care," Alison says. "Fluffums is family, and family means—"

"Ali," Hans says, "I know you love Fluffums, but Mom's right. It might be dangerous."

Jo snorts. "We've had Fluffums for months, and she's done nothing."

"I don't care if she's not a cat!" Ali's voice rises with every word. "She's ours, and I won't let you take her away!" She throws herself on the floor beside the crate and unlatches it before Hans can pull her back.

Fluffums leaps out of the crate and runs to the cat-scratching post, bounding onto its top and eyeing everybody cautiously. Small fangs stretch from her mouth, and two small horns have sprouted on her head. There's a ridge of spikes running down her spine.

Jo crosses her arms. "I've been researching, and I think she's a hodag."

Sam rolls her eyes. "Those don't exist."

"But it makes sense!" Jo jumps to her feet. "Dad found her in the Northwoods, and that's where they're supposed to live. They have horns and spikes and big teeth. That's the only thing she could be."

Sam and Hans exchange worried glances, and then look at their daughters.

"Even if it's true," Sam says, trying to keep her tone cool, "that only makes it more dangerous."

"She's not an *it*!" Ali cries. "She's Fluffums, and she's ours." She flies across the room and pets Fluffums between the horns; she purrs loudly, rubbing her head against Ali's hand.

"Besides," Jo says, "if she is a hodag, think of what this means. We could post pictures on social media and become famous."

Worried glances again, but Hans tilts his head to the side.

"No," Sam says.

"She has a point."

"I can't—"

"I'll manage the account." He shrugs.

"But—"

Hans raises his hands and his eyebrows. "Let's give it a shot, okay? See where it goes."

Sam sighs. "Just promise me, the moment things go wrong, you stop."

"I promise."

It has been nearly six months since I'd seen Erika Shepard and about four months since her story had appeared in print. She arrives at our small office looking disheveled and haggard. I wonder if she has been eating well, but haven't the heart to ask. I welcome her inside, and she takes a seat in the lounge. Her shoulders slump, but there's a fire in her eyes.

"I found her," she says.

I open my mouth, about to ask who, but then I recall her missing daughter—she'd come back with the real story, I'm sure of it. I grab my notebook and pen from the side table and wait for her to continue.

"There's a social media account that popped up," she says. "Called itself hodag-in-the-city. Just a bunch of images, but I recognized Ash at once."

Ms. Shepard explains that the hunter who'd shot her had taken her daughter home as some sort of sick prize, and his family has been treating her like a run-of-the-mill house cat. When her ferociousness came in, the family must have realized what she really was.

"If she's showing her hodag traits, she could transform any day. I couldn't let that happen, so I—I had to—" She closes her eyes and breathes heavily.

I clear my throat, trying to urge her back. Her eyes flick open, pure fire raging within them. For a moment, I imagine what she might look like in her beast form—the giant fangs, the horns, the spikes on her back. For the first time since I'd met her, I'm afraid.

"Erika," I say slowly, softly, "what did you do?"

Her hands tremble, and I brace myself for what she's about to say.

—Anita Cortez, "Hodags in the City," originally printed in *Otherworldly Occult Facts and Timelines Almanac*, vol. 9, issue 1, page 15

April

Spring is in the air—and winter and summer, depending on the day. Fluffums is curled up on the couch beside Hans. Sam and the girls have gone out to pick up pizza, and Hans scrolls absently through his phone. Fluffums's social media account spiked in interest right after he made it, but then people kept commenting "Hoax!" and "This sucks!" so they lost a lot of followers. The girls have been incessant about posting, though, and won't let the page die.

Hans reaches out and pets the hodag right between her horns. It amazes him how he's adjusted so easily to the horns and even the spikes along her back. She keeps growing, too, and he wonders how big a hodag is supposed to get. The one he'd shot ... it seemed huge.

A pang of guilt flashes through him. He'd killed her mother (father?) and taken her from her home. But hadn't they given her everything they could? And the girls loved her so much.

He lifts his head at the sound of the key turning in the lock and watches as Sam comes in, carrying two large pizza boxes, followed by the girls. Jo has a bag of sodas, and Ali's carrying a pint of ice cream. Next to him, Fluffums perks up, jumps off the couch, and rubs up along Sam's leg. The hodag's hair has gotten coarser; Hans wonders how it'll feel in the summer when they wear shorts. He wonders how big she'll be by then.

Hans gets to his feet and takes the pizza boxes, kissing his wife on the cheek as he does so. They carry everything into the dining room, and Sam takes the ice cream to the kitchen and returns a moment later with a stack of plates.

"Can you grab the red pepper?" Jo asks, and Hans goes in search of it. He hears a knock on the door, and Ali says, "I'll get it."

He's just found the red pepper flakes and walked back into the dining room when Ali screams.

The plastic jar drops from his hand as he bolts into the living room, right on Sam's heels.

Sam grabs Ali and pulls her away from the woman at the door. Hans throws himself between them, but the woman just stands there, unarmed, saying nothing.

Hans takes a moment to hear what Ali's screaming: "No! You can't have her!"

His head whips around in search of Fluffums, and he sees the hodag across the room, watching everything, staring at their visitor, grunting.

The woman has chestnut hair and is dressed in jeans and a blue T-shirt, a light-brown jacket hanging open. She crouches and holds out her hand. "Here, Ash, Mama's here."

Sam's shushing Ali, both of them backing away, and Hans knows he needs to say something, do something—anything.

"Who are you?" he finally says.

The woman stands up and faces him. Her face is blank at first, then he sees her eyes changing colors, pupils stretching into slits like cat eyes. Her right hand shakes, and she grabs it with her left to keep it still.

"You shot me," she says, her words icy. "And then you stole my daughter."

Sam has forced Ali into the other room. Jo holds her by the arm, and they're peeking into the living room. Sam steps beside Hans, glancing back and forth between him and the strange woman.

"What's going on?"

"Just what I said," the woman answers. "He shot me and stole my daughter." She crouches again and whistles. "Ash, come here."

"Fluffums—" Ali calls out.

Jo throws her hand in front of Ali's mouth and then shrieks when Ali bites her.

Ali flings herself across the room, skidding to a halt and scooping up Fluffums into her arms. "You can't have her!"

The woman's arm twitches wildly, and when Hans looks at her face, he sees her teeth lengthen into fangs.

"Ali," he says, "let her go."

"No! You can't make me!"

"Make you?" The woman laughs. "I can make you."

Sam screams as the woman rushes forward, her slender limbs thickening as coarse fur sprouts from her skin, bursting apart her clothes. Strong claws spring from her fingers and cut through the carpeting as she hurtles toward Ali.

The girl's screams are cut short as she's thrown back against the wall. Jo's screaming now. Sam's screaming, too, running toward Ali's broken form slumped on the floor by the TV.

Hans wishes he had his gun, but it's safely locked away, and he's frozen in place, barely registering what's going on around him.

He's not thinking when he steps in front of the door and spreads his arms.

The woman—the monstrous hodag—wheels around.

His eyes widen as she rushes toward him.

"It was the girl." A tear puddles in Erika's eye and drips down her cheek.

I must've gone ghost white, too stiff to capture her exact words in my notebook.

"Not the girl I'd struck down, but the other one. She pushed her father out of the way and turned toward me, and I saw on her face—I saw—" Erika swallows a sob and dabs her eyes with her sleeve.

I offer her a box of tissues, but she waves it aside.

"Her face was so full of love—love and fear. In a heartbeat, I realized Ash hadn't been afraid when I arrived. She hadn't even been confused. She'd seemed ... happy. Not just happy that I'd arrived, but happy before I'd gotten there. And the other one, the taller one ... She hadn't been trying to keep a mother from her child, but to hold on to someone she loved."

Her tears flow freely for a few moments, and neither of us speaks.

Finally, my mouth dry, I scrounge around for whatever words I can find.

"And the one you struck—?"

"More scared than anything else. I am a mother. I would never hurt a child."

"And your daughter?"

"She's safe."

I scribble some notes, and when I look up, Erika has dried her face.

"So what's next?"

"The girls asked if they could babysit." Erika laughs, and for once, it seems a sound of joy. "I've never considered the possibility. So we'll see." She sighs. "But I'm thinking, after Ash can control her human form, perhaps we'll move here. Growing up was so lonely for me. I don't want that for Ash. She wouldn't be so alone here if someone knows our secret."

Our conversation veers away from the supernatural to topics of motherhood and rent prices in the city, the bad housing market and rampant inflation. For a moment, I forget I'm talking with a monster. Then I realized she isn't a monster at all. Sure, she isn't human—at least, not all the time—but she is as much a person as you or me.

Maybe, someday, she'll be my neighbor.

Or maybe she'll be yours.

—Anita Cortez, "Hodags in the City,"
originally printed in *Otherworldly Occult Facts and Timelines Almanac*, vol. 9, issue 1, page 16

About the Author

Darren Lipman is an award-winning high school math teacher who hopes to become an award-winning author. His fiction has appeared in *Literally Dead: Tales of Holiday Hauntings*, the *Fairy Tale Magazine*, and *Space and Time*. He lives in Milwaukee, Wisconsin, with his Alaskan Klee Kai, Hoonah, in a house full of overflowing bookshelves. Find him online at thewritingwolf.wordpress.com.

Faceless
by Tanya Hales

Dear Sariah,

Welcome to your new life. We hope you are settling in nicely. You may remember little from your time of being Faceless, but that is for the best; your new experiences will be much more pleasant.

The girl you've replaced is Sariah Wilson. All her memories will soon emerge. In the meantime, trust your instincts, and you will naturally act and react as she would. Soon, you will fully integrate into her life.

We must urge you to keep all your actions in alignment with the things she would do. You will know what those things are. If your actions deviate too far from hers, you risk losing your ability to maintain her identity. You will become Faceless once more, and the human Sariah will return and reclaim her place in her life once more.

If that happens, we may never find a new place for you in the human world.

The DAS will not contact you again. If we ever see you as we go about doing our work, we will pretend not to know you. But know that you are not alone. There are many doppelgängers like us, quietly going about our new human lives. You will know them by their auras. Do not acknowledge them but allow their presence to bring you satisfaction that we who were once Faceless do not remain so forever.

After you read this letter, dispose of it as quickly and covertly as

possible. Do not burn it, as that may draw too much attention. We recommend flushing or shredding.
    Sincerely,
    The Doppelgänger Ascension Society

March 3

Dear diary,
    I burned the letter.

    It turns out that it was the kind of thing Sariah would do. She did it often, writing journal entries and poetry, and then burning them carefully in the flames of candles she kept in her room.

    The first memory I had after coming to was watching the flames lick the corner of the letter while I held it. As the fire ate away at it and blackened remains fell into the wax, a worry nagged at the back of my mind. What if I set her home ablaze?

    Yet, the action felt so natural, because it was exactly what Sariah would do.

    And I am Sariah now. Sariah is me.

    It's been three days since I woke up as Sariah, and the DAS was right. After assuming my place in her life, I didn't have to wonder what to do. I just knew her schedule instinctively.

    Wake up. Pull on the new Wonder Woman socks her best friend, Bella, gave her. Go downstairs without bothering to change out of her nightgown since Dad would already be at work and Kim and Greg were away at college. Eat Lucky Charms cereal, leaving most of the marshmallows for last. Get dressed and apply just a few swipes of mascara. Check on Mom and see she's still asleep after her night shift in the hospital. Scroll through Instagram videos featuring ferrets, since Sariah was determined to convince her mother they should get one. Realize it's time to go. Get into the patchy black 2010 Corolla parked under the sycamore. Drive to school and make it through another day as a high school senior.

    Never mind that I've never driven a car in my life. That I've never eaten marshmallows before. That the closest thing I'd previously seen to a ferret were the weasels that darted through the dark woods I once called my home.

But I don't live in a forest anymore. My bed is no longer damp moss. I wear clothes. I have a car. I have a face.

Just like the DAS said, Sariah's memories have emerged. At first, I acted purely upon instinct, but now I'm understanding why Sariah did things the way she did.

Last night was her eighteenth birthday. Everything was already in place for her four closest girlfriends to come over for cake and movies. The laughter and conversation felt so natural and happy.

When I was Faceless, there was never such unrestrained light and happiness.

As I opened the gifts each of them had gotten for Sariah, memories flashed in my mind of how Sariah met each friend, how their relationship developed and trust formed. The experience was so unexpectedly warm that I had to go hide in the bathroom so no one would see my tears.

Sariah wouldn't have cried in that moment, so I had to compose myself quickly. Anything too out of character would risk my ability to maintain her identity.

After dessert, we watched movies. First, a chick flick, then a horror film.

It featured a family staying at a cabin in the woods while a pale, bony monster lurked in the trees.

I hated every moment, but I giggled, gasped, and shrieked on cue.

The monster reminded me too much of myself. Not Sariah, who I've become, but the real me. The nameless, Faceless creature from the woods, lurking on the edge of human society, longing for a life, but always remaining separate. Humanoid, yet inhuman.

The doppelgänger. The double walker.

I had friends then, fellow Faceless I loved, inasmuch as I was able to love. I remember one close friend I always wandered through the woods with, because his presence made me feel safe. The DAS helped him assume a human identity about a year ago. I wonder where he is now, and how he's enjoying his life as a human.

I miss him.

Everything about my old life feels foggy now. I know I had emotions then, but they all seem so distant and muted compared to this bright, saturated life.

I should probably burn this journal entry as soon as possible, but Sariah usually waited a day or so before burning pages from her diary, and I must be her in every way I can.

March 6

Dear diary,

I feel like I've begun to fully take on Sariah's traits now. Her memories are mine. They don't even feel like they ever were hers. It's like I've always been Sariah Wilson, daughter of Abby and Colton Wilson, sister of Kim and Greg, lover of science and computer classes, hobbyist baker, and closet superhero nerd.

This should be amazing. It's something I've always dreamed of. But I keep feeling something nagging at the back of my mind. Thoughts of the woods, of damp leaves and red toadstools. Memories of curling up next to the bony bodies of fellow doppelgängers for warmth, our arms curled around our knees.

I hate that I can't stop thinking about what I used to be. That disgusting, pale, Faceless creature. The being who knew there was one single human out there whose aura was the right fit, whose face belonged to me if only I could find a way to take it. The creature who was helpless to do so without the aid of the DAS.

I won't ever be helpless again. This life is mine now. I won't do anything that might make me lose it.

I can't express how grateful I am that Sariah broke up with her boyfriend a few weeks ago. He was terrible, and it would have been awfully painful needing to maintain that relationship.

Bella, Amy, Claire, and I have plans to go downtown tomorrow. I look forward to seeing the city with my own eyes for the first time.

March 7

I saw him. I know it was him.

One minute, I was walking down the street with my friends, and the next moment, I locked eyes with a random stranger I've never seen before.

He was around my age, with deep brown eyes and well-maintained dreadlocks.

Sariah had never met him before, but I instantly knew his aura.

Every person's aura has a color and vibration. And his aura of purple and gold, with the resonant vibrations of a wooden wind chime, felt more familiar to me than my own.

It was the new face of my dearest friend from my old life.

He gave me the smallest smile as we passed each other on the sidewalk, but that was it. He didn't turn back to speak with me; nor did I. I can't.

I'm Sariah, and I don't know him. Not anymore.

March 8

I can't stop thinking about him. I can't stop wondering what his name is, who he is now, and how much he remembers of our time together in the woods.

Everything was so simple in those bestial days. Collecting berries with our long, bony fingers, taking down deer and feasting on them, spying on camping humans together, smelling their fear when they realized something unknown and unseen was watching them.

Back then, my friend used to carve designs in dead wood with his claws. Looking back on his art with the knowledge and perspective I have now, I'd say it was primal and primitive, but the repeating designs and symbols were genuinely beautiful.

Is he able to create art in his new role? Or is it too out of character for his current identity?

Neither of us are who we were back then. I know I need to forget him. My friends noticed I've been acting strange and distracted, and that's unacceptable. If I make too many mistakes, Sariah will steal her life back from me.

March 15

I found him again.

I went downtown with my friends, and I saw him working at a coffee shop. I couldn't go in and talk to him. Sariah hates the smell of coffee and never would have entered. I just watched him through the glass for a moment until it was time to walk away.

March 15 text exchange

>Bella: Hey, what's up? Are you mad at me?

>Sariah: Whaaaaat? Never.

>Sariah: Have I been acting weird?

>Bella: Super weird. Like, brooding and stuff, lol

>Sariah: No way. Just stressed about school.

>Sariah: Okay, fine, I might be a little grumpy. XD But it's not because of you.

>Bella: I think you've been single too long.

>Sariah: It's only been one month since I broke up with Jack, lol

>Bella: Yeah, that's basically forever, so this is an

emergency. I'm going to find you a boyfriend ASAP ;)

March 21

Today, we went into the coffee shop.

Bella made it happen. It wasn't me. Well, not mostly. I mentioned I was thirsty. And I really was. I may have timed my announcement for when we were walking past the coffee shop, but it was Bella who decided we should go in, which meant I didn't have to initiate the action by doing anything out of character.

And there he was, making and serving coffee. I couldn't stop staring.

Bella, Claire, and Amy got drinks while I hung back at a table with some water, basking in the sense of his familiar aura.

I tried to figure out how Sariah would go about interacting with him, but I knew she wouldn't. She wasn't the type to start conversations with strangers.

When the girls returned with their drinks, Bella noticed me watching him. She grinned and whispered to me, "Is it his eyes? Or the shoulders? You've always liked skinny guys with broad shoulders."

I laughed awkwardly. I could hardly say that it was his aura, noticeable only to me, that I was obsessing over, so I leaned into the Sariah instinct and said, "Shut up."

Just then, he approached our table, holding a tray. His name tag read Spencer.

He smiled. "I just wanted to make sure you all tried our cookie samples while they're hot. They just came out."

His eyes met mine, and my chest grew warm. He'd gone out of his way to come over so he could talk to me.

Before I could think of what to say, Bella jabbed a thumb toward me. "This is perfect for Sariah. She hates coffee, but she loves cookies."

Spencer chuckled. "We might have a bit of a star-crossed situation, then, since I'm a coffee barista and also gluten intolerant."

I blushed at the implications of the term "star-crossed," but I felt like I had no voice to speak. Sariah wasn't good when she was put on the spot.

"There are gluten-free cookies," Claire told him. "What really matters is how you feel about superhero movies."

He laughed sheepishly. "I haven't watched one in years."

Sariah would have lost all interest in him then, but I didn't. Still, I was stuck now, stalled by Sariah's personality, so I just took a cookie and thanked him, and he returned to his job.

At that moment, I hated myself. Or hated Sariah. Or both.

My friends chatted, but I kept stealing glances his way, wondering if he was still thinking about me too.

Bella poked me and whispered, "You seriously think he's cute, don't you? Want me to give him your number?"

I knew Sariah would instantly refuse Bella's offer, but I clamped my mouth shut. I stared at Spencer, the body that now housed the soul of my dearest friend.

I opened my mouth and choked out, "Yes."

Bella grinned, jotted my number down on a napkin, and jumped up to deliver it to him.

I couldn't do anything except stare at the table as a wave of vertigo rushed over me. I gripped the edge of the chair, feeling like I might fall off and sink through the floor. Sounds seemed to reach my ears from a great distance.

It was the consequence of not maintaining Sariah's identity, I'm sure of it.

But then everything snapped back into focus and clarity. I stayed in control of my new body.

Bella returned to our table. She sighed as she sat down. "I gave him your number. But he says he's already interested in someone else."

I blinked. "Oh."

I'd never considered he'd be so determined to faithfully play his new role that he might reject my attempts to reconnect.

My friends reassured me they'd help find me someone better.

The Sariah in me was satisfied with that.

But I wasn't.

March 23 text exchange

UNKNOWN NUMBER: HEY. IT'S ME, FROM THE COFFEE SHOP.

UNKNOWN NUMBER: I KNOW I SAID I WAS INTERESTED IN SOMEONE ELSE, BUT I'M NOT. SPENCER WAS. BUT SOMETIMES I STILL HAVE MY OWN FEELINGS, AND THOSE FEELINGS HAVE BEEN MISSING YOU LIKE CRAZY. HOW ARE YOU DOING?

SARIAH: :D :D :D

SARIAH: YOU'RE ACTUALLY TEXTING ME! I CAN'T BELIEVE IT!

SPENCER: YEAH! I'M NOT GOING TO LIE, I FEEL A LITTLE WEIRD RIGHT NOW, BUT I THINK IT'S WORTH IT. :)

SARIAH: WEIRD, LIKE A SENSE OF VERTIGO? THAT'S HAPPENED TO ME, TOO, WHEN I'VE DONE SOMETHING A BIT OUT OF CHARACTER, BUT IT WENT AWAY QUICKLY. I'M SO GLAD YOU DECIDED TO CONTACT ME! I'VE SERIOUSLY MISSED YOU SO MUCH!

SPENCER: YOU'RE SARIAH NOW, RIGHT? IT'S PRACTICALLY A MIRACLE THAT WE ENDED UP IN THE SAME CITY.

SARIAH: RIGHT? WE'RE SO LUCKY.

SARIAH: OH, AND YES. :) SARIAH WILSON. EIGHTEEN YEARS OLD. HIGH SCHOOL SENIOR.

SPENCER: GOOD TO MAKE YOUR RE-ACQUAINTANCE. ;) I'M SPENCER JOHNSON. TWENTY YEARS OLD. BARISTA AND COLLEGE DROPOUT, LOL. KIND OF SUCKS HAVING TO follow the path our human selves set in motion, right? No way I would have dropped out. I'm way too stubborn for that. XD

Sariah: For real. XD But if we can at least talk like this, it'll make everything so much better. I know we're not supposed to discuss our lives as Faceless, but not having anyone to talk to about it has been so lonely.

Spencer: Well, I'm here now. :)

Sariah: I've missed your aura so much. When we were near each other at the coffee shop, it felt so safe and familiar.

Spencer: I know what you mean. Seeing you again was great. It feels kind of like my soul was meant to be near your soul.

Sariah: Exactly!

Sariah: I need to get to bed now to stay in character and all that, but can I text you in the morning?

Spencer: Definitely. :)

March 24

Dear diary,

The vertigo came again last night after I texted Spencer, but it wasn't too bad. I just lay in bed, basking in the joy of being reconnected with my best friend, and the weirdness in my head, hearing, and vision went away after a few minutes. I'm sure I can handle it and maintain my identity.

I'll figure it out because there's no way I'm giving up Spencer now that I've found him again.

March 24 text exchange

> SARIAH: So. What's your favorite thing about being human? :)
>
> SPENCER: I have to choose just one? That's not fair.
>
> SARIAH: No, you can text me as much as you want, lol
>
> SPENCER: XD
>
> SPENCER: I'll pick the first thing I think of and say that it's being able to cuddle with cats in a cozy bed.
>
> SARIAH: You have cats? Lucky. My parents don't approve of pets.
>
> SPENCER: Yep. Three of them.
>
> SARIAH: I bet they're a little more cuddly than the bobcats and mountain lions we're used to. :P
>
> SPENCER: For sure. They still bite, though. XD
>
> SARIAH: I'm still in bed too. I agree that it's amazing.
>
> SPENCER: It would be hard to go back to life in the woods.
>
> SARIAH: Unbearable.

SPENCER: THAT MIGHT BE A LITTLE STRONG. I MEAN, WE KNEW DOPPELGÄNGERS WHO WENT BACK TO BEING FACELESS.

SARIAH: NOT WILLINGLY. THEY FAILED TO MAINTAIN THEIR HUMAN IDENTITY AND LOST THEIR CHANCE.

SPENCER: NOT ALL OF THEM WERE UNWILLING. I KNEW A FEW DOPPELGÄNGERS WHO RETURNED BY CHOICE. THEY SEEMED HAPPY WITH THEIR DECISION.

SARIAH: DID WE EVEN FEEL HAPPINESS BACK THEN?

SPENCER: OF COURSE WE DID. I THINK THERE'S SOMETHING ABOUT BEING HUMAN THAT MAKES US NATURALLY DESPISE OUR OLD LIVES, BUT WE HAD SOME BEAUTIFUL EXPERIENCES. AND I WAS ALWAYS HAPPY WHEN WE WERE TOGETHER.

SARIAH: I WISH WE COULD BE TOGETHER NOW.

March 26

Dear diary,

Sariah had a sleepover with the girls last night. Things are good but I'm distracted. I often find my mind wandering, wishing I was talking to Spencer instead of the girls. Bella, Claire, and Amy are Sariah's friends, whereas Spencer is mine.

At the sleepover, we talked about our worst fears. My greatest fear is of being nameless, Faceless, and without a life of my own again.

But obviously I couldn't say that, so I relied on Sariah's instinct and said that my worst fear is spiders. Can you imagine that? Me? Afraid of spiders?

But no human can see my secret truths. Not ever. I get to be human now, but I don't get to be me.

March 28 text exchange

> SARIAH: What do you think people would say if they saw all our weird texts?

> SPENCER: We'd just tell them we're really into role-playing. LARPing or whatever.

> SARIAH: That's not what LARPing is. :p

> SPENCER: Oh yeah? And who made you the LARP expert?

> SARIAH: Apparently the DAS, since they gave me the identity of a proud nerd.

> SPENCER: The DAS would probably be mad we keep talking ...

> SARIAH: Do you think they even care what happens to us now that they've finished their job of helping us get faces?

> SPENCER: I'm sure they care enough because they want to help us maintain our new identities, right?

> SARIAH: Yeah. Probably.

April 2

Dear diary,

The more I text Spencer, the more oddly separate from my body I feel. Every day, it seems to get a little worse. I can only text him while I'm sitting or lying down now.

I was hoping it would get better over time, but what if it doesn't? I'll just have to figure out a way to handle it.

April 3 text exchange

> SARIAH: Want to meet up sometime? It'll be so good to spend time together in person.
>
> SPENCER: Yeah, let's try it. There's a cool art gallery near where I work. We could go there together after I finish at 6.
>
> SARIAH: That sounds great! I haven't done something like that yet. Should I eat beforehand, or should we get something while we're out?
>
> ...
>
> SARIAH: Did you see my last text about dinner?
>
> SARIAH: I hope your vertigo isn't as bad as mine is right now. I feel awful. Gotta push through it, though, right?
>
> ...
>
> SARIAH: I really hope you're doing okay

April 4 text exchange

> SPENCER: We can't meet up. I can feel it. Doing so

will make me deviate too far from Spencer's path.

Sariah: Oh. OK. I understand.

Spencer: My grasp on his identity is getting pretty precarious, and I bet the same is true for you. We should probably stop talking to each other. You have your new friends. You'll be fine.

Sariah: But none of them are you. You're the only one who truly knows my soul.

Spencer: I've thought long and hard about this. Please don't make it harder than it needs to be, or else I'll have to block your number, for both our sakes.

Spencer: I know you'll be safer without me in your life too.

April 4

I never cried when I was Faceless. I never felt devastated, never felt this gaping emptiness that makes me feel like I'm going to be sucked into myself, like I'm a black hole. There is no light in me anymore. I am alone.

My only choice is to be Sariah in every way now. It's what I should have done from the beginning.

April 17 text exchange

Mom: Time to come home, Lovey. It's almost midnight.

...

Mom: I know you read my text. It's 10 past. Come home.

Sariah: It's the weekend.

Mom: That's why I let you stay out until midnight instead of 11.

Sariah: I'm eighteen now. You don't get to give me a curfew anymore.

Mom: You're still in high school, and I'm still your mother. I won't stop loving you and trying to keep you safe just because you're legally an adult now.

...

Mom: Please at least tell me where you are.

...

Mom: Can you respond and let me know you're seeing my texts?

...

Mom: I love you. Just be safe.

Sariah: Jeez, I was just watching the new Batman movie with Claire. Fine, whatever. omw

---

April 18

Dear diary,

I can't talk to my mom. I can't tell her anything about the real me. I hate acting like a brat to her, but it's what Sariah would do.

Sariah didn't know what she had, and I just have to go along with it.

Back when I used to daydream about being human, I didn't know it could be so painful.

April 22

Dear diary,

I wonder what the real Sariah is experiencing. Now that I stole her life, she's the Faceless one, alone in the dark woods. It must be horrible to leave a warm human life to be trapped in that state.

Every day, I try so hard to be her, but I feel like I'm living a lie.

My friends aren't really my friends. My family doesn't love me. They only care about Sariah. If they knew who I was, they would hate me. They would try to drive me off. Maybe even try to kill me.

They'd just want the real Sariah back.

April 26

Last night, I made a plan.

I need to contact the DAS. I feel so stuck right now, and they're the only ones who can help. Out of all doppelgängers, they're the ones who are most artfully integrated in human society. Their job is to understand patterns in human behavior so they can help their fellows steal human faces.

They're the only ones I can turn to. They're the only people who can tell me how I'm supposed to maintain my role as Sariah when it's making me so miserable.

April 29

I've made posts on all the cryptid forums I can find. I made posts on social media using anonymous accounts. I basically posted adverts calling out the Doppelgänger Ascension Society and asking them to please contact me.

Everyone on the Internet must think I'm writing nonsense, but the DAS will take it seriously. They won't like the attention I'm drawing to them.

They can't ignore my posts forever.

May 15

Two weeks, and no word from the DAS.

I did everything I could think of to get their attention, and nothing.

Tonight, I even drove to an empty parking lot and screamed their name into the darkness until my voice went hoarse and the vertigo got too bad. I lay on the asphalt for who knows how long, tears streaming down my face.

The DAS doesn't care about me. They didn't lie when they said they'd never contact me again.

Now I'm stuck, a doppelgänger trapped in a human world, and I've never felt more alone.

May 18

I'm writing this in my car right now, and I think this is the end. It's so dark. My hand is shaking so bad I can barely hold the pencil.

Today, I was desperate to go somewhere familiar since I felt like I was losing all sense of self. So I got into my Corolla and drove to the woods. My heart was pounding, and I knew I was on the verge of a breakdown as I drove.

After an hour, I reached the edge of the woods. It was already dark, but I drove into the forest down a dirt road, looking for any familiar landmarks from my old life, but I saw nothing.

I was driving for only a minute when I started shaking so bad that I had to stop the car.

I've ruined everything.

I can feel myself slipping completely, the world around me spinning. I'm dizzy and nauseous. Sariah would never go out into the forest alone like this. It would terrify her.

Whatever I do, I won't be able to recover from such a huge deviation.

It's over.

May 18 text exchange

SARIAH: PLEASE ANSWER MY CALLS, SPENCER. PLEASE.

SARIAH: I'M BEGGING YOU. I HAVE NO ONE ELSE I CAN TURN TO. I NEED YOU. I DON'T THINK I HAVE MUCH LONGER IN THE HUMAN WORLD. I DON'T KNOW HOW TO BE SOMEONE I'M NOT. I DON'T EVEN KNOW WHO I AM ANYMORE. I NEVER KNEW THIS WOULD BE SO HARD, AND I THINK I'M READY TO JUST GIVE UP, BECAUSE ANYTHING IS BETTER THAN BEING SO COMPLETELY ALONE LIKE THIS.

SARIAH: I MISS YOU. I MISS YOU SO MUCH.

SPENCER: TELL ME WHERE YOU ARE. I'M GOING TO COME GET YOU.

SARIAH: NO! THEN YOU'LL JUST END UP LIKE ME.

SPENCER: MAYBE I DON'T CARE ABOUT THAT ANYMORE. THESE PAST FEW WEEKS HAVE BEEN THE MOST LONELY, PAINFUL TIME OF MY LIFE. MAYBE I DON'T WANT TO BE HUMAN IF IT MEANS I DON'T GET TO BE WITH YOU.

SARIAH: YOU DON'T MEAN THAT.

SPENCER: NOW YOU'RE THE ONE NOT ANSWERING MY CALLS. I'M IN MY CAR. YOU CAN'T STOP ME.

SARIAH: YOU CAN'T RUIN YOUR LIFE LIKE THIS!

SPENCER: I MEANT WHAT I SAID. WHEN I GET TO YOU, I'M GOING TO HOLD YOU IN MY ARMS LIKE I SHOULD HAVE DONE THE MOMENT I FIRST SAW YOUR HUMAN FORM. I'M GOING TO REMIND YOU WHO YOU ARE, THAT YOUR SOUL IS THE MOST PRECIOUS THING IN THE WORLD TO ME. NOW PICK UP AND TELL ME WHERE YOU ARE. I'M NEVER LEAVING YOU ALONE AGAIN.

Dear Sariah,

You don't know me, but I feel like I know everything about you, as I've glimpsed so many parts of your life.

I'll spare you most of the details, but I wanted to leave you this letter, explaining a few things before I go.

Walking in your shoes these past couple months has been so enlightening. I got to do so many things I've never done before. But the best part was experiencing the love of so many people who didn't even really know me. But they thought they did, and that gave me the perspective to know that they love you so much.

Your parents, siblings, and friends would do anything for you. Don't take them for granted. You have so much to be grateful for.

I've learned the same is true for me. I always looked forward to the day I would be human, but I already had everything I needed. I was loved too. I just needed perspective to see it.

Live intentionally, Sariah. Pursue what matters and appreciate the immensity of the love and friendship in your life.

I'll leave this note on your dashboard where I know you'll find it. You'll never meet me, but I want you to know I'm grateful for you.

I'm reentering the woods with the person I love now. I'd be lying if I said I wasn't terrified, but being able to make my own choices is what I want most, and knowing what he's willing to give up to be with me is the best gift I've ever been given.

I'll be Faceless, but I'll be me, and I'll be loved.
It turns out that's all I ever needed to be happy.
Sincerely,
Your doppelgänger

About the Author

When Tanya Hales was a baby, she enjoyed books by chewing them to pieces before eventually moving on to the higher art of reading. Tanya splits her time between her work as a writer, an illustrator, and a mother, all of which she loves intensely. She now lives in Utah with her family, illustrating coloring books, writing YA fantasy, making cute stickers, and daydreaming constantly about imaginary worlds.

About the Editors

Lisa Mangum has worked in publishing since 1997. She has been the Managing Editor for Shadow Mountain since 2014 and has worked with several *New York Times* best-selling authors. While fiction is her first love, she also has experience working with nonfiction projects.

Lisa is also the author of four national best-selling YA novels (The Hourglass Door trilogy and *After Hello*), several short stories and novellas, and a nonfiction book about the craft of writing based on the TV show *Supernatural*. Her latest book *Write Fearless. Edit Smart. Get Published.* was released November 2024.

She has edited several anthologies about various magical creatures, pirates, and food for WordFire Press. She regularly teaches at writing conferences, including hosting a writing weekend in Capitol Reef National Park through UVU. She lives in Taylorsville, Utah.

Jessica Guernsey writes fantasy and sci-fi short stories. With a BA in journalism from Brigham Young University and a MA in Publishing from Western Colorado University, her work has been published in magazines and anthologies. By day, she crushes dreams as a slush pile reader for multiple publishers. Frequently, she can be found at writing conferences. She isn't difficult to spot; just look for the extrovert. While she spent her teenage angst in Texas, she now lives on a mountain in Utah with her family and a bossy mini schnauzer. Discover more stories at jessicaguernsey.com.

If You Liked ...
If you liked Weird Wilderness, you might also enjoy:

Other WordFire Press Titles by Lisa Mangum

A Bit of Luck: Alternate Histories in Honor of Eric Flint
A Game of Horns: A Red Unicorn Anthology
Dragon Writers: An Anthology
Eat, Drink, and Be Wary: Satisfying Stories with a Delicious Twist
Hold Your Fire: Stories Celebrating the Creative Spark
Of Wizards and Wolves: Tales of Transformation
One Horn to Rule Them All: A Purple Unicorn Anthology
Undercurrents: An Anthology of What Lies Beneath
X Marks the Spot: An Anthology of Treasure and Theft

Our list of other WordFire Press authors and titles is always growing. To find out more and shop our selection of titles, visit us at:

wordfirepress.com